MW00618920

It Gets Dirtier

Eric B Crime Novels, LLC

Note: This book is a work of fiction. Names, characters, places and incidents are products of the author's imagination or are used fictitiously. Any resemblance to actual events, locale, or persons living or dead, is entirely coincidental.

Published by: **Eric B Crime Novels, LLC**
Eric B Crime Novels, LLC
P.O Box 345
Wilmington, DE 19899

Revised Edition Copyright date: 2016
ISBN 978-1-944151-22-5

It Gets Dirtier by: Wasiim

Edited by: Navimjan Services LLC
Cover design by: Street Knowledge Publishing Services

All Eric B Crime Novel titles are available at special quantity discounts for bulk purchases for sales promotion, fund-raising, educational, or institutional use and book clubs.

www.streetknowledgepublishing.com

Printed in Canada

A note from the author

Although this is a work of fiction I want it to be noted that these things can really happen. The decisions YOU make can affect your family, friends and everyone else you may be around. The streets have no heart and bullets have no names. Yes, I want you to be entertained by my work, but please also take a deeper understanding of the things that take place in this novel. Examine each character, the decisions that they make, and watch how the consequences unfold. Don't let it happen to you.

Thank you for your support. I hope you enjoy the book. Please email me at wasiim302@gmail.com for any feedback you'd like to give. Also I'm available on Facebook: wasiim.young and you can find me on Instagram under @wasiim_young
Thank You,

Kenneth Young a.k.a.
Wasiim

First and foremost, I want to thank Allah for giving me the talent, skill and patience I needed to complete another book. I thank Him for everyone one who has supported me and read my work. I would also like to thank Him for allowing me to humble myself so that I could learn more about writing and become a better author.
Ameen

Chapter 1

"Sinnamon, get come here now. I need you to help me with something." Sinnamon's mom Betty yelled from her bedroom.

"I'm trying to fix Shaquan's bottle, mom." Sinnamon yelled back from the kitchen.

Only ten years old, and still a baby herself, Sinnamon had a lot of responsibilities. After her father abandoned Sinnamon and her mother five years ago, they were forced to get public assistance and move to Riverside Housing Projects in Wilmington, Delaware. During her struggles, Betty gave up on life, and began getting high. She started out smoking weed and sniffing coke here and there. She eventually got caught up, and began using harder drugs, and got strung out on Lady Heroin. She ran the streets all day and night selling herself to get high, leaving Sinnamon to fend for herself. Even though Betty was a junkie, she never sold her food stamps she received from the state. There was always food in the house, even if it was only bread and cold cuts from the corner store that Sinnamon often walked to get herself.

About a year and a half ago, one of Betty's many tricks got her pregnant, and she gave birth to a baby boy. Although drugs were found in the baby's bloodstream, Betty eventually got him back from the state's custody, only to leave the responsibility of dealing with Shaquan on young Sinnamon. Only God knows how she manages her living situation, and is still able to attend and do good in school.

"Sinnamon, I said get in here now. If I tell you again, I'm gonna fuck you up. I need you." Betty yelled a second time.

"She gets on my nerves, Shaquan. I'll be right back. Don't fuss." Sinnamon said to her brother as she sucked her teeth, and made her way to Betty's room, already having an idea of what her mother wanted.

"Baby, help me fix this string around my arm. I'm too weak." Betty said as soon as Sinnamon walked in.

"Why you always gotta make me do this Mom?" Sinnamon asked as her eyes watered up. She hated seeing her mom shoot up Heroin in her veins.

"I'm sorry Sinn baby, but I need this. Mommy's not feeling well, and I need you to help me." Betty said, really regretting putting her daughter through the torturing process so many times. But she had to get high.

Reluctantly, Sinnamon began to wrap the old string around Betty's arm as Betty got her heroin filled needle ready for her fix. Tears began to stream down Sinnamon's pretty cinnamon face as she watched the liquid in her mother's needle go from a dark yellow urine color to red, then disappeared into Betty's veins. Betty's pain immediately began to ease and she began to smile.

"Thank you baby," she said as she began to nod off. She tried to wipe the tears from Sinnamon's face, but Sinnamon pushed her hand away and went back to tend to Shaquan.

"It won't be like this forever Shaquan. I promise." You won't have to go through what I go through. I'm gonna go to school and do good. Then I'll get a job and we'll be ok." Sinnamon said still crying as she fed her five month old baby brother.

5

Sinnamon's talk with Shaquan was cut short when she heard a banging at her front door.

"**Boom, boom, boom**....." The door sounded like thunder causing both Sinnamon and Shaquan to jump.

"Betty please let me in." A man on the other side of the door said in a desperate tone. His cries however fell on death ears because Betty was in her room too high to move.

Sinnamon stared blankly at the door while Shaquan cried. The constant banging kept scaring him. Sinnamon started to open the door but knew better. Opening the door was a big no-no in Betty's house. Betty taught Sinnamon early on to never open the door even if she knew who was on the other side. Just like now, Sinnamon recognized the man's voice. It belonged to Betty's boyfriend Sam.

Finally on his last limb Sam tried his luck with the door. He twisted the knob and was relieved when the door popped open. Quickly he ran inside, shut and locked the door. A smile broke across his face, and he wiped the sweat from his forehead with the back of his hand. Once again he cheated death, or another vicious beat down.

Sam opened his hand, and praised the bundle of Heroin that he managed to scandal from one of the hustler's only minutes ago.

"Where ya momma at girl?" Sam asked as he sat at the table with Sinnamon and Shaquan. He was still out of breath.

"In her room." Sinnamon said simply. She didn't like Sam to much. "You know you shouldn't just come into people's houses. My mom didn't invite you in."

"And you know you shouldn't sass no grown man." Sam said as his eyes wandered around Sinnamon's small frame. He rested his glance on her small but shapely thighs, and got a hard on.

Sinnamon looked to the ground, Sam's stares made her uncomfortable.

6

It Gets Dirtier

"What cho momma doin' in her room that she ain't hear me banging on the door like a mad man." Sam looked towards the back room. He figured Betty was high and out of it. Once again his eyes rested on Sinnamon. At the age of 43 he had a sick fetish for little girls, and always had an eye on Sinnamon. He watched as she filled out little by little over the years. Now he had her to himself for the moment.

"Tender little thing ain't cha." Sam rubbed his rough dirty hands across Sinnamon's soft face, then down to her small inner thigh. Sinnamon jumped from his touch.

"Don't be scared." Sam smiled at Sinnamon brightly, showing his gums in the front. The sight of his black gums made Sinnamon's stomach turn.

Sam calmed himself down long enough to prepare his high. Everything he needed was conveniently in his pockets. Knowing he didn't have much time, Sam removed one of the bags of heroin from the bundle, and dumped the contents onto a large spoon. Looking down at the empty bag he read the words 'death wish' stamped in bold print. This was the dope everyone was going crazy over.

Unlike Betty, Sam didn't need any help to tie up. He had a piece of rubber wrapped around his arm in a blink of an eye. Using a lighter and a little water Sam got his dope right and sucked it into his needle. He plucked at his arm a couple of times and then sunk the needle into his waiting vein.

Sinnamon watched as all Sam's worries seemed to disappear. His face wore a smile, and his eyes seemed glazed over. Sam enjoyed his high briefly, then fixed his eyes back over to Sinnamon. He stroked his manhood as he eyed her and hoped she didn't put up much of a fight. He grabbed Sinnamon by the arm and tried to guide her to the floor.

"Get off me," Sinnamon yelled as she tried to fight Sam off.

"Shhh girl, you gonna wake ya momma." Sam spoke in a low aggressive tone. He covered Sinnamon's mouth with his dirty hand.

It Gets Dirtier

Sinnamon opened her mouth and bit down hard.

"Awww shit you little bitch." Sam moaned out in pain. He smacked Sinnamon in the face with force busting her lip.

He moved in on her, pinning her small body against the table. Almost knocking Shaquan, who was in his car seat, down. As they struggled Sam lowered his pants exposing himself to Sinnamon, and then he ripped her tights and panties off.

"Mommy help me please," Sinnamon screamed out to Betty, but she was still out of it.

"Smack." Sam back handed Sinnamon on the cheek, causing her face to turn forcefully to the right. Her eyes landed on a small steak knife. The second she felt Sam's penis touch her flesh, she picked up the knife and jabbed it two times in his neck, hitting a major artery. Sam's blood squirted all over Sinnamon's face painting it bright red. Sinnamon felt the warmth from Sam's blood all over her face and body, she watched fearfully as his blood continued to pump out from his neck. Even with him wrapping both of his hands around his neck, blood still managed to squirt out at Sinnamon. Finally he collapsed dead at her feet.

Looking down at Sam's body, Sinnamon dropped the knife and backed away. She raised her hands to her face in shock, and stared at Sam's body. She wiped her face, then stared blankly at her bright red hands, and screamed at the top of her lungs.

Chapter 2

Years Later...............

"I refuse to be late to school my first day," Sinnamon said to herself as she hurried and got herself and her brother Shaquan together. Sinnamon was seventeen and on her way to William Penn High School to start her senior year and she was excited.

It had been a long road for Sinnamon due to the hardships she suffered over the years. Because she lacked family support and was living in poverty, Sinnamon's living conditions were rough. She secretly stayed with her little brother in the projects for the last two years because of her mother's addiction to heroin. The only time her mother would actually show her face was around the first of the month when the welfare check was due to come. The only good things she did for her two children were allow them to keep the food stamps. Everything else she kept.

"Boy if you don't put your shoe on the right foot and stop playing," Sinnamon said in a motherly tone that she'd gotten accustomed to using when dealing with Shaquan, "You see I'm running late."

Shaquan smiled at her "sorry mommy, I mean Sinnamon; I'm tryin to hurry up."

It Gets Dirtier

"You can call me mommy if you want, I may as well be your mother." Sinnamon helped Shaquan with his shoes and kissed him on his forehead. "I love you." Sinnamon told him.

"I love you too Sinnamon" he replied, happy to feel loved.
Although he was only 7 he understood his feelings well. Going through so much with his mother, Shaquan really needed all the love Sinnamon gave him.

"I'm so glad I'm done with school this year; hopefully I'm able to get a well-paying job. I would love to get us some new clothes." Sinnamon told her brother as she got dressed in an old pair of sweat pants, tee shirt and a run-down pair of Tims.

There once was a time that Sinnamon dreaded the first day of school and would often try to skip the first few days because she knew all the other kids would be coming in with their new gear and she would always stand out. But now she didn't even care. Her attitude was "so what, if they tease me. I'm going to do well in school and go to college, and eventually pursue a career as a lawyer." Then she would be wealthy and she would have the upper hand.

Although money and nice clothes were foreign to her, natural beauty was a close friend. Sinnamon had the most flawless cinnamon colored skin one would ever see. Even during her stages of puberty, she never had a blemish and her skin-tone complimented her chestnut brown eyes perfectly. As far as her facial features, her beauty was comparable to Jada Pinkett-Smith and Eva from America's Next Top Model.

Although she only wore sweats and other loose clothes, anyone could see that she had a hell of a shape. Her stomach was perfectly toned because she worked out often to release stress. She also had thick dancer's legs and a perfectly phat round ass that could only be described as stripper material.

To top things off, she had perky, full C-cup breast that were normally covered by her long thick black hair. It's sad to say that even though she was highly intelligent - maintaining at least a 3.5 grade point average and had the beauty that many would go through numerous surgeries to attain, she lacked confidence tremendously. She always felt as though she wasn't good enough, that's why she never took any interest in boys. Well that and the fact that she basically has been a full time mother to Shaquan since the age of ten.

Sinnamon missed out on most of the things kids grew to cherish. Christmas and other holidays were just regular days to her. No one ever taught her how to ride a bike, play jump rope, skate or anything. She didn't even have friends. The only things she had were Shaquan and her love for learning in order to get a better life.

"Come on Shaquan, you have to go to Ms. Jones so I can catch my bus". Sinnamon told Shaquan as she gathered her things and headed for the door to meet Ms. Jones in front of her house. Ms. Jones was Sinnamon's next-door neighbor and the closest thing to a family member she knew of besides her brother and mother.

"Thank you so much for taking Shaquan to school for me Ms. Jones, I really appreciate it. I don't know what I would do without your help." Sinnamon hugged the older woman.

"Its fine honey, you just make sure you stay on honor roll and graduate on time," Ms. Jones said in a warm voice.

"I will Ms. Jones!" Sinnamon took off for the school bus.

At the bus stop, the usual adolescence jokers greeted Sinnamon.

"I like your outfit," a girl name Janeen blurted out with a laugh when Sinnamon arrived at the bus stop. Janeen was a fairly nice looking 18-year old girl that couldn't stand Sinnamon before she even met her. Most of the girls Sinnamon grew up around couldn't stand her. She never understood the cause of the hatred she received, so she always assumed it was because she was so poor.

In all actuality they were really jealous of her because of her beauty, Sinnamon would have never guessed it though.

"I know right, her outfit is definitely a bomb! And the run down Tims go perfect," one of Janeen's friends cracked.

It Gets Dirtier

Sinnamon was already used to things like this, and just smiled itoff and continued to wait on the school bus. She knew deep down in her heart that one day she would be on top and they would all be envious of her. Besides the few jokes Sinnamon was abused by about her clothing, her school day was going perfect. She had all honors classes and she liked all of her teachers. Things couldn't have been more perfect for Sinnamon. When she was in her classes, the world outside didn't matter. She had no one to ridicule her because she was in a classroom full of white kids that didn't bother her; they rarely ever acknowledge her presence, which was fine by her. She was in her comfort zone and wished she could be in school all dayand night.

During lunchtime, Sinnamon's day took a turn for the worst when she ran back into Janeen and her crew.

"Sorry, but bums can't sit at this table bitch." Janeen spat coldly when she reached the table Sinnamon was sitting at. Trying to keep her cool, Sinnamon ignored the comment and quietly continued to eat.

"Bitch, I know you heard me, now get the fuck out of my seat." Janeen said with force. Taking a deep breath, Sinnamon got up from the table. It took everything she had for her not to lash out at Janeen. All of her suppressed anger and frustration was dying to come out, but she kept her composure.

"You can have your table," Sinnamon said simply and began to walk away, but that wasn't good enough for Janeen. She wanted to continue the pettiness and it frustrated her terribly that Sinnamon wasn't getting out of character. Janeen stuck her foot out and tripped Sinnamon causing her to fall face first onto the ground. Sinnamon's lunch was all over her face and shirt.

"I hope that wasn't your outfit for tomorrow," Janeen said smartly and high-fived one of her girls.

The students at the surrounding tables were in tears of laughter. Pulling herself up from the ground, Sinnamon looked around and felt

12

embarrassed for the first time in years. Janeen ruined her day for no good reason at all. The more Sinnamon thought on the situation, the more her anger began to take over. She was ready to give Janeen the fight she obviously had been wanting.

"Why do you always have to fuck with me Janeen? I never did anything to you. I swear you're so fucking childish!" Sinnamon screamed with tears in her eyes as she wiped the food from her face. Sinnamon's sudden rage shocked everyone. Anyone that knew Sinnamon never heard her raise her voice, let alone curse, so they knew a fight was in the making.

"Bitch, who the fuck you talking to." was all Janeen could say. She had been tormenting Sinnamon for years and not once, did she ever see this side of her.

"I'm talking to your immature ass Janeen. What, you wanna fight or something? Is that why you're constantly picking on me? If so, you can get your fight if that will stop you from harassing me." Sinnamon looked around for teachers then continued, "Well, the teachers aren't around, so what do you want to do because I'm sick of this shit," Sinnamon said boldly.

With her girls backing her 100 percent, Janeen was up for the challenge and approached Sinnamon with her back up. Knowing they were going to jump her, Sinnamon still didn't back down. She felt this would be the only way to get people to leave her alone. She also knew she could take at least handle two of them with ease. Growing up in the projects, Sinnamon had her fair share of fights and was actually good with her hands. She fought knuckle up like a man and wasn't with the scratching and hair pulling; she was ready to box.

"I know what, you bitches ain't going to jump my peoples," a girl Sinnamon never saw a day in her life, said as she stood by her side.

"Bitch, you wanna keep fucking wit her, square up one on one."

"And who the fuck are you?" one of Janeen's girls asked.

"Don't worry about it, but like I said you bitches ain't bout to jump my girl, so what's good," the girl said.

13

It Gets Dirtier

Sinnamon was shocked that someone was actually trying to help her. It was unbelievable to her so she just stood there. Being an opportunist, Janeen saw that Sinnamon wasn't on point, and took a swing at her. Lucky for Sinnamon, she was swift on her toes and side stepped the attack then countered with a number of right and left hooks that all connected squarely with Janeen's face. Seeing Sinnamon going to work on their friend, Janeen's girls were hesitant to come to her aide. None of them were trying to feel anyone of the blows Sinnamon was laying on Janeen. The unknown girl on the other hand was so excited by Sinnamon's attack that she joined in by punching one of Janeen's friends square in the nose, causing blood to fly instantly. The scene was quite brutal, especially for a girl fight.

After a while, the fight was broken up by a number of teachers and security guards. All the girls were escorted to the main office. Left behind in the cafeteria were pieces of hair and blood. Sinnamon left feeling satisfied with her victory. She now only wanted to know who this unknown hero was.

Chapter 3

"So why did you help me?" Sinnamon asked the unknown girl as they sat alone waiting to be seen by the principal.

"Cuz I can't stand people like them. You were mindin' ya own business and they just wanted to pick on you, thinkin you're weak." She stopped and laughed, "You showed them though! I ain't never seen a girl fight like that. You were looking like Lela Ali or somebody." Sinnamon shared the laugh with her.

"So what's your name?" Sinnamon asked.

"Essence."

"That's a nice name; I'm Sinnamon, spelled with an S."

"I know your name, I be around ya way sometimes and I saw you all summer long when I was chillin with my boys in riverside. You got a son right?" Essence quizzed.

"You might as well say I do, but he's actually my little brother."

"Damn girl, you must always have him then, cuz everybody from around ya way thinks he's yours. Well, everybody I asked anyway."

"You asked about me? Why?" Sinnamon was shocked.

"Cuz you seem cool, I don't know nobody and I don't like these bitches style around here. Besides that, you remind me of myself a couple years ago."

"What do you mean?"

"You keep to yourself, and handle ya own." Essence became quiet; she was trying to figure out how to word her next statement without hurting Sinnamon's feelings.

"I also can tell you got it rough like me," Essence said sincerely.

"You can't possibly have it half as bad as me, I mean look at you." Sinnamon looked Essence up and down, taking in her expensive clothes and beautiful features. "You have on nice clothes, and you're gorgeous, and probably come from a well off family or something."

"I wish." Essence waved her hand at Sinnamon. "These clothes cost me nothin, so don't be fooled and I'm from the projects just like you. I moved here last year from Chester, because my mother got killed for stealin drugs from some petty ass hustler." Essence spoke of her mother's death with little emotion.

"So who do you stay with now?" Sinnamon asked.

"To be honest, I swing from house to house. I was staying with my older sister at first, but she started acting funny, thinking I wanted her sorry ass man. Now I just stay wherever I can. I don't have any friends like that, so I mainly just chill with the local hustlers." Essence explained.

Sinnamon was shocked to hear about Essence's living situation and couldn't believe how she managed to keep herself up. Sinnamon began to wonder if she should ask Essence to stay with her.

"Ms. Dupree, step into my office please." The principle interrupted the girls' conversation. Sinnamon slowly got up from her seat and followed the tall man into his office. "Have a seat please," he said politely.

"Mr. Lacefield, I apologize for my behavior in the cafeteria, but..."Sinnamon began as she sat down.

"No need to explain Sinnamon, I spoke with a few of your teachers and a few students, so I know you and your friend didn't start that crap in my school. Lucky for you, the air is a little clear

16

otherwise; you would be leaving in a police cruiser for assault. I hear you pack a good punch." Mr. Lacefield chuckled.

"So, does that mean I can stay in school?" Sinnamon was hoping for the best. She never had any discipline problems in school and wasn't trying to get anything on her school record. She had already begun applying for college and knew that matters like fighting could affect her possibilities of being accepted. "

"Ms. Dupree, I took a glance at your files and see that you have never caused any problems in this school. It's also noted that you are one of our top students, but some disciplinary action must take place. If I don't suspend you, it will look as if I'm showing favoritism." The principle sighed.

"But Mr. Lacefield that can mess up what I worked so hard for. I'm really looking to get some type of scholarship and go to college soon. Can you please bend the rules just once?" Sinnamon begged with tears in her eyes.

Mr. Lacefield was touched by Sinnamon's' emotions and began to think. Being a black man that made it out of the hood, he was pleased to see one of his own trying as hard as he did. "Listen Sinnamon, I admire your passion for learning and I wish you the best of luck, but I still have to do something." He stopped and picked up a piece of paper off his desk.

"I'll disregard this suspension paper." He sent it through his shredder. "But I need you to stay home for the next five days, so it can at least look as though I did something. You're a bright young lady and I'm more than sure your teachers will allow you to make up your assignments upon your return. You just make sure you don't make me regret this."

"You won't Mr. Lacefield. I promise. Thank you so much."
Sinnamon was relieved that things worked out in her favor.

"I'm glad I could help you." Mr. Lacefield said with a big smile. He felt very good about helping Sinnamon out. It was clear that this young woman would be going places.

"Do you have a way home?"

"No."

"Well here, take these bus passes and catch the city bus home. And make sure you stay out of trouble." He gave Sinnamon a couple of bus passes and sent her on her way. "By the way, keep this between us. I don't want anyone coming in my office saying I'm not doing my job properly."

"Okay Mr. Lacefield. Thanks again." Sinnamon said before leaving the office.

"How many days did you get suspended?" Essence asked Sinnamon at the bus stop.

"Five."

"Me too, and I'm pissed. I know I'ma miss a lot of work. Shit, my teachers were already passin' out homework and it's the first day of school." Essence wasn't as high ranked of a student as Sinnamon, but she made sure she got her work done. She too, had dreams of going to college one day, despite the odds.

"I'm not trying to miss any assignments either, but my teachers seem to be nice, so I'm assuming they'll let me make everything up," Sinnamon said.

"Maybe, but you do know that technically, bein' that we were suspended, they don't have to." Essence always thought the worst.

"Yeah, but we'll be fine." Sinnamon looked over at Essence, "so where are you going now?"

"I'm not even sure, hopefully, one of my peoples are around so I can chill with them. But then again, it's nice out so I might just take a walk." Essence replied.

"Well you can come with me if you want. I'm about to go home and clean up or something, I guess."

"That's what's up. If you want, we can head to the mall later on".Essence said.

"I don't have any money and I'll have my brother by then anyway."

"You don't need any money. I'ma put you up to a few things and ya brother can help with the plan, to tell you the truth." A sly smile came across Essence face. Sinnamon agreed with the trip to the mall, although she didn't really want to go. She hated to be seen in public and by the way Essence mentioned her plan, she assumed that it was something that could get her into trouble. The only reason she agreed was because she really didn't want to be left alone and had a need for friendship.

On the bus ride home the girls shared their life stories and realize they had a lot in common. It was a whole new experience for Sinnamon to actually converse with someone of her age group. Normally, the only conversation she got was from her brother, Ms. Jones, and the teachers in her school. Only thing about her life she left out was what happened with Sam years ago. She never discussed that with anyone.

"You got something to eat in here?" Essence asked as Sinnamon let them into the small house.

"Yeah, I may not have any furniture or anything else for that matter, but the fridge is always full. Help yourself," Sinnamon said proudly.

If Essence never told Sinnamon about her childhood growing up, Sinnamon would have been embarrassed to entertain her company in the empty roach infested house.

"That's what I'm talkin bout." Essence looked into the full refrigerator. "You want something?" Essence began to pull things out.

"I'ma beast on the stove."

"Yeah, what are you about to make?" Sinnamon asked.

"I'm 'bout to cook a full course meal in this piece. I ain't have no home cooked food in a minute."

As Essence prepared the meal, she and Sinnamon continued to share their stories. The two of them clicked so well you would have thought they had known one another all their lives. They were

19

building a friendship fast and to someone that didn't know any better, they could pass for sisters.

Essence was no more than 3 inches taller than Sinnamon with beautiful eyes that were hazel with a tint of green. She was built almost identical to Sinnamon, but just a tad bit thicker. She even had long beautiful hair like Sinnamon with the exception of the honey-blond streaks that complimented her caramel skin perfectly. Essence also had a classy style with her appearance. Every piece of clothing she had was stylish, even down to her underwear. Feeling that her looks were her best asset, she felt she had to keep herself as close to perfect as possible. Her wardrobe consisted of strictly name-brand clothes and she rarely wore sneakers or boots like Tims. She always had on some type of stilettos. Essence was so anal about her clothes that she wouldn't wear panties if she didn't have a matching bra. Her nails and toes stayed perfectly manicured, thanks to her own talent. Everything about her spelled "Diva".

"I wish I could be movie-star pretty like you," Sinnamon said suddenly as they ate.

Sinnamon had been admiring Essence the whole time they were together. The statement caught Essence off guard and shocked her. She thought to herself, that Sinnamon couldn't possibly think she was ugly. Sinnamon was one of the prettiest girls she had ever ran across. She may have needed help with clothing and style, but she even looked pretty in rags.

"I mean, don't think I'm gay or anything," Sinnamon noticed Essence looking at her funny, "I'm just saying I wish I was pretty. I don't even like going out in public." Sinnamon said sadly.

"You gotta be joking. When was the last time you looked in the mirror?" Essence took Sinnamon by the hand and led her into the small bathroom. "Now look in that mirror and tell me what you see." Essence said forcefully.

"Someone not worth looking at."

It Gets Dirtier

"Sinnamon, you must need glasses or something. Look at yourself." Essence took Sinnamon's hair out of her ponytail and combed it out. "You have beautiful eyes, long pretty hair that jealous bitches like Janeen buy at Rash's. Shit, earlier you said I was gorgeous, and you look like me in many ways. I personally think you have me beat and trust me, that's hard to do cuz I'm one of the sharpest women on this planet."

Essence spoke with cockiness. "You just need to get past the self consciousness cuz you are beautiful Sinnamon. And I can tell through them baggy ass sweats you have on, your shape is on point."

"No one else seems to notice." Sinnamon turned away from the mirror.

"Don't be afraid to look at yourself. Fuck what them other people say. They just hatin cuz they don't look nowhere near as good as you and they try hard. You are pretty without effort. You probably can't even wake up with an ugly face." Essence joked, making Sinnamon smile. "And look at your smile, girl, you look like you live with a dentist or some shit."

"Girl you are too funny." Sinnamon laughed. "But do you really think I'm pretty?" Sinnamon questioned, while noticing some of her beautiful features for the first time.

"I don't think, I know. How about this, I know you gotta go meet your brother at the bus stop soon, so while you handle that, I'ma go get you something to wear for when we go to the mall. What you wear, about a size eight in jeans, and small in shirts?" Essence asked.

Speaking of the jean size was something new to Sinnamon. She only wore baggy sweat pants and she never even bought them. Ms. Jones would often give her the old clothes she ran across.

"I never been shopping for jeans, but I do wear a small in shirts and if it's any help, I wear medium panties." Sinnamon told her.

"I'm pretty sure you wear a size 8, so don't worry about it. What size shoe do you wear?"

21

It Gets Dirtier

"These are a size four and a half," Sinnamon answered, referring to her boots.

"I'll get everything together and watch, you'll be Diva-fied, just like me". Essence said as she went out the door.

*****

"Why don't we, why don't we, why don't we fall in loooovvvvve....." Ameri screamed through the speakers of the '95 Acura Legend that Essence was pulling up in front of Sinnamon's house with.

Hearing the loud music out front, Sinnamon naturally looked out of the window. The car was one she saw before, but never on her block. It was a white coupe, sitting on 18" rims. The windows were tinted, so it was hard to make out the driver and the system was on point. When Essence jumped out with two big bags in her hands, Sinnamon's jaw almost hit the floor. She immediately ran to the front door.

"Girl, whose car do you have? I thought we were going to ride the bus. And what's in this heavy behind bag?" Sinnamon grabbed one of the bags Essence was carrying.

"Ya clothes and shoes, and that's my boy Dolo's car. He lives around the corner from here. He be lettin' me push his shit sometimes because I be boostin' clothes for his daughter and girl." Essence told her.

"You got all this stuff for me?" Sinnamon asked in disbelief as they walked into the house.

"That's not even a lot; it's only four or five outfits and a bunch of panties and bras from Victoria Secret. The bags are so heavy because of the shoes, belts, and accessories." Essence explained.

"See look," Essence dumped the bag she had on Sinnamon's bed. Sinnamon did the same and her eyes lit up with delight as she admired the clothes and colorful accessories. This was the first time Sinnamon possessed new clothes since the 7th grade. Sinnamon was so happy before she knew it, she found herself thanking Essence with a big hug and tears of appreciation.

"No one has ever been this nice to me."

"Don't worry about it, you're going to be the sister I never had." Essence assured her. "You all emotional girl." Essence chuckled. It touched her to bring so much joy to someone else. Essence may have done things that were morally wrong to get what she had, but she also appreciated and liked the act of giving. Growing up, no one ever really helped Essence with anything. Everything she owned, she stole, cheated, or had sex to get. Now, she wasn't a straight out whore, but there were times she felt she had no choice but to spread her legs. During winter nights, a motel room was way better than outside.

"Come on, let's get you diva-fied so we can hit the malls." Essence looked around. "Where's Shaquan?"

"In his room coloring."

"Well we gonna hook him up tonight too. Wait 'til I show you how I do my thing. I be coming outta stores with winter coats and more shit."

Essence began to comb out Sinnamon's hair.

"You're not scared to steal?" Sinnamon asked. Just the thought of it made Sinnamon's stomach flutter.

"I used to be, but after a while, I over came my fears because I had no choice. I either had to steal or go without and I wasn't trying to do without. I steal for food and shelter. If it wasn't for this hustle, I'd be somewhere stripping or turning tricks for a living, and I'm too good for that."

Sinnamon knew exactly how Essence felt. She always knew if she was more confident with herself, she would've been sliding down a stripper poll at the age of 14 if she was able to get over on the Manager about her age. After about a two and a half hour make over, it was seven o'clock and Sinnamon looked like a totally new person. One look in the mirror, and Sinnamon was in tears again. Never in a

23

million years would she have pictured herself looking like she was. She literally looked as if she just stepped off the cover of a magazine.

"Look how big ya butt is," Essence was looking at Sinnamon's perfectly round backside.

"I know you ain't talking, you're thicker than me." Sinnamon replied.

"Yeah, but my ass don't stick out that far. You're gonna need some sort of male repellent for that thing. You're gonna turn some heads!"

After putting the last touches to Sinnamon's new look, the girls grabbed Shaquan, Essence's buzzer bags and got into the freshly detailed Acura and pulled off. Essence turned the radio up blasting 'Baddest Bitch' by Trina.

The trip to the mall was an experience the two of them would never forget. Sinnamon received so much attention, that she was overwhelmed and scared. She didn't know how to respond to the sudden change.

"Girl you better holla at one of these fine niggas." Essence told her.

"Yeah right, I wouldn't even know what to say, besides that, I don't even have a phone." Sinnamon really didn't want to interact with the men who were trying to get with her.

"Suit yourself, scaredy pants, I'ma get mine". Essence teased.

The girls hit the Concord and Christiana mall, stealing over a thousand dollars worth of Express, Gap, Kids Gap, Wet Seal, and Children's Place clothes. The two of them would take turns in the store stealing. One would steal, while the other would fuss with Shaquan as he ran wild and pretended to cry. They had a ball and no one working in the stores seemed to suspect anything.

"Come on, let's go in Macy's." Sinnamon began to walk in the direction of the big department store. She loved boosting already.

"Yeah, and guess where ya'll be if you try ya luck in there." Essence said.

It Gets Dirtier

"Where?" Sinnamon asked cluelessly. She didn't know how tight the security was in the store.

"Turnkey! They don't play in there. That's why I stick it to the small stores. We'll make money off them all day."

The mall was starting to close and it was time they made their way home. Sinnamon was floating on cloud 9, thinking of her new found friend, new look and new moneymaking scheme. For once she felt she finally had a life and things were looking good for her. Essence was the breath of fresh air she needed. The way she felt things couldn't get any better.

Chapter 4

Over the next few days, Sinnamon and Essence continued to hang tight, forming a bond that people normally took years to form. Sinnamon convinced Essence to move in with her, and at night they would just sit up and talk until daybreak. Then, in the evening, they would hit up the malls and continued their stealing spree. To her own surprise, Sinnamon was a natural.

During the course of their 5-day suspension, they worked on some schoolwork and Sinnamon's confidence. With the new clothes, a manicure, pedicure and hairdo, Sinnamon was at the top of her game and for the first time she felt she looked good.

"I can't wait to go back to school tomorrow. I feel so good about myself, thanks to you." Sinnamon told Essence as they laid on Sinnamon's bed talking.

"Them bitches gonna be sick when we walk in there tomorrow. I can't wait to see ya girl Janeen's face. She not gonna believe how you came up."

"Nobody is, but truthfully, I don't really care. I'm just happy, feeling good inside."

"I bet you like the attention though," Essence teased.

"Actually, I don't. Men are so freaking perverted." She thought back to Sam.

"Men are so freaking perverted." Essence mocked Sinnamon's proper voice and nudged her. "You talk all white and shit."

"No, I don't talk white. It's called proper English. Just because I'm from the projects, doesn't mean I have to sound like it."

"You trying to say I talk ghetto?" Essence asked defensively.

"You can at times."

"Fuck you." Essence acted as if she was offended.

"Don't get mad." Sinnamon tossed a pillow at Essence.

"I guess I talk like that because of the people I hang around." Essence explained.

"Yeah, that can happen."

"So what are you wearing tomorrow?" Essence asked.

"I think I'm going to wear these low rise skinny jeans from Abercrombie with this cream ruffle shirt from Express."

"And what shoes?"

"I have to get used to wearing those darn heels, so I might wear those brown flats."

"Don't wear them with that shirt; you better throw on those leopard print peek toe pumps. You'll look real cute in that."

"Your right, but they hurt my feet."

"Sometimes it hurts to look good."

"So when's the next time we can go shoe shopping?"

"We can only go once or twice a month. We go too much, Tammy's going to get indicted." Essence laughed thinking about Tammy and their scheme.

Tammy was a woman that Essence did business with. Being that Tammy was the manager at Aldo's, Essence would give her free clothes and in exchange Tammy would allow Essence to get 5 pair of shoes for the price of one.

"We should see if we can hook up with another shoe connect." Sinnamon suggested.

27

"That would be nice, but people like that are hard to come by."

"Maybe we'll run into someone."

"If not, we're still alright. We make a nice piece of change off the clothes anyway. We both got at least three hundred and some change."

Essence added up the money in her head.

"It feels so good to have money in my pocket." Sinnamon smiled to herself.

"I know that's right." The two of them continued to talk as they did every night until eventually they fell asleep.

The next day at school went exactly as Essence predicted. All eyes were on them as they sashayed their way through the halls together. A few of their peers even mistook Sinnamon as a new student. Her teachers were even amazed by the improvements.

"Well Sinnamon, don't we look nice today." Sinnamon's English teacher commented.

"Thank you." Sinnamon replied with a smile. She was really feeling herself today. With all the compliments and stares she received, it was hard for her not to get a big head. She knew she was the shit. At lunch, Sinnamon and Essence found an empty table and sat down and in a matter of minutes, it was filled by young men eager to get a chance with one of the two beauties.

"What's up ma? Can I holla at chu for a minute." A young man asked, making Sinnamon blush.

"Boy, if you don't beat it. I know you see us talking." Essence snapped.

"Damn, what chu her bodyguard?" The boy retorted.

"No, I'm her sister and you ain't wanna talk to her last week, so don't now."

"Whatever." The boy walked away feeling defeated.

"Niggas in here are so fucking lame." Essence huffed.

"I know, all they want is sex. That's why I'm not trying to talk to anyone. I'm not going to have sex until I'm married." Sinnamon said.

"You're crazy. You saying that shit now cuz the opportunity hadn't presented itself yet. In time, you'll see. Nigga's are going to be coming at you left and right. Wait till you hear of the sick shit they say." Essence spoke as they ate.

"I can imagine." Sinnamon already had a taste of some of it at the mall.

"You see that bitch Janeen yet?" Essence smiled suddenly.

"No, did you?"

"Did I!" Essence eyes lit up with excitement. "You messed that poor girl's face up bad. Her eye is still swollen and black. She should be in here now, right?"

"I think this is her lunch period. She was here when we fought." Sinnamon looked around the cafeteria.

"Let's go find her so she can take a good look at the champion." Essence put her fist in the air in a fighting stance.

"You're crazy; I'm not going out my way to see that girl. I don't need any more problems with her or her friends." Sinnamon didn't want to ruin her day.

"The way you whipped her ass, I can guarantee you, she won't be steppin' to you any time soon." Essence laughed.

"I did give it to her huh?" Sinnamon threw a playful combination.

"Come on, I know she's around here." Essence looked around.

The two girls got up and began to walk through the lunchroom.

The students were studying their every move as they walked by gracefully with Essence leading the way.

"There she goes right there." Sinnamon whispered to Essence.

She felt butterflies in her stomach, because she really didn't want to fight again.

"Hi Janeen," Essence taunted her with a wave. "Don't you look nice today. I see that eye of yours is really healing well." Essence smirked when she and Sinnamon walked past.

"Hi Janeen" Sinnamon managed to get out, before busting out laughing.

It Gets Dirtier

Janeen was furious to see Sinnamon looking way better than she was and then to top it off, she rubbed it in her face with her teasing laughs. Janeen finally got the chance to see how it felt to be the butt of a joke and she didn't like it.

"You'll get yours." Janeen mumbled. She put her head down and walked past.

"Well you already got yours." Essence laughed.

The next couple of months were about the same with the two girls. They tore the malls up for clothes and aced everything in school. Things couldn't have been better, until they got a snag in their plans. They began to get careless with their stealing and returning clothes, and began to get red-flagged. The pressure was on. Every store they normally hit was on to their scheme.

"Damn, what the fuck are we going to do Sinn?" Essence asked frustrated after leaving the Granite Run Mall in PA. "That's the third mall today. Everywhere we go, these people be breathin' down our necks."

"I know, but we should have seen it coming. I mean look how much we stole from them. I'm just glad we haven't been arrested." Sinnamon looked at the brighter side of things.

"You right, but things are going to be tight without that money. I don't know about you, but I like cash." Essence complained.

"Yeah, but money isn't everything Essence. Look, we have a place to live and food in the refrigerator. We'll be alright, stop buggin'." Sinnamon was content with the changes in her life. She had a new look, her house was finally furnished and Shaquan was happy with the toys he had.

"What are we going to do about clothes and money?" Essence asked.

"We have winter clothes, a lot at that. As far as the money, I couldn't tell you because I haven't the slightest idea. But with your hustle and bustle mind frame, I'm sure you'll figure something out. I'm alright personally. I'm use to not having money."

"Fuck that, we too good looking to be use to not having shit.

It Gets Dirtier

Women like us are supposed to be on somebody's damn magazine cover or some rich person's wife. We don't have to struggle, don't you understand that?" Essence exclaimed.

Sinnamon didn't like when women took that attitude on things. She always felt in her heart that women could go out and get their own if they put the work in and tried. She felt too many women her age give up too fast on their dreams in order to satisfy a man.

"Essence, you don't make any sense. As women, we can get the same things men have, so why do you feel we need them for something. And why the hell do you think we need to be eye candy for some horny men to get money. You have to think past that. We're young and getting educated and we have things going on for ourselves. You helped me to realize that, so why don't you see it?" Sinnamon didn't understand Essence's logic.

"I feel you Sinnamon, but the point is we'll never get good jobs right now. You know that, cuz if it was possible you'll be working and you know it. The only things we can do is use our looks and do hustles to get money."

Sinnamon got quiet, thinking about what her friend just said. It was true that she herself had tried to get plenty of jobs and fell short. It just seemed that with her availability and lack of experience, she always got turned down. It's sad to say, but it's like that for most inner-city youths. They try to get jobs to escape poverty, but get turned down because of their age or because they're not "qualified enough".

"So what do you suggest?" Sinnamon asked.

"I have an idea, but I'm not sure if you'll like it." Essence was thinking about the plan she came up with as she drove down I-95.

"What is it?" Sinnamon knew it could mean nothing but trouble.

"Well...," Essence hesitated "I say since we're right there in the projects, we could let the hustlers that we know cook and bag up crack at our house."

31

"Are you out of your mind Essence? I don't even know any ofthose guys like that." Sinnamon said frantically.

"Well they know you and it's not like they would try to do somethin' to us. There's no need to flip." Essence tried to calm Sinnamon down.

"I'm not worried about them doing something to us, it isn't legal and if the police come in our house, me and my brother will go into some foster home or something." Sinnamon's heart raced just thinking about being separated from Shaquan.

"It's not like we'll have to do it long. And if somethin' did go down, all we have to do is run if we got sent to a foster home. Remember I would be going right with you." Essence reminded Sinnamon that she was in the same position.

"What about my brother?"

"We'll find a way to get him too, but right now, I'm pretty sure he's gettin use to dress'n nice, going on field trips, and bein' able to have money on him." Essence was trying to win her argument. She really felt what Sinnamon was saying, but her instinct to survive kicked in and common sense went out the door. Survival was all Essence knew her whole life, and money was her key to survive.

"Sinnamon look, I worked too hard and fought too long to get where I'm at now, and I'm not tryin to lose my place. I'm young, smart, and sexy and I'm going places. I'm not tryin to give up my youth just yet. So trust me on this one, we can do that until we get things right with ourselves. It shouldn't take long." Essence really meant what she said.

Sinnamon thought on things for a moment. She knew allowing drug dealers into her home was a bad idea, but she also knew the money would be good and easy to make. So going against her own good judgment, she began to feel Essence's idea. The monster, known as greed, got the best of her.

"I'm with it Es, but only for a little while. We need to work on another plan." Sinnamon said.

"We'll work on somethin." Essence grinned. She was happy that Sinnamon agreed to go along with her plan. "But for now, I have the perfect nigga in mind to be our first customer."

"Who?"

"The boy Esco from Concord Ave. I heard he's doing it big"

Chapter 5

"Esco, this is my girl Sinnamon, Sinnamon, this is the guy Esco I was telling you about." Essence brought Esco into the small apartment. He was carrying a book bag full of cocaine.

"I know who she is. I've seen her around." Esco talked with a smooth tone. He took Sinnamon's hand and shook it lightly, while staring her in the eyes.

"Nice to meet you." Sinnamon spoke shyly. She felt uncomfortable because of the look Esco gave her. Sinnamon knew of Esco from him being around the projects from time to time. She found him attractive but would never approach him. She figured he was way out of her league.

Esco was a slim, brown skinned man, about 6 years older than Sinnamon. He stood at 5'10" and wore his hair in styled braids that Sinnamon found to be a turn on. The days Sinnamon saw Esco with his hair not done, she wanted to ask him if she could braid it, but never got the courage. Esco was a known lady's man. He had smooth dialogue and was respected in the streets. Women all throughout the city wanted a shot with him. They knew his money was long and any woman that he dealt with stayed in the latest designs. Although Esco was a known baller, he kept things simple and humbled himself. Instead of riding around in a Benz or something else spectacular that he had the money to buy, he drove around in squatters, and rental cars. Esco disciplined himself a long time ago to never drive a car for more than a month until he was out of the game.

"Well now that the formalities are out of the way, I'd like to get to business." Essence broke Esco and Sinnamon out of their trance.

"Okay, so how ya'll want to do this?" Esco walked into the small kitchen, looked around and put his book bag on the counter. He expected the kitchen to look bad and have roaches running everywhere, but Sinnamon and Essence kept the maintenance up in the house to perfection. Not only was the kitchen clean, but everything matched as well.

"It's basically how I told you over the phone. You and your peoples can come over here, cook your coke, bag up or whatever...."

"Sit down with me a minute." Esco interrupted. He pulled out seats for the two ladies at the kitchen table.

"First off, no one will be comin' in here but me. Too many niggas runnin in and out will draw too much attention. Second, did you tell anyone else about this?" Esco looked directly at Essence.

"I only told you so far." Essence answered.

"Well good, you won't be tellin' anyone else either." Esco spoke strongly. "I'm only doin' this for ya'll cuz I feel ya'll must be hard up for cash to be willin' to let niggas ya'll don't even know like that in here with drugs and whatever else they choose to bring in here. You young girls don't think shit through, that's cool though. Ya'll just need some proper guidance."

Sinnamon and Essence were both embarrassed by Esco's remarks. Sinnamon gave Essence an "I told you so" look, and then put her head down as Esco went on. "This drug game ain't nothin' to play around with. You have to move with caution no matter how small a part you play in it. One false move and it can be the end. Most the niggas I grew up with either lost their life or their freedom behind this shit. My boy Gage just got fifty-six years not too long ago because somebody planted a bunch of shit in his house. That could've been ya'll if ya'll fucked with the wrong niggas."

Esco was sincere with his words. He knew if someone else was there and the police raided the apartment, the average nigga would let the girls take the charges. That's how the game goes. It's every man for himself when it comes down to it. That's why Esco rolled alone most of the time. He had a few guys he was cool with from his hood, but outside of that he only chilled with women. Between grinding and spending time in the studio rapping, his free time was limited. The other reason Esco decided to help Sinnamon and Essence out was due to his attraction to Sinnamon. She wasn't of age at the moment, but he knew in due time, if she was guided right, she would make the perfect wife.

"This is what I'm willing to do for ya'll". Esco pulled out 2 knots of money. "This is off G.P. to hold ya'll over for the time being. Don't go crazy with it." He handed the girls the money. Which turned out to be two thousand a piece. "Every month, I will pay all ya'll bills and take ya'll grocery shopping and from time to time, I'll take ya'll up New York so ya'll can throw that shit on. Plus, I'll give ya'll fifteen hundred pocket change and teach ya'll a little bit about this game. The only thing I need from ya'll is to not tell anyone about our arrangement and ya'll have to do good in school. Agreed?"

"Agreed." The girls answered in unison.

"And don't have no niggas in here. Now follow me in the kitchen. I'ma teach ya'll how to cook up coke.

* * * * *

"So what do you think about Esco? I saw you staring at him all gogglily eyed and shit." Essence teased Sinnamon. They were in Sinnamon's room watching the show 'Girlfriends' on UPN.

"I was not looking at him like that." Sinnamon said innocently.

"Whatever bitch," Essence rolled her eyes. "You ain't gotta lie to me. That nigga fine and you know it. I get the chance, I'ma fuck the shit out of him."

36

"Girl you are so nasty. You don't even know him like that but that's your stuff."

"I know and I'm alright with that. I'm not just some whore that fucks everything with a dick, but a bitch has needs." Essence was on the defense.

"I'm glad I'm not like that." Sinnamon mumbled.

"So what, you're the last virgin in Wilmington; that don't make you no better than me." Essence felt like Sinnamon was trying to down her and she hated being viewed as a whore. "Why haven't you had sex yet anyway?" Essence asked after a long pause.

"Never really had the desire, or the opportunity. I never even went out on a date." Sinnamon let out a soft sigh. She always wanted to let loose deep inside, but didn't have the heart.

"Hell, we're about to change that. I know some niggas that'll take us out anytime I ask." Essence quickly rushed towards the phone and began to dial numbers.

"No, wait! Don't do that." Sinnamon begged. She leaped off the bed and began to tussle with Essence over the phone. "I'm not playing Essence."

"Can I speak to Dez," Essence was showing all her teeth, she was smiling so hard. She went into a corner of the room and guarded herself and the phone from Sinnamon.

"I can't fucking stand you." Sinnamon fumed. Essence couldn't help but laugh. She found it so funny when Sinnamon cursed.

"Remember my girl you and E said ya'll saw me with?" Essence paused and waited for a response. "Well what's good this weekend? We tryin' to go out."

Sinnamon continued to give Essence the evil eye as she set up the date. She was scared to go on the date, because it would be a new experience for her, although deep down inside she was excited. Sinnamon sat on the bed with her arms folded, thinking about the date until Essence got off the phone.

It Gets Dirtier

"Why did you do that Essence?" Sinnamon whined. She flung the pillow at Essence's head. "You know I'm shy."

"I know, but you can't be forever. You're young and it's time you start having fun and stop acting like somebody's damn grandma. Besides, somebody's gotta clean those coochie cobwebs out eventually and it won't get done if you don't mingle."

"Whatever." Sinnamon rolled her eyes with a smile. "So where are we going?"

"You'll see this weekend." Essence answered with a mischievous grin on her face.

Chapter 6

"Where are ya'll goin', getting' all sharp?" Esco questioned the girls from the kitchen. Ever since they made their deal a few days prior, he's been at their house almost every day, and was playing the big brother roll to a T.

"Look at you all nosey." Sinnamon joked. She got a kick out of having a man showing some concern about her well being. Having Esco around filled a void in Sinnamon's life that's been empty since she could remember.

"I ain't playin'. I know ya'll going out with some niggas. I wanna know where ya'll goin in case somethin' happens." Esco said seriously. He had genuine concern for the girls. Also, he was a tad bit jealous to know Sinnamon was going out on a date. He didn't want anyone to ruin what he knew was a good girl.

"Well if you must know." Essence appeared from out of the bathroom. "A couple of my friends are takin' us out to dinner and a movie."

"I hear that. Pass me that tray of ice that's in the freezer." Esco asked Essence when she walked into the kitchen. He was almost done cooking up a key of raw cocaine and needed the ice to harden it up.

It Gets Dirtier

"That shit stinks." Essence frowned up her face. She opened the freezer and grabbed the ice.

"No it don't, it smells like money." Esco grinned as he watched his mixture harden and turn white.

"How do I look?" Sinnamon stood in the entrance of the kitchen. She was wearing her hair down. She had on a tight blue and black corset top, a black fitted blazer jacket, and a pair of dark blue skinny jeans. The jeans hugged the curves of her backside immaculately. She topped it off with a pair of black knee high boots, and silver accessories.

Esco stared and sucked in her beauty momentarily. Everything about Sinnamon spelled perfection and for a moment, he was going to try his hand, but had to remember she wasn't 18 yet. When he thought about her only being 17, it messed his head up because of her maturity. None of the women his age or older was on her level, both physically and mentally.

"You look nice." Esco finally spoke.

"Nice." Essence frowned. "My girl looks like a star nigga."

Sinnamon blushed. It was still fairly new to her to get compliments. "Well I'm ready if you are."

"Well come on, they should be around there by now. We were supposed to meet them 10 minutes ago." Essence looked at her watch.

She and Sinnamon grabbed their coats and headed for the door.

"Why ya'll gotta walk to meet them niggas somewhere?" Esco questioned.

"Because we don't have a car and you said you didn't want us bringin' nobody to the house, duh." Essence laughed and she and Sinnamon walked out the door.

"Smart ass." Esco yelled through the door.

The girls were set to meet Essence's friends at the KFC on Governor Prince, which was about a five-minute walk from where they lived. On the way they received the normal catcalls from the local hustlers that stood on every other corner. Essence had on a short brown leather jacket that didn't cover her backside and with her runway walk, any straight man would have stared. She wore a pair of light blue jeans that looked painted on. She had on a mock neck caramel cashmere sweater with brown and gold accessories. And topped it off with a pair of brown stilettos.

"Bout time." Dez said when Essence and Sinnamon approached. Dez and Essence embraced briefly and then shared a soft kiss. Dez was a tall dark-skinned man with long corn rolls. He was leaned up against his '96 Black Cadillac Deville that sat nicely on 22" rims. He was dressed in a black snorkel coat, dark blue jeans, and a black Chucker - low cut Tims. He wore his jacket open, displaying a 32" white gold Jesus piece chain that glistened from the store's lights. Hanging from his lips was a lit blunt. He looked like the poster boy for 'Thugs R Us.'

"Where's E?" Essence looked around for Dez's friend.

"His fat ass went in the store to grab something to eat."

"Damn, ain't we about to go to dinner?" Essence asked.

Hearing the word fat, Sinnamon frowned her face up and gave Essence a dirty look. A million thoughts floated around her head. She wanted her first date to be with someone at least halfway attractive.

"Let me go see what's taking this nigga so long." Dez walked towards the entrance of the store.

"Why do I have to get the fat one Essence?" Sinnamon snapped as soon as Dez entered the store.

"Calm down girl. E is not some big fat nasty looking dude. You know I wouldn't do you like that. He's cute, see look." Essence pointed to Dez and E as they came out of the store.

E was carrying a large soda and sipped from the straw as he approached Sinnamon. Sinnamon quickly took inventory of her date. E was a big man but far from fat and out of shape as she pictured. He had a light brown complexion and stood at about 6'2", and weighed in at a solid 235. He was referred to as fat because he had a potbelly.

41

It Gets Dirtier

E was wearing a navy blue and white Yankees fitted cap and a blue and white button up shirt. He wore a dark blue pair of Rocawear jeans, which laid nicely on his brand new 6" butter Timberland boots. His jewelry consisted of a 32" styled link chain with an iced out cross pendant that hung just below his belly button. He also sported an iced-out Jacob watch that had a blue leather band. He gave off a serious "I got money Aura" about himself.

"How you doing Miss?" E smiled after taking a sip from his Sprite. "You look even better up close." E's eyes explored Sinnamon from head to toe, then from toe to head.

"I'm doing well." Sinnamon blushed like a schoolgirl as E continued to compliment her.

"Ya'll can talk in the car, I'm ready to go. It's cold out here."

Essence rubbed her hands together and made her way to the passenger seat of the Cadillac. The rest of them followed suit and got in the car. Dez took the wheel and they pulled off.

"So where are we eatin' and what movie are we goin' to see?" Essence questioned minutes later. She glanced in the rear view mirror to check on Sinnamon. Whatever E was saying put a big smile on her face, so she knew her girl was pleased.

"Well, we was thinkin' about orderin from Apple Bee's take out and shooting to our spot. We just copped a new apartment by the Wilton. We moved to Stonebridge and Apple Bee's is right there. We got the big screen with surround sound and the official bootlegs off of the computer. Ya'll gonna think ya'll in the movie theater." Dez boasted.

"You with that Sin?" Essence turned around to face Sinnamon.

"It doesn't matter." Sinnamon answered. It didn't matter where they went to her. Only 15 minutes went by and she was already feeling E. She was hoping to get to know him better. He was being the perfect gentleman.

"That's all it is then." Dez said. He was already driving on 13 headed towards the apartment.

It Gets Dirtier
* * * * *

"Wow, this apartment is nice." Sinnamon exclaimed when she entered. She and Essence looked around and was surprised to see that two young men could have such a decorative place. The walls of the living room were filled with beautiful black art that matched perfectly with the chocolate leather furniture. Their coffee table held an array of magazines from Black Mens to Smooth to XXL. Their two end tables had stylish lamps and each had a mahogany framed picture of their mothers.

Sizing up the TV, the girls guessed it to be a 63". It was a hi-definition TV by Sony. The surround sound speakers were strategically placed throughout the front room unnoticed. On one side of the TV shelf, it held well over 250 DVD's, while the other side held a nice sized stereo and a Play Station 2 game system and games.

"I'm impressed." Essence admitted.

"So where do you want me to take the food." Sinnamon questioned. She didn't want to sit it just anywhere because everything was so organized.

"Let me have it." E took the bags to the kitchen. The girls made themselves at home in the front room, as E and Dez fixed everyone's plates.

"The foods' ready." Dez told the girls, as he and E brought them their plates.

They all sat down and enjoyed their meals, along with a nice conversation. The setting was perfect. Dez and E already had the night planned. They had soft music playing in the background as they ate. Sinnamon was loving the dating thing.

"Ya'll smoke or drink?" Dez questioned after the meal.

"I haven't smoked a blunt or had a drink in like a month." Essence thought about the last time she had a drink or smoked.

"Well, I don't." Sinnamon spoke up. Drugs and alcohol weren't her thing.

"Roll somethin' up." E blurted out. "I don't mean no disrespect to ya'll, but I'ma enjoy my smoke."

Dez walked into the kitchen and returned a second later with a vanilla Dutch, a jar of weed, a bottle of Remy VSOP, and a bottle of Moet.

"Grab some glasses from the cabinet for me." Dez told Essence. He put everything on the table, then began to crack the Dutch open. Essence returned with the glasses and sat one in front of Sinnamon. She then popped the top of the Moet bottle and poured herself and Sinnamon a drink.

"Who is this glass for?" Sinnamon looked at Essence as if she was crazy.

"For you."

"I told you I do not drink."

"Girl, if you don't relax, its only Champaign. It's not gonna get you drunk." Essence was putting pressure on her friend without even realizing it. She just wanted Sinnamon to enjoy herself.

Sinnamon looked at the bubbling liquid for a moment. Deep down inside, she didn't want to drink it, but at the same time, she didn't want to spoil the night. She looked at Dez and E, laughing and joking as they threw back shots of their Remy and passed their blunt around.

"It's not gonna hurt you baby girl." E assured her.

"Just relax and enjoy yourself." Essence took a shot of the Remy, followed by a sip of Moet.

Sinnamon picked up the glass and put it to her lips. She took a sip and to her surprise, it wasn't that bad. She giggled as the bubbles tickled her nose.

"I told you it wasn't that bad." Essence said as she took the blunt from Dez. She took a drag and coughed lightly. "This shit hits hard." Essence tried to get herself together.

"That's that Betty." Dez laughed. Although Essence was hip to the streets, she didn't know what Betty was. Betty is liquid PCP.

Users mix it with spearmint leaves or weed, while others dip their cigarettes in the liquid; they're called dippers. The effects of Betty are so strong some people get highs that they never come down from.

Essence passed the blunt to Sinnamon. Normally Sinnamon wouldn't have anything to do with drugs, but seeing the drink she had wasn't that bad, she felt the blunt wouldn't be either. She looked at it, then took a deep drag from the blunt.

"Hold that shit in." Dez watched Sinnamon inhale the smoke. The smoke filled Sinnamon's pure lungs and almost immediately, she began to feel the effects of the drugs. She took another drag that caused her to cough. The smoke rushed from her nose and mouth as her body jerked. Her eyes began to tear up as she tried to catch her breath.

"This is too much for me." Sinnamon passed the blunt back to Essence. High from the blunt, Sinnamon and Essence began to feel a little loose. Sinnamon found herself throwing back straight shots of Remy and smoking like she was a pro. Everyone was having a good time, laughing at Martin's stand up show, 'Runtellthat'.

"Oh my God guys!" Sinnamon suddenly jumped up from the sofa.

"We have to catch the red rabbit!" The PCP from the blunt had Sinnamon hallucinating. She turned towards Essence and the guys. They all looked at one another and thought Sinnamon was playing and broke out in laughter. Sinnamon stood there confused. She didn't find anything funny.

"What are you guys waiting for? We can get a million, maybe even billions if we catch the red rabbit!" She crotched down and waved an imaginary carrot.

"Here rabbit, rabbit, rabbit," she cooed, and suddenly, she made a run for it. Sinnamon began to run and dive around the apartment, trying to catch the red rabbit.

Essence, Dez and E sat there in disbelief. Neither of them had ever seen anyone bug out like that. Essence looked at the blunt she had in her hand and quickly put it out. "Get her Dez!" Essence screamed.

"That's ya girl. I ain't gettin up. I'm stuck." Dez laid back in his seat and looked towards E. "E, you wanna fuck her. You better go get ya pussy before she hurt herself."

E gave Dez a "Fuck You" look and went after Sinnamon. He was high as well, and pissed that Dez mixed their haze with Betty. He would've never given Sinnamon something like that. He began to feel bad.

"What the fuck did ya'll do to me and my girl? I can't feel my legs."

Essence smacked Dez in the back of the head.

"I told you we was smoking Betty." Dez said defensively.

"And what the fuck is Betty, Dez?" Essence sat on the sofa with her arms folded.

"Wet, love boat, PCP, whatever you want to call it." Dez began to say the other names for Betty, hoping that maybe she would catch on.

"Pop!" Was the sound of Essence's fist landing square on Dez's jaw.

"Nigga, are you fucking crazy? I don't smoke no shit like that." She continued to swing wildly at Dez. She was regaining all her senses now, and she felt stupid. A long time ago her sister told her not to smoke weed with just anybody, and to watch carefully when another person rolled the blunt. She should've known what she was smoking.

"Calm down girl. It ain't that deep." Dez exclaimed through laughter. He didn't think the matter was that serious until he saw the tears coming down Essence's eyes.

"It is that deep. You got my girl buggin' and shit." Another effect of PCP was that it played off of someone's emotions. If you're real mad, you're likely to act violent and if you are down you may cry.

46

"Baby.... baby, I'm sorry." Dez tried to restrain and comfort Essence at the same time. He held her in a tight bear hug, then lifted her over his shoulder and took her to his room. At the same time, E was trying to get Sinnamon to come out of the bathroom. She was sitting next to the toilet after throwing up seconds earlier. The convulsions from throwing up had Sinnamon sweating like a basketball player.

"Come on baby girl, you need to lay down." E said in a soothing tone.

"No! Leave me alone. You didn't want to help me find the rabbit. Now I'm going to be poor forever." Sinnamon began to cry.

Seeing that Sinnamon wasn't budging, E decided to grab a fan so she could get some air. He didn't want Sinnamon to pass out from the heat. For some reason, PCP made people sweat tremendously. E plugged the fan up and placed it in the entrance of the bathroom. He turned it on medium and made sure it blew directly on Sinnamon. She immediately felt a sense of relief. E left, so Sinnamon could have a minute to herself and walked back to the living room to talk to Dez. He wanted to let Dez know that he was wrong for giving the girls PCP. Normally, he wouldn't care, but he saw the innocence in Sinnamon every time he looked in her light brown eyes. There was something special about her.

When E made it to the living room, he saw that it was empty. He figured Dez took Essence into his room and went in that direction. He was about to bang on Dez's door, but heard Essence's soft sexual cries.

"That nigga ain't shit." E mumbled to himself then went into the kitchen and poured Sinnamon a glass of milk. He heard someone say that milk can bring your Betty high down. When he made it to the bathroom, Sinnamon was sitting directly in front of the fan, in all her glory. E didn't know if he wanted to look or turn his head. The gentleman in him made him turn away, but the young man in him had him taking peeks. He couldn't help but get a hard on. Sinnamon was butterball naked with her legs cocked open. Small chill bumps covered her perfect body. The cool air also made her small nickel sized nipples erect and they stood out like little erasers. Taking a peek in between her legs, E admired how perfectly shaved Sinnamon's womanhood was. Every strand of hair was gone.

"You're gonna fuck me aren't you?" Sinnamon looked up at E with those innocent eyes that he found so special. He wanted to say hell yeah, but he was better than that.

"Nah baby girl, I would never take advantage of you. You ain't in your right mind right now. Drink this milk; it'll help you feel better." E gave Sinnamon the milk and she quickly drank it. All the throwing up and sweating had her feeling dehydrated. The milk made her feel better, but she was still out of it.

"Come lay down." E said gently. He had his back towards her so he wasn't staring.

"I can't get up, can you carry me?" Sinnamon spoke with the softest voice.

"This shit is crazy." E mumbled. He scooped Sinnamon in his arms and cradled her to his chest. She rested her head on his shoulder. As he walked her to his room, she began to softly kiss his neck. Her touch sent chills down his spine.

"My pussy feels funny. It's making my thighs all wet." Sinnamon said in a bedroom voice.

When E reached his room, he laid Sinnamon's naked body on his queen-sized bed. He wanted badly to join her, but decided against it. He went into one of his drawers and grabbed a big tee shirt for Sinnamon. As he helped Sinnamon put the shirt on, she grabbed his hand.

"You see how wet my pussy is. Doesn't it feel funny?" Sinnamon purred. She rubbed E's hand in her softness. He enjoyed the feeling briefly, then stopped himself. "Don't you want to have sex with me?" Sinnamon looked at E puzzled when he snatched his hand away.

It Gets Dirtier

"Baby girl, you just don't understand how bad I do, but right now ain't a good time. You still feeling it and shit. We'll talk about it in the morning. You need some rest." E tucked Sinnamon in his bed, kissed her on the forehead and left the room. "Damn," E huffed when he shut the door behind him. "A nigga gonna get blue balls in the morning." He made his way to the living room and crashed on the sofa for the night.

Chapter 7

Sinnamon was awakened by the smell of turkey sausage and eggs. She sat up in the large bed, stretched and let out a soft yawn. She looked around and took in her surroundings. It was evident that she wasn't home. She began to recount the night and was wondering how she ended up with just a tee shirt on and nothing else. Being slightly hung over, she began to feel nauseated. She got out of the bed and searched the room for her clothes. She saw them nicely folded on E's large dresser. She didn't recall taking off her clothes and was slightly embarrassed when she saw her panties and bra folded on top of her clothes.

"Thank God Essence gave me those new panties and bras." Sinnamon was relieved that she didn't have on her normal grandma style bloomers that were old and worn out. She now understood why Essence always stressed to be sure they wear nice underwear. Sinnamon could hear Essence now. "You never know what will happen."

"I know that's right." Sinnamon mumbled as she struggled to put her jeans on.

"Wake up baby girl." E said loudly as he was carrying a tray of food into the room. He was expecting Sinnamon to be in the bed asleep.

He was trying to do the breakfast in bed thing. "Oh shit, my bad." E quickly backtracked out the door. Once again, he caught Sinnamon with her ass out. "Just let me know when you are dressed."

Sinnamon covered her breast with her arms. Her Cinnamon colored face turned red from embarrassment. She wasn't comfortable with anyone seeing her body. After getting dressed, Sinnamon took a seat on E's bed.

"You can come in." She called out to E.

"I apologize for barging in on you. I made you breakfast." E entered the room and handed Sinnamon the tray of food, then took a seat next to her. "How you feeling?"

"My stomach feels a little crazy and I have a headache, but I'm cool. This food looks good." Sinnamon looked down at the tray. She wanted to eat, but wasn't sure if she would be able to hold it down. She looked at E and wondered if he took advantage of her or not.

"Where's Essence?" Sinnamon asked after swallowing a mouth full of food.

"In there with Dez. They're still asleep." E answered. He found himself staring at Sinnamon as she ate.

"Why are you staring at me like that?"

"I don't know." Sinnamon caught E off guard. "You're just so beautiful." Sinnamon placed her fork down and sat her tray of food on the bed. She turned to E.

"So beautiful that you had to get me drunk and high to have sex with me;" Sinnamon snapped. She made the conclusion that E had sex with her. Her anger turned into tears. "I was a virgin."

"Hold on now baby girl." E put his hands up as if he was surrendering. "I didn't touch you. You was trippin' off that shit we was smokin', threw up and stripped naked. I ain't have nothin' to do with that. All I did was try to help. I put a tee shirt on you and put you in the bed. I slept in the livin' room." E tried his best to talk smoothly. He didn't want to come at Sinnamon in any way that would make her feel disrespected.

Sinnamon stared blankly at E not knowing if she should believe him or not. The previous night was a blur to her. All she knew was that she woke up in a man's bed, basically naked. "Where's Essence?"

Sinnamon felt the need to question her friend.

"I told you her and Dez are still in his room sleep." E answered calmly. Sinnamon jumped from the bed and darted out the room. She found Dez's bedroom and opened the door without knocking. She stopped in her tracks when she saw Essence on the bed on all fours, and Dez behind her, pounding away. E was right behind Sinnamon. In a sexual trance, Dez and Essence didn't notice their spectators. Essence gripped a pillow for dear life and buried her face in it.

"Damn, this shit feels good." Essence muffled voice could be heard through the pillow.

"Give that pussy to daddy." Dez panted. He knew he was performing well.

"Essence, I need to speak with you for a minute." Sinnamon put her game face on. She had her arms folded across her chest and was staring directly at Essence. Essence hesitated momentarily. She didn't want to get up because she was almost at her climax, and was pissed by the interruption. But by the look on Sinnamon's face, she knew she had to go talk to her.

"Well, can ya'll shut the door so I can get dressed?" Essence gave them a 'hurry the fuck up' look.

Sinnamon and E left the room. Sinnamon made her way to the living room with E trailing closely behind. He still felt the need to explain himself. He didn't want Sinnamon to look at him as some type of rapist.

"Sinnamon, I swear to God, I didn't touch you. I would never take advantage of you like that." He thought about telling her how she was coming on to him, but felt that would only add insult to injury. "Look me in my eyes when I talk and you'll see that I'm telling the truth."

It Gets Dirtier

Sinnamon looked E in the eyes. Deep down, she felt he wouldn't do her like that but after last night, she wasn't so sure. She needed to speak to Essence for insurance. She also wanted to know why her girl left her on her own in the condition she was in. Before Sinnamon could respond to E, Essence walked in.

"What's up Sin?" Essence was now dressed in her jeans and one of Dez's tee shirts. E left the room so the two of them could be alone.

"So what's up?" Essence asked again. She sat next to Sinnamon.

"Did E have sex with me last night?" Sinnamon's voice was soft like a child's.

Essence wasn't really sure herself. The only thing she could say was that when she went to use the bathroom, E was sleep on the couch and she didn't hear them. "I don't think so. I saw him on the couch last night. Were you that smashed that you don't remember?"

"You saw how I was Essence." Sinnamon spoke in an even tone. She was pissed. "You know I never smoked or drank before. Why would you leave me by myself like that? You're supposed to be my girl."

Essence began to feel guilty and didn't even know how to respond to Sinnamon. All she could do was stare blankly at her seeing the hurt and disappointment in her face.

"Say something." Sinnamon spoke loudly.

"I'm sorry Sinnamon. I am ya girl. I don't know what I was thinkin last night. I don't know what to say." Essence said honestly.

The girls talked the situation over briefly and came to the conclusion that Sinnamon still had her virginity. They made a pact, never to abandon one another again in any type of situation. Anything could have happened. They sealed their pact with a hug.

"You ready to go home?" Sinnamon asked.

"Yeah, let me tell Dez we're ready." Essence left to go get Dez.

When Essence left, E walked in. He was determined to get things right between himself and Sinnamon. He really wanted a second date and more.

53

"Can I talk to you for a minute?" E asked.

"For what?" Sinnamon spoke with little patience. She was still upset that E got her high. She didn't even consider that it was Essence, and not him that pushed the drugs and alcohol on her. It didn't matter to him if she smoked or not.

"Sinnamon, I just want to make sure things are clear about last night. I didn't and would never take advantage of you. I'm sorry that I even allowed you to smoke after you said you didn't." He paused a moment and looked deeply in Sinnamon's eyes. His eyes alone said how much he wanted her and Sinnamon could see it. "I know you don't know me too well and last night wasn't such a good night, but I wanted to know if you'd let me take you out again. This time, to a nice spot without all the extra shit."

"I don't know about that." Sinnamon broke the eye contact.

"Well, let's at least exchange numbers. You can't say we weren't vibin' on our way out here."

Sinnamon smiled slightly. "I guess we can do that." She had to admit to herself that she was feeling E's conversation in the car.

"E, ya boy act like he ain't tryin' to get up right now. Can you drop us off?"

"Yeah, I got ya'll." E said smoothly, and then grabbed his keys and they hit the door.

Once outside, Sinnamon and Essence walked to the Caddy, while E went in the opposite direction. "Where ya'll goin? My car's over here." E clicked the alarm to his new Infinity Q-45. It was cream, had a light tint and was sitting on 22" rims. He didn't have it a full two weeks yet, so the t-tags were still on.

"Damn, I see you ballin'." Essence said as she got in the car. "I try."

Essence and Sinnamon arrived in their neighborhood a little after 10 a.m. When they walked to their block, they we're surprised to see Esco's car was out front. He never parked directly in front of the house. When they walked in, they spotted Esco laid out on the couch, and Shaquan was in front of the TV playing play station.

"Get up boy." Essence shook Esco's leg to bother him. Esco turned over half asleep and looked at the girls through his blood shot, half shut eyes. He flipped open his cell to check the time and to see if he had any missed calls. He was up to the wee hours of the night waiting for the girls to call him. He was hot.

"Where the fuck was ya'll at all night? Ya'll couldn't call and let me know what was goin' on. I been up all night waitin' for ya'll little ass's to call." Esco snapped. He was fully awake now.

Essence looked at him as if he lost his mind. She didn't have anyone telling her what to do in a long time and couldn't figure out why Esco thought he could. She was a grown woman in her eyes and didn't have to answer to no one.

"You got it fucked up nigga. You gave us a couple dollars to use the crib, but you ain't runnin' shit. You ain't my father, my dude, we ain't even fuckin. So why you trippin'?" Essence wasn't trying to hear his shit.

"I don't give a fuck about that shit you sayin'. Ain't neither of ya'll grown and like I said before, ya'll need guidance. I ain't sayin' ya'll can't do ya'll, but it would've been common courtesy to call me and let me know ya'll was cool. I do actually care. I view ya'll as my sisters. Then to top it off, ya neighbor came by this mornin' to drop Shaquan off. It's a good thing I was here, but ya'll ain't think about that." Esco had the tone of a father. A million thoughts were going through his head. He really did care about the girl's well being, but even more, he wanted to know what Sinnamon was doing all night and with who?

Sinnamon and Essence sat quietly. They knew Esco was right, especially Sinnamon. She never slipped when it came to Shaquan because she practically raised him. This was the first time they didn't sleep in the same house.

It Gets Dirtier

"Your right, we should've called." Sinnamon was smiling because she could tell Esco really cared.

"And we would've been home last night, but we don't have a car and the niggas we were with was drinking." Essence was trying to make any excuse she could.

"I would've came and got ya'll, but ya'll don't have to worry about that no more." Esco dug in his pocket and pulled out a set of keys.

"Ya'll can have the Buick." He was referring to the Blue '95 Buick Road master that was parked out front. "Not too many people saw me in it, so it's straight. The insurance is good and it runs like new." He tossed the keys to Sinnamon.

"Are you serious?" Sinnamon asked in disbelief. She looked at the keys that were in her hand.

"Yeah, and when I get up, we're goin' to the mall so ya'll can get cell phones. I need to make sure I can keep in contact with ya'll, and ya'll will be able to call me whenever you need me." He was talking to the both of them, but was staring at Sinnamon.

Essence snatched the keys from Sinnamon. "Come on girl, let's go for a ride!" She was out the door before Sinnamon could respond.

"Thank you Esco." Sinnamon said with a smile. She reached out to him and gave him a big hug. Esco held on a little longer than she did. She felt good in his arms.

"Come on Shaquan." Sinnamon grabbed Shaquan's arm and they made their way to the car.

Chapter 8

By the time the summer hit and school was over, Sinnamon changed to a totally different person. She still maintained a 3.5 G.P.A., and loved school, but she changed as a woman. With the help of her new friends E, Essence and Esco, Sinnamon was fashion on two feet. She dressed everyday as if she was going out and knew she looked good. Her newfound confidence did a lot for her.

After their first date, Sinnamon and E hooked back up and E won her over. He spoiled her with frequent shopping sprees, dates to expensive restaurants, trips on the weekend and more. She was in heaven. Sinnamon was so wrapped up in E, that she began to neglect Shaquan and didn't spend as much time with Essence. Essence was happy that Sinnamon was happy, but still felt a little envious. Sinnamon had two men that were doing well in the drug trade, competing over her and didn't even notice it. Anything E did for Sinnamon, Esco out did him. Esco wanted Sinnamon to know she didn't need E for anything. He took care of her, Shaquan and Essence. Only problem was Sinnamon overlooked all Esco did because she viewed him as a brother. Essence knew what was going on though, and E was beginning to catch on too.

"So what are your men doing for you this weekend for your birthday?" Essence asked Sinnamon.

It Gets Dirtier

They were in Sinnamon's room the Wednesday before Sinnamon's birthday weekend. She was turning 18, but you would've thought she was going to be at least 21.

"I only have one man." Sinnamon rolled her eyes at Essence. She was tired of hearing Essence say Esco was feeling her.

"When are you going to open your eyes girl? That man is in love with you. I don't see how you don't see it."

"Esco is like my brother girl. He does things for you too."

"Yeah, but not half of the things he does for you. I'm just ridin' off your coat tail." Essence explained.

Sinnamon stared at Essence blankly, and then broke out in laughter. "Girl, you are so crazy. That man doesn't want me. He has so many women chasing him and like I said, he calls me his little sister. Besides, I'm too young for him anyway." Sinnamon tried to reason.

When Esco first started to come around, she had a crush on him, but never would admit it. And for a moment, she felt he had a thing for her too until he started acting like her father.

"You are a trip!" Essence threw her hand in the air. "He's what, two years older than E. I've been around niggas like them since I was like 14 and can't think of one nigga like them that didn't have a young girl. Besides that, you'll be 18 soon and niggas are draftin' us young girls early. They like'em fresh out of high school. So stop being in denial."

Sinnamon thought a moment, and then began to reflect on some things. Esco did look at her like he wanted her from time to time. Not only that, but E was beginning to complain about Esco's strong presence as well. He hated Esco being at Sinnamon's house so much and he wasn't even allowed over there. He asked Sinnamon several times to move in with him. He even moved out of the apartment that he and Dez shared and bought a 3-bedroom town-house for him and Sinnamon. He was sprung.

"Well even if Esco did want me, I couldn't be with him. I love E."

It Gets Dirtier

Sinnamon looked at Essence, then to the ground. Deep down she felt something about Esco. She just wasn't sure what it was.

"What I don't understand for the life of me, is how you got both of these grown ass men going, and didn't give neither one of them any pussy. I thought I was the pimptress, I guess I need to take notes from you. You sure you ain't fucked them niggas." Essence joked. She was trying to change the mood now because she could tell Sinnamon was really beginning to think about what they were talking about. Sinnamon gave a half smile and put her head back down. Things were beginning to become clear and she knew she needed to do something before it got out of hand. She would hate for something crazy to happen between E and Esco.

"You ok."

"Yeah, I'm cool. I'm just thinking about what I want to do for my birthday." Sinnamon lied.

"Well make sure you free Saturday night, because I already made plans for us and we're going to have a ball. Wait 'til you see what I picked out for us to wear. We gonna be sharp." Essence booked Pharaoh's nightclub for a surprise party, thanks to Esco. The best thing about it was that Esco managed to link up with Oskino, and he agreed to perform. Esco, Bucko and Murder was set to open up for him.

"Where we going?" Sinnamon was excited. Essence always had tricks up her sleeves. There was never a dull moment with her.

"You'll see." Essence smiled.

* * * * *

"Put this blind fold on." E pulled Sinnamon to him and tied a bandanna around her eyes. It was Friday, June 1st...Sinnamon's birthday and E had a surprise for her.

"Why do I have to go through all this?" Sinnamon sucked her teeth and snatched the bandanna off. She really wasn't in the birthday mood. Her mind was on other things. For one, her mother didn't show up at the house as she normally did, and she never missed Sinnamon's or Shaquan's birthdays. Then to top it off, it was the first of the month and the check was in the mail. Sinnamon felt something must've been wrong.

Sinnamon was also having problems with Esco and Essence. They were beginning to get tired of Sinnamon leaving Shaquan with them so she could run around with E. Esco was even more pissed when one of his boys told him that E had Sinnamon in the car with him while he was making drug transactions. Esco felt that wasn't a place for a woman, especially Sinnamon.

"Come on now girl. I'm tryin' to do something special for you. Stop buggin' and put the blind fold on." E insisted. He could tell something was bothering Sinnamon and knew his surprise would cheer her up.

Sinnamon let out a loud sigh. "Okay, come on." She took the bandanna and reluctantly put it on. Once the bandanna was secure around Sinnamon's eyes, E took her by the hand and guided her outside.

"You ready?" E asked.

"Yep.".

"Surprise Baby!" E took the bandanna off and Sinnamon couldn't believe her eyes. She sat in silence for a minute, staring blankly. She couldn't believe that in front of her eyes was a pearl pink, CLS 500 Mercedes with a big bow and tag that had her name on it.

"Oh my God! Oh my God!" Sinnamon finally responded. She turned to E, who was dangling the keys to the car from his hand. Sinnamon rushed him and embraced him with a hug that knocked him to the ground. "Thank You! Thank You! Thank You! I love you soooo much."

Sinnamon planted kisses all over E's face as they laid in E's front lawn.

"You're welcome baby girl. I told you you're not going to have to worry about anything while you are with me. I got you. Now, let me up and go take your car for a spin." E sat up and handed Sinnamon the keys. Sinnamon didn't hesitate; she snatched the keys and jumped in the car falling in love with it immediately. It was equipped with a TV/Navigation system in the dash and TV's in the headrest. The seats were customized in cream colored leather with pink stitching. The driver's seat had Sinnamon's name engraved in it. The 22" floater rims with the pink background made it the hottest car in Wilmington. Sinnamon pulled off, headed towards her house.

"Essence, where are you?" Sinnamon called Essence from her cell phone.

"Home, why you sound so happy?" Essence replied.

"You dressed?"

"Yeah."

"Well, be out front, I'm about to come get you." Sinnamon hung up before Essence could say anything else.

Essence walked into the bathroom to touch herself up. She figured Sinnamon had some shopping money and wanted to hit the malls. She didn't mind that at all because Esco had just paid them for the month and she was itching to spend her money. "Esco can you watch Shaquan?" She yelled from the bathroom. He was in the living room playing Playstation with Shaquan.

"Don't I always got him?" Esco answered smartly.

"Don't get mad at me." She said defensively.

"My bad homie. Just tell Sinnamon she need to be in a little early tonight cuz I need to talk to her and I'm not babysitting. I got a few things I need to take care of.

"Okay." Essence walked out the front door. When she stepped out, she admired the pink Benz as it slowly turned the corner and floated up the block. "That shit is official." Essence said to herself. She wondered who was driving and tried to make out the driver. When the car stopped in front of her, she got a clear view and ran to the passenger side when she saw it was Sinnamon.

"No that nigga didn't buy you this car!" Essence was just as excited as Sinnamon. They were really riding in style now. "You gotta give that nigga some pussy now." Essence said as she got into the car

"I might." Sinnamon pulled off with huge smile. "I might not."

"Girl, you are somethin' else. If my nigga would've bought me some shit like this, he would've got fucked in this bitch." Essence was admiring the inside of the Benz.

"I bet he would have." Sinnamon laughed.

"So where are we going?"

"The mall."

* * * * *

"So what did you want to talk to me about?" Sinnamon asked Esco. She and Essence had just returned from their trip to the mall. Before Esco responded, he thought about what he wanted to say. He had to make sure he chose his words carefully, so Sinnamon wouldn't get mad at him. He had a lot on his chest and he needed to get it out.

"Sinnamon, when I first came around here, it was because I wanted to make sure you and Essence had some type of guidance. Ya'll are both some beautiful young women and I know niggas be comin' at ya'll left and right, and I don't want you to be steered in the wrong direction."

"What are you trying to say?" Sinnamon didn't know what Esco was getting at.

"That nigga E ain't right for you." Esco said bluntly. He decided that beating around the bush wasn't going to cut it. But his statement caught Sinnamon off guard. She loved E and she knew he loved her too. So she didn't know what possessed Esco to tell her that E wasn't right for her. She narrowed her light browns at Esco. The fierceness in her eyes cut through his soul.

"Where do you get off telling me my man isn't right for me. You're not my father Esco, you're not even my brother so you're going to stop acting as if you run me. I see why E doesn't like me around you. What you like me or something?"

It Gets Dirtier

"Sinnamon, you can't even see it can you?" Esco walked close up to Sinnamon. "The love I have for you runs way deeper than homeboy. You need to stop and think about ya relationship and I ain't hatin', cuz that's not my style. I'ma boss nigga, but I want to open ya eyes to some shit.… When the last time that nigga offered to take you and ya brother out?" Esco struck a nerve with that one. "Sinnamon, since you started messin' with that nigga, you stop spendin' time with Shaquan. Essence and me always got him. Ms. Jones don't even like takin him no more cuz you never pick him up when you supposed to. He's your responsibility."

Sinnamon put her head down as Esco spoke.

"I applaud the nigga for keepin' you fresh and happy, but it's more to it than that Sinnamon. If he wants you in his life, he needs to accept Shaquan too. And that nigga needs to stop takin' you with him when he makes his drug runs.

"Who told you that?" Sinnamon was shocked Esco knew because she didn't tell anyone about that, not even Essence.

"It don't even matter Sinnamon. You just make sure nobody else tells me no more shit like that, because next time I hear it, I'ma say somethin' to him when I see him." Esco was breathing down her throat now. He lifted her face by the chin and forced her to look in his eyes. A tear rolled down her face and he wiped it away with is thumb.

"And yes, I do like you." Esco kissed her passionately and held her in his arms.

Sinnamon didn't know what to do. She wanted to pull away, but felt something in the kiss that she couldn't let go of. This kiss was a lot different from the one's she shared with E. This one had a lot of power with it. Esco released Sinnamon from his grip. They stared at one another for a moment. Although they were silent, there was so much said through their eyes. Esco gave Sinnamon one last kiss on the forehead and walked out the door.

Once she was alone, Sinnamon took a seat on the couch and began to sob. She was young and confused. She knew she was in love

63

with E, but wasn't sure how she felt about Esco. She was sure she felt something, she just didn't know what it was.

Chapter 9

Sinnamon looked at herself in the mirror one last time. It was Saturday night, and she and Essence were getting dressed to go out. Sinnamon didn't know the party was for her, but she knew it was supposed to be live and she had to look good. Tonight Sinnamon decided to let the skin show. It was hot and she wanted to make it hotter with the outfit she chose. She had on a black Valentino mini pencil dress that complemented her curvaceous hips and backside. She sealed the deal with a pair of red Christian Loubuotin peek toe stilettos. Wearing her hair down, and her Gucci shades, Sinnamon looked like a celebrity. She sat in the mirror a moment longer to apply her favorite Mac lip-gloss, giving her full lips a nice shine. Once she was satisfied, she grabbed her red Marc Jacob clutch and went into the living room where Essence was waiting.

"Bout time." Essence jumped up from the couch. She had been waiting for Sinnamon for about 45 minutes.

"You know I had to make sure I looked right." Sinnamon turned around so Essence could see her.

"You look good, but if E see you, he's gonna kill you."

"I'm not worried about him right now."

"If you say so." Essence took a couple steps back. "How do I look?"

"Fly, but not as fly as me." Sinnamon teased. "Sike, you look good girl. We are going to have the girls at the club hating for real." Essence wore a cream and red Miss Sixty's silk baby doll dress, with a pair of cream Jimmy Choo straps with four inch heels. Even though the dress was not tight it still exposed Essence firmed legs and natural curves. "I ain't done yet, I just grabbed a pair of Channel glasses last night." She grabbed the glasses from her handbag and put them on.

"What you think?"

"I think we look like runway models!" Sinnamon slapped hands with Essence. With that, they hit the door and jumped in the Benz. The girls arrived at the club in a quick ten minutes. Based on the parking availability, the party was packed already and it wasn't even quite ten o'clock yet. Sinnamon found a parking spot and she and Essence gave themselves a look over one last time. They got out of the car and made their way into Pharaohs. Before pulling up, Essence called Esco and gave him the cue so the plan was in motion. Entering the building, the girls saw that the security was tight and the music wasn't playing as loud as Sinnamon thought it would be.

"What's up with the music?" She asked a bouncer, as he let her in. He just shrugged his shoulders and Essence couldn't help but to laugh.

"What are you laughing at?" Sinnamon asked.

"Nothing, just come on." Essence wanted to hurry up and get the surprise over before she ruined it.

"Surprise!" Everyone yelled at once when Sinnamon and Essence walked into the club. Sinnamon almost jumped out of her skin. She was so scared that she placed her hand over her chest and inhaled deeply. She had to regain her composure.

"Why didn't you tell me?" Sinnamon smacked Essence's shoulder. She had a big smile on her face.

"Esco made me promise that I wouldn't say anything." Essence told her. Sinnamon got butterflies in her stomach at the mention of Esco's name. She had been avoiding him since their kiss.

"He's not here is he?"

"Why you say it like that? He threw the party, so of course he's here. He's supposed to perform." Essence was unaware of Esco and Sinnamon's kiss.

"Shit....," Sinnamon mumbled. She knew she would have to face him now. Esco had been calling her all day to give her a birthday gift. She just didn't answer the phone. The kiss they shared really spooked her out.

"What happened between ya'll?" Essence questioned.

"I don't even want to talk about it, it's a long story. I'm ready to leave." Sinnamon turned to leave and ran smack into Esco's arms.

"You look nice, beautiful." Esco looked Sinnamon up and down.

"I've been trying to give you this all day." Esco pulled a medium size gift bag from behind his back. "I hope you like it." He passed the bag to Sinnamon. "If you get the chance, I'd like to talk to you later on, but right now I'm 'bout to take the stage to open the show." Esco planted a soft kiss on Sinnamon's forehead and walked away.

"What's in the bag?" Essence asked, being nosey.

"I didn't open it yet." Sinnamon said sarcastically.

"Well, open it." Essence shot back.

"Come on, let's leave."

"You must be crazy. This party is about to be jumpin'. Stop bugging'. Whatever got ya panties in a bunch forget about if for the moment. It's your party girl. Enjoy yourself," Essence encouraged. "And open that gift so I can see."

"Okay, okay!" Sinnamon pulled out a large velvet box. When she opened it, what looked like the twinkling of the stars was staring back at her.

"Daaaaaaamn!" Essence exclaimed.

"These are beautiful." Sinnamon had to admit. She didn't want to accept them, but diamonds are a girl's best friend, and she was staring at well over ten karats of Ice. Esco bought Sinnamon a three piece set. There was an Iced out watch from Jacob, a necklace with a diamond heart pendant, and a pair of diamond earrings to match.

"Well, don't just stare at it, put that shit on. As a matter of fact, let me help you." Essence grabbed the box and removed the jewels. In no time, Sinnamon was officially iced out. "Trina's not the diamond princess no more." Essence said loudly. She was ready to party now.

"Go, Go, Go, Go, Go shorty." The DJ was mixing up Fifty Cent's in the club. "Where the birthday girl? At the count of three, everybody say Happy Birthday Sinnamon." The DJ said into the Mic. "1,2,3" "Happy Birthday Sinnamon!" Everyone in the club screamed.

"Go shorty, it's ya birthday. We gonna party like it's ya birthday." Fifty rapped. After "In the Club" went off, Esco took the stage. He was dressed in a white tee that was airbrushed. The background had a brick design, with the words, "Concord Ave" written in the bricks in graffiti; courtesy of Abdul Kareem. On the back of the shirt was the words RIP Magic. That was Esco's cousin. He also had on a pair of Authur Maurice jeans and all white shell tops Adidas. He kept it basic, with the exception of the jewelry. He had on a 36" iced out style link chain with a huge medallion, similar to Nas's Queen's Bridge chain. The only difference was that Esco's chain had the word Backstreet on it. He also had on an iced out watch and pinky ring. You could see the ice sparkle from the stage lights.

When Esco got the mic in his hand, the DJ put on a beat from a recording that Esco did with Overtime Records. The beat was jumping and the crowd was familiar with the lyrics because everyone was bumping the mix tape in their cars. Everyone crowded the stage as Esco began to rap.

"I ain't even gotta lie...you see the truth in me...I can get a gun if I...don't beat you brutally." Esco was in his zone. After Esco's solo joint, his boys, Bucko, Murder and Smooth took the stage with him. They were killing the stage and the crowd was feeling them.

"I see ya peoples doing they thing." E crept up on Sinnamon and wrapped his arms around her then kissed her neck.

"Hey baby." Sinnamon said. She wasn't really paying E any attention because she was so into the show.

"Damn, you ain't happy to see a nigga?" E stopped, and got a closer look at Sinnamon. Being high and drunk, he didn't register everything he saw until then and his temper began to boil. "What the fuck I tell you about wearin' skimpy shit like that?" E spat. He grabbed Sinnamon by the arm and pulled her to the side. "And, where the fuck you get that jewelry from?"

Sinnamon dropped her head to the ground. She didn't want to argue with E at the moment. She was enjoying her party and didn't want to ruin it. To top it off, Esco was there and would quickly check E if he heard him yelling at her the way he was.

"Answer me!"

"Esco gave it to me for my birthday."

"Well give it back."

"Why?"

"Why? What the fuck you mean why? You don't need no nigga but me buyin' you shit. I'm 'bout sick of that nigga. He gonna make me put somethin' hot in him in a minute." E began to let the alcohol talk for him.

"He's my brother, E." Sinnamon whined.

"I ain't tryin' to hear that shit. You heard what I said." E was interrupted when the music was cut off and Esco began to speak.

"I don't be doing shit like this." Esco started. "But I got one more gift for my home girl Sinnamon. Marzet, you ready?" Esco called out to another one of Wilmington's unknown talents. Marzet was a tall brown skinned man that had a voice and style similar to Jaheem. When Marzet took the stage, Esco passed him the mic. "I'm ready." Marzet told the DJ.

It Gets Dirtier

"See this shit I'm talkin' bout." E was boiling. The DJ put on the instrumental version of Usher's Lovers and Friends. Marzet began to replace Usher's vocals. Sinnamon could feel herself getting dizzy and had to find a seat. Her nerves were getting the best of her and she didn't know what to do. She knew something was going to go down when she saw the anger in E's eyes.

"This nigga must think I'm some type of sucker." E spoke out loud. He was embarrassed and felt he had to do something now. Esco forced his hand. It was bad enough he received a threatening phone call from Esco earlier that day. Esco called him and told him that he better not ever make a sale in Sinnamon's presence again. E was willing to let that go because no one else knew about it, but this was straight up disrespect. To make matters worse, Esco was the one who invited E to the party.

"You know what Sinnamon, I ain't even gonna flip and mess ya party up. By tomorrow morning though, ya shit better be packed and at my house. You ain't stayin' nowhere near that nigga again." E was in Sinnamon's face and she could smell the Remy Martin on his breath. "Do you understand me?" He said forcefully.

"Yes."

Chapter 10

"How you goin' to let that nigga play you like that couzin?" Dez asked E. Dez, E and Dez's cousin Spoon were riding in E's Q-45 on their way to E's house. Spoon was a down south cat from ATL. He was in Wilmington because he was on the run for attempted murder and robbery. His M-O was home evasions and he was an expert at what he did. He wasn't that big of a man, only standing at 5'7" and weighing in at 155 pounds soaking wet. He maintained a low profile and didn't speak much. His skin was real dark and almost matched the all black clothing he wore every day. He kept a black fitted cap over his baldhead and kept it pulled down over his eyes.

"Yeah man, I thought you was all way trill with ya shit nigga."
Spoon spoke with a southern accent. E stopped the car abruptly, causing himself and his passengers to jerk in their seats.

"What the fuck was I supposed to do, pop the nigga in front everybody? Tell me that nigga. I ain't no bitch, so don't get it fucked up Spoon. You don't even know me nigga. I just ain't no dumb nigga, and I ain't goin' to jail for no bullshit." E fumed.

"Who the fuck you talkin' to bruh! You should've been poppin' that shit to that nigga that was hollerin' at ya shorty in front of everybody. You bitch ass nigga." E's words didn't sit too well with Spoon. He thought about pulling out his titanium 38 that was tucked on his waistline and killing E right there in the car.

"Chill ya'll." Dez interrupted. He saw the argument going in the wrong direction.

"Fuck you mean chill. This nigga talkin' like he want it to pop off. We can get it crackin'. I'm real trill with mine." Spoon fumed.

"It ain't even that deep ya'll. We all cool in here. That nigga Esco is the problem. We need to handle that nigga instead of beefin' with each other." Dez tried to reason with E and Spoon. He knew Spoon was a real live wire and didn't want him to get set off. E was Dez's boy but he was going to have to ride with his cousin if things got hectic. Spoon took a deep breath to calm himself down.

"My bad cuzin. I'm wit ridin' on that nigga." Spoon was itching for some type of action.

"Well then, that's what it is. We gonna catch that nigga tonight." Dez said.

* * * * *

"So what do you think gonna happen after that stunt Esco pulled?" Essence asked Sinnamon. The party was over and they were on their way home.

"I don't know. I just hope Esco doesn't do anything to my baby. He's cool and everything, but he's really beginning to spook me out." Sinnamon paused for a moment. "I'm moving with E tonight." She turned to Essence when she made her last comment.

"I can understand that. That might help the situation. Does E know Shaquan gonna move with ya'll?" Essence asked.

"He will, and he has no choice really."

* * * * *

"We gonna hit the studio tomorrow. We need to put some shit together." Esco was talking to the boy Marzet that serenaded Sinnamon at the party. He was dropping him off at home. Marzet stayed right around the corner from Sinnamon.

"What time?" Marzet asked.

It Gets Dirtier

"I'ma pick you up at 11 am sharp. Make sure you up nigga." Esco slapped hands with Marzet as he got out of the car.

"I'ma be up. Good lookin' out for puttin' me on. I've been tryin' to get out there a while now." Marzet was smiling from ear to ear. Tonight was his first time singing in front of a large crowd and he knew with Esco's help, he could do a lot more because Esco was plugged in.

As Marzet shut the door, shots were fired and Esco's back window shattered. Marzet and Esco weren't sure where the shots were coming from. Esco slipped low in his seat, then grabbed his baby 9MM from under his seat and cocked it back. Marzet ducked low and moved to the front of Esco's car. He pulled a snub nose .357 from his waistband and prayed silently. He wasn't one that got into many altercations, and the only reason he had a gun on him was because he went out to a club and knew the niggas in Wilmington didn't know how to act at times. At almost every party, a fight breaks out that leads to bloodshed.

Esco peered in the rear view mirror to see where the gunfire was coming from. Shots were still being fired at his car, so he saw the fire from the guns that were aimed to kill him. He knew it was at least two shooters and assumed it was E. Esco quickly slid from out the car and ran to the front of it where Marzet was.

"What type of shit you got me in?" Marzet asked Esco. Marzet clutched his gun in his hand.

Esco ignored Marzet's question and stood up to return fire. After firing three rounds at his intended targets, he crotched back down.

"You got a gun nigga, is you gonna bust it or not?" Esco looked at Marzet like he was crazy. "Come on nigga."

Marzet and Esco both began to return fire. All the gunfire made the small block sound like a mini war zone. You could hear shells drop everywhere as the gun battle went on. Nearby cars were filled with bullet holes.

It Gets Dirtier

"It ain't over nigga." E yelled as he limped back to his car. In the mist of the shooting, he was struck in the calf. He didn't feel it until he tried to run. "I'ma kill you nigga." He yelled over his shoulders.

"Damn." Esco was hot that he didn't have an extra clip. He wanted to light E's ass up real good. "You aiight nigga?" Esco asked Marzet.

"I'm cool."

"I'ma kill that nigga, word I am." Esco said more to himself than to Marzet.

"We still going to the studio tomorrow?"

"Yeah man." Esco had to smile at that.

* * * * *

I should've been moved. There's too much going on around here. Sinnamon heard gunfire in the distance. She was in her room packing her stuff to move to E's. Essence was in the other room packing Shaquan's things. Sinnamon was serious about moving. She knew if she didn't the gunfire she just heard could be at her doorstep soon. Little did she know, it already was.

"Well, I'm all done." Essence appeared at the entrance of Sinnamon's room.

"Can you start taking the bags to my car? I'll be done in there in a minute." Sinnamon was stuffing the last of her things in a suitcase. After Sinnamon felt she grabbed everything she needed, she looked around her room to make sure she didn't miss anything. When she was satisfied she had everything, she began to load her car up. Within a half hour, everything was in Sinnamon's car and she was set to move.

"You sure you're ready to do this?" Essence asked. She and Sinnamon were in front of Sinnamon's car.

"I'll miss the house but I really have no choice. There's just too much going on right now and I don't want to be the cause of any more drama." Sinnamon said half-heartedly.

"Well don't act funny now that we ain't roomies anymore."

Essence gave Sinnamon a hug. "I'ma miss you too baby." Essence kneeled down and kissed Shaquan on the forehead. After saying goodbye, Sinnamon drove off. It was almost 4 a.m. in the morning and she was leaving what she called home for the first time. She began to wonder if everything would work out. After Sinnamon pulled off, Essence went in the house and sat on the couch. She was sad that her roommate was gone. She had grown attached to her over the time they lived together and she was really hoping Sinnamon didn't stop talking to her as much now.

"Where Sinnamon?" Esco scared Essence when he came into the house.

"She just left, why?"

"Where she go?"

"After that stunt you pulled, she said she's movin' with E. She don't want any trouble to start between you and him."

"Shit!" Esco spoke out of frustration. He sat on the couch next to Essence and removed his 9MM from his waist, and sat it on the coffee table.

"Well, it's too late to stop the trouble. That nigga just shot my car up while I was in it. You ain't hear the shots? That shit happened right around the corner." Esco put on a pair of gloves and removed a box of bullets from underneath the couch. He popped the clip out of his gun and began to reload it.

"What you 'bout to do?" Essence asked. She was watching every move Esco made. She felt like she was part of a movie and loved every minute of it. She wanted to ask Esco for a gun so she could ride with him.

She didn't like E anyway.

"I'ma put somethin' hot in that nigga." Esco cocked the gun back.

* * * * *

"Baby you home?" Sinnamon called out as she entered E's house. He gave her a set of keys when he first got it. Sinnamon began to look around the house. "Baby, where are you?" She questioned again. She figured he was there because his car was parked out front.

"Naw shorty. E at the hospital." Spoon appeared from out of nowhere. Sinnamon jumped and dropped her bags. She quickly pulled the pepper spray that she carried out of her pocketbook. "Chill shorty, I'm Dez's cuzin. They sent me out here to get the guns E had in here. Him and ya other dude shot it out earlier." Spoon chuckled and walked up on Sinnamon. "That pussy must be real good shorty." Spoon said in a rough whisper. Spoon presence didn't sit well with Sinnamon. He made her feel uncomfortable and she wanted him to leave, but needed to know what happened.

"What hospital is he at and why didn't he call me? Is he okay?"

"He at Wilmington Hospital." Spoon brushed past her. "You can ask that nigga why he didn't call you when you get there." He slammed the front door shut when he walked out.

Chapter 11

"Watch how I kill 'em now, Watch how I kill 'em" Esco was banging one of his new tracks, as he cruised Wilmington in a black Delta '88. He was dressed in a pair of black sweats, black tee shirt and a pair of baseball gloves. On his lap was a large .45 ACP handgun. In the back seat he had an AK-47. He was ready for war. It was a week after his shootout with E and he finally got the tip he was looking for. E was set to re-up in the next hour with a nigga name Cozy, who Esco grew up with. E was looking to grab 10 bricks of uncut cocaine in a secluded area. Cozy was cool with the set up because Esco was his people's and he was set to gain $180 thousand, and keep his coke. Esco didn't want anything but revenge. Esco reached Cozy in no time. They talked over their plan until it was time to meet E. He was going to be by himself when they met, so everything was perfect. Cozy offered Esco some of the coke but he turned it down. Esco had enough coke to make the entire Wilmington area look like winter, and had enough money to last two life times. People just didn't know he was holding so heavy. They knew he had money, but would never guess that most of the coke in Wilmington came from him. Even what Cozy was selling E, came from his latest shipment. Esco truly played the game like a chessboard, he was the king and like a smart player, he used every piece on the board to protect himself.

It Gets Dirtier

With the plan in motion, Cozy and Esco shook hands and went their separate ways. "I got my hammer in case shit don't go right." Cozy assured Esco.

"I'm cool, I got some big shit in the back seat if things get messy, but it won't...that nigga ain't built like that." Esco told Cozy, before they moved out.

Once at the buy spot, Esco parked his car and waited for the perfect time to strike. Just as planned, E pulled up in his Q-45 by himself.

"This nigga dumb as shit. He don't even switch cars when it's time to re-up. And nigga's wonder why they get indicted and shit." Esco thought to himself as he watched E's moves. He had his .45 clutched in his hand. The deal was sealed in less than five minutes. E jumped in his car and threw a large duffle bag in his back seat. He pulled off, satisfied with his purchase. He'd come a long way over the years. He thought back to when he was just a corner nigga, copping 8 balls for $90. He chuckled at the memory. His smile quickly faded when he saw Esco pointing a gun at him.

Esco pulled in front of E's car and jumped out so fast that E's only reaction was to slam on the breaks. That was a bad move! He had a better shot running into Esco's car. Esco was glad to see the fear in E's eyes. He wished he had a camera because the look on E's face was definitely a Kodak moment. He fired seven shots into E's windshield. The bullets sent E flying back in his seat. Esco quickly grabbed the duffle back out of E's car and threw it into his. He watched as the car drifted onto the side of the road. The job was done. Esco pulled off, laughing as he went to drop the coke off to Cozy, who was parked around the corner. Everything went as planned. So he thought.

* * * * *

"Can you explain why you had a loaded handgun and was wearing body armor?" A Wilmington Detective asked E as he lay in a hospital bed. He was banged up from the bullets, but was still

78

breathing. He was only hit in the shoulder, his vest caught all the other shots. The impact broke three of his ribs and cracked his sternum. E stared at the detective blankly. He was high from the medication, but knew not to speak to the detective. He was already cuffed to the bed, so it didn't matter what he had to say anyway, in his opinion. He had more than enough bail money, so he knew he wasn't going to see the inside of a prison cell. He was going to make bail and roll to Cali where his family lived.

"Where my lawyer?" E asked.

"He can't help you, only I can. You're facing some serious charges here and someone is trying to kill you. If you just tell me who the gunman is, you'll come out a lot better." The detective tried to sound sincere. He didn't care about E or his situation. He was looking for his next bust. "So who shot you?" He asked again.

"Roger Rabbit." E cracked up laughing. That frustrated the detective, causing him to turn red. He hated when victims didn't cooperate. Tucking his notepad in his pocket, he stormed out, almost knocking Sinnamon down when he walked out the room. As he was walking out, she was walking in. They stared at each other briefly.

"Tell your boyfriend to give me a call when he gets some sense." The detective said smartly to Sinnamon. She just rolled her eyes and made her way over to E.

"How are you feeling baby?" Sinnamon kissed E on the lips lightly. She was scared to touch him because he looked as if he was in a lot of pain. E was pleased to see Sinnamon at his bedside. Every time she walked into a room, she brightened up his day. He was truly in love with her, but wasn't sure if she was worth all the trouble. This was the second time he was shot over her. He began to feel it was her fault that he was laid up in the hospital, but it wasn't. Esco didn't shoot him because of Sinnamon, he shot him because E shot at him first.

"What happened baby?" Sinnamon asked.

E looked around to make sure they were the only ones in the room. Once he saw they were alone, he told her. "Ya little boyfriend shot me up earlier. I think my connect set me up."

Sinnamon wanted to lash out at E for his comment, but bit her tongue. She was getting tired of taking the blame for E's and Esco's beef. She never wanted any of it to happen.

"That's not my boyfriend E, so you can please stop saying that."

"Whatever Sinnamon, if you'd moved with me when I first told you, all this bullshit wouldn't be goin on. I told you a while back, that the nigga was diggin' you." He wanted to make Sinnamon feel guilty.

"Do you want me to leave?" Sinnamon had tears building up in her eyes. She felt like everything was her fault.

Looking into her light browns E melted. "I'm sorry baby." E reached out to Sinnamon.

She embraced him and began to cry, "I'm sorry baby. I should've listened."

"It's okay baby. I need you to do something for me."

"What's that?"

"Go downtown and post my bail. You have to pick up my mom up so she can sign the paperwork."

"Okay."

* * * * *

"Have you seen Esco?" Sinnamon asked Essence over the phone. She had just dropped E's mother back home after posting an 80 thousand dollar bail.

"Not since yesterday. Why? What's up?" Essence asked. She didn't hear about the second shoot out yet.

"He tried to kill my baby for no reason Essence, no reason." Sinnamon tried to keep herself from crying.

"Where you at?"

"On my way over there." Sinnamon was referring to her old spot, where Essence's now stayed.

"Well hurry up. I have to talk to you. We can't be talkin' over the phone about stuff like this. I'll see you when you get here." Essence hung up. She was kind of mad that Sinnamon would think that Esco tried to kill E for nothing.

Sinnamon pulled up five minutes later. When she entered the house, she embraced Essence with a warm hug because she needed the comfort. Her life was spinning out of control.

"Why is all this stuff happening?" Sinnamon sat down on the couch. "What's wrong with Esco? I thought me and him were better than this. Does he even consider what type of predicament he's putting me in?" Sinnamon vented.

"It's not even Esco's fault." Essence interrupted.

"How can you sit there and say that it's not his fault? E is laid up in the hospital right now. He would be dead if he didn't have a vest on." Sinnamon began to raise her voice.

"If it was up to E, Esco would be laid up in the hospital. I bet E didn't tell you how him and his boy shot Esco's car up after the party, while he was in it." Essence was now the one yelling.

The new information shocked Sinnamon. She knew E got shot that night, but he told her he did it himself when he was cleaning his gun. He never mentioned anything about Esco, and she forgot all about what Spoon told her the night she moved in. Sinnamon sat quiet for a moment. She wasn't sure how she wanted to react. She was mad that E lied to her and shot at Esco first.

"Well, what did you expect him to do after Esco disrespected him in front of all them people." Sinnamon had to defend her man.

"After all the shit Esco did for you, you gonna sit here and blame him for this shit? Ya nigga shot first. Him and Dez's dumb ass. I already told Dez about himself...that bastard. How they gonna shoot at someone we call our brother. Look at the bigger picture Sinnamon." Essence was now standing up over top of Sinnamon. Sinnamon jumped up to her feet and was now standing eye to eye with Essence. There was a lot of tension built up.

"Esco's not my damn brother Essence. When are you going to see the big picture? He's a cool person, but I have to side with my man. That's where my heart is."

"You sure that's where ya heart at? Your eyes say something different every time you see Esco. And he told me about ya'll kiss."

"You know what." Sinnamon picked up her pocket book and threw it over her shoulder. "I don't have to explain myself to you. I'll talk to you later." Sinnamon didn't want to face the truth. She left Essence standing in the living room.

"Look at you. Don't even want to hear the truth." Essence yelled as Sinnamon slammed the door shut. She flopped down on the couch in frustration.

Sinnamon peeled off, almost hitting another car that was pulling out. She had to swerve out of the way. After about five blocks, she pulled over and banged her fist against her steering wheel, and then rested her forehead on it. She began to cry hysterically. Once again, she was confused. She felt as if she was in love with two men and hated the feeling. Ashanti's "Rain on me" played through her speakers as she sat in deep thought. A piece of her wanted to run away with Esco, but a bigger portion told her to stay with E. He was her man and she could never be disloyal to him. She made a vow right then and there to ride with E through everything that came from this situation. Even if she herself had to pick up a gun and go to war with him.

Chapter 12

"Say word, that nigga still breathing?" Esco was in Cozy living room three days after the shooting.

"I bullshit you not. He called me and left a message talkin' cash shit. He don't know what he's gettin his self into, fuckin' with me." Cozy blew out a large cloud of weed smoke, then deeply inhaled another puff.

"So what, he think you had something to do with him getting shot?" Esco asked. He waved the blunt off when Cozy passed it to him. He wasn't in the mood to smoke. He was trying to put together a plan to put E down for good.

"I guess he do, but you know I don't give a fuck, long as he keeps it in the street and don't take it to the police, I'm cool." Cozy's main fear was catching a case. He didn't mind the beef part of the game, but now-a-days the so-called gangsters were getting shot and testifying.

"I hear that, but it won't even go that far. I got somethin' for that nigga." Esco stood up and gave Cozy a handshake and brotherly hug.

"I'ma get at you later on."

"Ah yo." Cozy called out to Esco before he left out. "If you need me, holla at me dawg. After this shit is handled, I need you to strap me with that babe Essence. She phat like duck butter." Cozy cracked a huge smile.

"I'ma call you tonight. I just might need you for this one." Esco shut the door behind him.

* * * * *

Three weeks later, Sinnamon was still trying to get her life back in order. She and E were still having problems over the situation with Esco. He questioned her every time she left the house and when she returned. Due to E's constant insecurities she couldn't even hang with Essence as she normally did. All of her time and energy went towards pleasing E and chilling with Shaquan.

Essence and Sinnamon still spoke over the phone everyday and based on the info that Essence gave Sinnamon, Esco was MIA. He came by maybe once a week to check on her and drop a couple of dollars off. She figured he wanted things to cool down in the city before he got cased up, which was partly the truth. E however, was living it up. With Esco absent he, Spoon and Dez had room to breathe. E had a new connect, selling him bricks for 15 thousand a piece and he was moving at least 20 to 30 a week with the help of Dez and Spoon. He wasn't even worried about his beef with Esco anymore. He bought himself a black bulletproof Range Rover and kept a vest on his chest when he was out in public. With him, Dez and Spoon armed at all times, E felt safe. The only worry that was in the back of his head was the fact that he had charges pending.

"You see this shit baby? Tony Montana status, ya hear me? I'm on top of the world." E, Sinnamon, Dez and Spoon were in E's basement, counting the week's profit with money machines. They had at least a quarter million in front of them. So you could imagine how much he had in the stash.

"Whoever said crime don't pay is a motha fuckin' liar." E slapped hands with Dez, then with Spoon. Spoon just looked at him. He still didn't like E after the night of the party. He didn't care how much money they made together, he didn't respect E and didn't feel he was getting all the money he should. It was him who turned E on to the connect down south in the first place. He felt like Tony Montana and E was Frank, and if he got the chance, he was going to snatch E's throne and his girl. The only thing stopping him was Dez. Dez and E were tight and Dez was satisfied with the increase in income. The monsters called greed didn't fill his spirit.

"Baby, I'ma be done with this shit after a few more flips." E suddenly announced. The announcement shocked both Dez and Spoon.

Sinnamon however, loved the news she was hearing. "Sinnamon, if you're ready, I'm trying to take our relationship to a new level. I'm talking marriage, kids, and the whole nine."

Sinnamon didn't respond. She was okay with marriage, but the kids would have to wait. She didn't want to put her dreams of being a lawyer to the side. She had a lot of schooling to do and then work. Kids would have to wait at least another ten years.

"So if you gonna retire, where that gonna leave us?" Spoon questioned.

"What chu mean, where's that gonna leave ya'll?" E stared at Dez and Spoon blankly. He wasn't worried about them. He figured they had their own money, and should be able to make their own moves.

"Ya'll got money. So I suggest ya'll either look to retire with me or find a way to make it without me. I put my work in this game and it's time I bow out gracefully. I ain't tryin' to be one of them niggas that refuse to stop hustlin' after havin' all the money and wind up doin' 25 to life in the bing."

Dez understood where his boy was coming from. He recalled saying how dumb niggas were that were millionaires and kept hustling and ended up with a boatload of time. He wanted to stop before it was too late himself, but he wasn't ready for retirement. He was busy spending his money on material things instead of saving for a hard time. He barely had enough cash in his stash to buy a few bricks, let alone take over E's connect and buy 20 or more.

It Gets Dirtier

Spoon stayed silent. He knew this day was coming. He had a nice piece of change in the stash, but still wanted more. Besides, to him, you were in the game forever and you definitely couldn't turn your back on your friends. So he wasn't feeling E's idea of bowing out. Not when he and Dez were still trying to do their thing. He planned to speak to Dez alone when he got the chance. He needed to know where Dez's head was.

* * * * *

"See, told you ya boy was a sucka." Spoon said to Dez.

They were on their way to their apartment. "He ain't worried 'bout us. He got his change up and now he's ready to roll." Dez sat in the passenger seat thinking as he stared out the window. He was contemplating his next move. He wanted to remain on top, because he was loving the life he was living.

"Nigga, is you listenin'?" Spoon looked over to Dez.

"Yeah, I hear you nigga!" Dez yelled suddenly. He was frustrated.

"What the fuck you gonna do, huh? Tell me that? We need to rob that nigga, so we'll be straight."

"I told you before, I ain't with that Spoon. That's my nigga. He played his part to the T. He never had to put us on in the first place. He was right when he said we should have money put away." Dez tried to reason.

"I ain't tryin to hear that shit. You just as soft as he is." Spoon began to push Dee's buttons.

"Watch ya mouth nigga. I put in hard work just like you did. I just ain't on no grimy shit like you. I can't picture robbin' my boy over a little bit of paper. Nigga, on some real shit, where would you be without him?" Dez looked in Spoon's direction to see if he was paying attention. "I thought you wouldn't have anything to say. Now if you lookin' for a stick, I'm with you...just not E. We should plot on that nigga Esco. He probably waitin' to catch us sleepin' anyway."

"I hear you nigga, but I still think ya boy doin' some sucka shit. Just give it some thought. Robbin' Esco would be a plus, but it's too

86

much work. We don't know too much about him. E, on the other hand, we know everything. I'm telling you, you need to think about that shit." Spoon really wanted to get E. Things were personal to him.

Chapter 13

A couple weeks later.....

"Bout time you got out the house." Essence told Sinnamon. They were walking around the King of Prussia Mall, doing some shopping.

"I know, E's just been buggin' a lot lately. He's scared that I might go around Esco or something." Sinnamon was swinging a Bloomingdales bag. She stopped in mid stride and looked for a place to sit. She wanted to talk to Essence about something personal.

"Let's sit over there." Sinnamon pointed to an open bench she spotted.

The two women took a seat and sat their bags down. They were silent for a minute and watched as people walked by them. Essence could sense Sinnamon was ready to drop something heavy on her, so she waited until Sinnamon was ready. She didn't want to rush her.

"My life is so crazy Essence." Sinnamon finally started. "Just last year, I was an ugly nobody. Not one guy ever complimented me or anything. Now look at me." Sinnamon opened her arms as if saying "Tah-dah." All the men I see now are eyeing me down. I have a boyfriend and another guy that really likes me, and I don't know what to do with myself. This is too much."

"What do you mean?" Essence wasn't sure what Sinnamon was trying to say.

Sinnamon looked over at Essence and made eye contact. "I feel like I'm going crazy right now. E doesn't want me to leave the house unless I'm with him, and I'm not used to that. Then, he and Esco are having problems and at times, I feel it's my fault."

"It's not your fault though. You know that." Essence spoke with a soft tone. "You have to understand, niggas are going to be niggas. Their beef probably goes deeper than what we think."

"I know it's not my fault, but I'm still in the middle of it. I don't know Essence." Sinnamon sighed. "Now E's talking about leaving the game."

"That's good." Essence frowned her face up and gave Sinnamon a confused look. She figured Sinnamon would love to hear that E planned to leave the game.

"Yes, that is really good, but he wants to get married and start a family."

"What's wrong with that?"

Sinnamon now looked at Essence with the confused frown. "Girl, I'm only 18, and I want to go to college, and start my law career. Nothing has changed with my plans for the future." Sinnamon paused for a moment. "Don't say anything to no one, but I feel something for Esco too. I don't know what it is but it's something there."

Essence cracked a huge smile. "I knew you were in love with that man."

Sinnamon gave Essence a playful shove. "I didn't say I was in love with him... but I do care. That's why I worry so much about them beefing." Sinnamon had really been thinking about the beef between E and Esco. She had a feeling in her gut that it wasn't over yet.

"So tell me this. If something were to go down between them, what would you do?"

"It depends on how far it goes."

"What would you do if E killed Esco?" Essence really wanted to know.

"To be honest Essence, I think I'd leave him alone. I would hate E for that. He knows I'm close with Esco, that's why he doesn't want me around him."

"What would you do if it was the other way around, and Esco killed E?" Sinnamon looked Essence straight in the eyes before answering.

"I'ma ride for my man."

"Meaning?"

"I'd shoot Esco."

* * * * *

"Listen, all we have to do is go in and out. This won't take long. He's in there by himself. I watched Sinnamon pull off like an hour ago. You ready?" One of the two masked men spoke, while they were in the back of E's house. E was in his kitchen making a sandwich.

"I'm ready." The other guy answered.

"At the count of three, I'ma kick the door down. You just run in with ya gun out and I'll take it from there. I don't want you to get ya hands dirty. This shit is personal for me."

"I got you."

"Okay. 1, 2, 3"

"Boom!" With one big kick, the door surprisingly came right open. The sound of the door scared the shit out of E. He fumbled with the jar of mayonnaise that he was about to put in the refrigerator. It crashed to the ground and shattered from the impact. The two intruders were in the kitchen within seconds.

"Don't move too fast, homie." The first intruder said when he came in the kitchen. E put his hands in the air to surrender. He had a small stash for a situation like this.

"The money is up stairs in my room. I'll take you to it. Just don't shoot." E said calmly.

"Boom!" The man who had the personal problem with E fired a shot, hitting E in his kneecap.

It Gets Dirtier

"Who said we was here to rob you?"

The pain from the gunshot caused E to drop to the ground. He rolled around in pain, cutting himself with the glass from the mayonnaise jar. He didn't expect to get shot. He took a look at the man, and then remembered-he still had beef with Esco. He felt like a fool for sleeping on his enemy. With all the time passing, he thought things were squashed between him and Esco.

"Come on Esco, you don't gotta do it like this. You can have that bitch man, and the money. Please, just let me live." E begged for his life. The man towered over E and let out a hideous laugh.

"Come on E man up, I thought you was gansta. Don't cry now."

"Come on man, I'm leaving the game! I'll be out ya way. I got a baby on the way man! Please don't kill me!" E lied. He would have told the gunman he was Jesus Christ, if he thought it would save his life.

"I'll take care of ya seed for you." The gunman removed his mask. E knew he was dead now. Before he could say a word, it was over."

"BOOM!" E took a shot to the face. His blood splattered on the gunman's face and he wiped it off with the sleeve of his hoodie.

"Damn man, you got blood all on me and shit." The man spoke to E. The other man with him had to turn the other way. The large Desert Eagle made E's face look as if it was melted. The gunman fired five more rounds, two of them blew half of E's face off. The other three landed in his chest, causing his body to jerk.

"Let's find the money." The man with the weak stomach said. He wanted to leave the body as soon as possible. He laid a few people down himself in his life, but this was the first time he was this close to death.

* * * * *

"Call me when you get in the house." Essence gave Sinnamon a hug and got out of the car. She then went to the trunk of the car and removed the few bags she had. Sinnamon watched as Essence fiddled with her keys before unlocking the house door. Once Essence was safely inside, Sinnamon blew her horn and pulled off. It was now a little after 10pm, and she knew E was gonna flip out on her, because he wanted her in by 9pm. Sinnamon was having a good night and wasn't in the mood for E's bullshit.

She began to think of how she could soften up E's mood. She already knew a home cooked meal was out of the question because of the time. She decided that tonight would be the night that she would finally give him some. On her way home, she stopped at the liquor store that was located on Concord Avenue, which was seconds away from the exit that leads to I-95. Sinnamon entered the store, hoping she didn't get carded. This was the first time she ever entered a liquor store. She figured, she looked old enough and decided to take a chance. As she approached the counter, she looked for the ashy green bottle that she always saw E and his friends sipping from. Being that it was Top Shelf liquor, she spotted it in no time.

"Can I get a bottle of your Remy VSOP and a bottle of Moet?" The Moet was for her. She remembered liking it the first time she hung out with E. The man behind the bulletproof glass grabbed Sinnamon's Moet but wasn't sure what size bottle of Remy she wanted.

"What size Remy ma'am." He spoke in an Indian accent.
Sinnamon wasn't sure how to label the size of the bottle so she pointed to what she called the medium size bottle. It turned out to be a pint. The cashier put the bottles in a bag, then in the slot part of the bulletproof window that spins around to the customer. Before turning it, he looked at Sinnamon hesitantly. "Can I see I.D. please." Sinnamon's face began to turn red because she could feel the people in line behind her. She began to pretend to look for her I.D.

"It's cool cuz, she with me." A familiar voice said behind Sinnamon. She turned around and spotted Esco smiling down at her. She was happy to see him. Not only did he just save her from embarrassment, but also it's been so long since she laid eyes on him. Esco stepped in front of her to pay for the liquor. Sinnamon took that as an opportunity to check him out. It didn't surprise her to see him dressed plainly in a black tee shirt, black sweat pants, and a black pair of low top Timberland boots. The only thing that stuck out was his expensive chain and watch.

Esco grabbed Sinnamon's bag along with a bottle of Remy and 6-pack of Corona's for himself. He then walked Sinnamon out to her car.

"So, what brings you to the liquor store?" Esco questioned, once they were outside of the store.

"About to celebrate" Sinnamon spoke shyly.

"Celebrate what?"

"Mind ya business." Sinnamon teased. She had a big smile on her face.

"So it's like that now." Esco smiled back. It felt good for him to see Sinnamon again. They talked for a couple of minutes before Sinnamon remembered that she was supposed to be mad at him.

"So what's up with you and E? I need you guys to squash your beef Esco. You know that's my boyfriend. You and I are supposed to be cool, so please don't continue to put me in an awkward position."

Esco chuckled lightly. "Sinnamon, I ain't even worried 'bout that nigga anymore. He ain't on my level, but I still dig you." It was really hard for Sinnamon to look into Esco's eyes, so she put her head down. He lifted up her head with is pointer finger.

"Esco please, don't go there." Sinnamon snatched her head away softly. Her eyes once again, met the ground. "I have to go."

"I understand." Esco gave Sinnamon her bags. "You still my baby though. If you need me, you know how to reach me." Esco opened Sinnamon's car door for her, then shut it behind her when she was safely inside. He then watched her pull off.

"Damn, she bad." Cozy told Esco when he got in his car. He was parked across the street from where Sinnamon was parked.

"I know man. I'ma get her eventually." Esco spoke. He cracked open a Corona and passed Cozy one. Then, they pulled off.

It Gets Dirtier

Chapter 14

When Sinnamon pulled up into E's garage, she parked her car and sat there for a moment. She was surprised E wasn't blowing her phone up, being that she was two hours late for her curfew. She began to think of a story to tell E if he began to question her. Talking to Esco had her feeling slightly guilty, but she was relieved to know he wasn't worried about his problem with E anymore. That lifted a lot of weight from her shoulders. Now, all she had to do was shake off the feelings she had for Esco.

Sinnamon grabbed her bag of liquor and got out of the car. She popped her trunk and removed the bags she had, which contained a few pair of shoes that she brought. On her way to the front door, she saw the TV flickering in their bedroom and hoped E had fallen asleep. If so, she would take a quick shower, and throw on some sexy under garments to entice her man when she woke him up.

Sinnamon entered the house quietly. When she didn't hear E scream her name, she knew he had to be asleep. She quickly made her way up stairs and into their large bedroom. To her surprise, there was no sign of E. The TV was on and the bed was unmade, as if he'd been in it. Sinnamon grabbed the things she needed for her shower and stripped down to her birthday suit. She took a glance in her large mirror and admired her womanly frame. She noticed the hair around her love was beginning to grow back. She grabbed her razor and the rest of her things and went into the bathroom. Still, there was no sign of E.

"Maybe he's in the basement." Sinnamon spoke out loud. She began to fiddle with the knob that controlled the shower water until she found the perfect setting. With the shower water running and the steam filling the bathroom, Sinnamon covered her hair with a shower cap and got into the steaming water.

After a good shave and nice bath, Sinnamon got out the shower and dried off in the bedroom. She put on a tropical scented lotion that she knew E liked, and then put on a Victoria Secret's black and royal blue lacey thong set. The bra complimented Sinnamon's C-cups by sitting them up a little more than they would be naturally. Sinnamon turned slightly in the mirror to make sure her thong was on properly. Her soft butt cheeks made the back piece of the thong disappear. The only thing visible was the decorative bow that rested on top of her butt. The thong was designed so that when you untie the bow, the thong fell off. Sinnamon sealed her sexy get-up with a pair of black Stilettos that tied up her calf. Sinnamon looked at herself in the mirror after getting ready and was pleased with what she saw. She took a deep breath, grabbed the Moet and Remy, and then headed to the kitchen to get glasses. From there, she planned to go to the basement and seduce E.

When Sinnamon made it to the kitchen, her whole life changed. She couldn't believe the horrible scene that lay in front of her. She had a flash back of Sam's bloody body.

"Oh my God! E, No!" Sinnamon cried when she spotted E's body lying on the kitchen floor. Half of his face was literally blown off, and he was unrecognizable. The only thing left that was still intact was his right eye, which remained open, part of his forehead, half of his nose and a portion of his mouth. Pieces of his face were caved in from the impact, and the other parts of body tissue painted the tile on the kitchen floor. E's head laid next to the mess from the mayonnaise jar.

It Gets Dirtier

The combination of mayonnaise and blood made a pinkish custard. The yellowish color of his fatty tissue and brain was exposed and hanging from his head. Blood also splattered on the nearby walls and refrigerator. Before she knew it, Sinnamon found herself at the sink throwing up. The gruesome sight of E's body was too much for her to bear. She couldn't believe he was gone. After throwing up a few times, Sinnamon finally got her stomach together. She kneeled down next to E's body and began to cry as she talked to him. "Who did this to you baby? Why now?" Sinnamon screamed. She looked towards the sky and questioned God's decree. "Why did you take him from me God? Why? Please send him back God! Please send him back!"

Sinnamon spotted the Remy bottle that she dropped at the entrance of the kitchen. She opened it and took a big gulp, hoping to drown the pain as she sat next to E and talked. She spoke on how they first met, when he bought her the Benz, all the way up to the present moment. She realized how much she loved E.

"I would've married you baby." Sinnamon's words began to slur. The liquor was taking affect. "I know who fucking did this to you, and I'm going to get him for you baby. I promise." She pictured Esco on the Ave, in his all black. No wonder he wasn't worried about the beef anymore, Sinnamon thought to herself. She got up and staggered to the phone that was plugged in the kitchen wall. With a shaky hand, she began to dial the number to Essence's cell phone.

"What's up girl?" Essence answered.

"E's dead!" Sinnamon blurted through her tears. Essence immediately felt Sinnamon's pain.

"What happened?" Essence didn't know what else to say at the point. The news came as a surprise to her.

"I don't know. I came home, got in the shower, and, and, and...." Sinnamon was crying so hard, it was hard for her to breath.

"Sinnamon, take some deep breaths and calm down. I'm on my way out there, okay?" Essence spoke with a mothers' tone.

"Okay." Sinnamon sniffled. A small stream of snot flowed from her nose as she cried. She hung up the phone and made her way back to E's body. This time, when she sat with him, she rested his mangled head on her lap. His blood stained Sinnamon's thighs and arms. She wasn't even affected by the gruesome sight anymore. She was in a trance. Sinnamon began to drink the bottle of Remy again. This time she drank it fast, as if it was only water. When the bottle was empty, she threw it across the room. She ran both of her hands through her hair, causing it to mess up. Her head was spinning and filled with thoughts of revenge. She knew Esco was responsible for E's death. For a second, she thought about calling the police and having Esco arrested, but she felt that wouldn't be enough. He needed to die a horrible death like E did.

"I promise, I'm going to get him." Sinnamon looked down at E and ran her fingers across his waves. She was interrupted from her trance when the doorbell rang. Sinnamon gently lifted E's head from off her thighs and placed it gently on the ground. Drunk, she stumbled to the door. When Sinnamon opened the door, Essence looked at her bloodstained friend momentarily. She wasn't sure if Sinnamon was injured or not, due to the amount of blood on her body.

"Are you okay?" Essence finally embraced Sinnamon with a tight hug. They kept their embrace for a few moments as Sinnamon cried her eyes out. "Did you call the police?" Essence asked. She shut the front door.

"No."

"Stay right here, I'm going to run upstairs and find you something to put on so we can call them." Essence paused and studied Sinnamon as she walked back to the kitchen. Sinnamon was almost falling all over herself. "Have you been drinking?"

"Yesh." Sinnamon slurred.

Essence shook her head and began to climb the steps. She felt bad for her friend. She could tell Sinnamon was taking the murder hard. She wondered if Sinnamon had witnessed the murder or not.

98

Then wondered who did it. Her first thought was Esco. In Sinnamon's bedroom, Essence looked through Sinnamon's things and found a robe for her to put on. She went downstairs and into the kitchen, where she found Sinnamon sitting next to E, with a bottle of Moet to her lips.

"Oh my God!" Essence stopped in her tracks. She turned her head from the sight of E. It was too much for her, but she knew she had to be there for her friend. She took a deep breath, kept her vision focused on Sinnamon, and preceded to enter the kitchen.

"Here, put this on." Essence helped Sinnamon put on the large robe. She strained to lift Sinnamon's weight off the floor. Being drunk, Sinnamon wasn't cooperating too much. Once Essence had Sinnamon on her feet, she tied the robe and walked her to the living room. She couldn't stay in the room with E's body.

After sitting Sinnamon on the couch, Essence pulled out her cell phone and called the police. She found Sinnamon's address on one of E's magazine that was on the coffee table and gave it to the dispatcher. After telling the dispatcher what happened, they assured her that help was on the way.

"Why did Esco have to do this?" Sinnamon said out loud when Essence hung up the phone.

"How do you know it was him?"

"I just know." Sinnamon snapped. "And I'm going to kill him."

"You can't do that."

"Well I am. You'll see."

The two women talked things over until they could see the blue and red lights flashing in the windows. Essence didn't know what to think. She didn't want Sinnamon to try to do anything to Esco, but at the same time, she felt where she was coming from. She would ride for her man too. The only difference was that Sinnamon wasn't that type of person. Essence could see Sinnamon getting herself killed trying to go up against Esco and began to wonder where that would leave her. Essence never knew Sinnamon wasn't a stranger to murder.

It Gets Dirtier

Chapter 15

After E's death, Sinnamon went through some major changes. She was no longer the innocent young girl that she was prior to the murder. She was now, a mad woman on the hunt for revenge. Her plan was to kill Esco by any means necessary. She felt that not only did he kill E, but he killed her new life as well. How was she going to maintain without E?

"He probably thinks I'm going to run to him now." Sinnamon told Essence. They were in Sinnamon's old spot on the couch the day after the murder. Sinnamon couldn't return to E's house at the time. It was just too much for her to bear.

"Sinnamon, why do you have it set in your head that Esco did that shit. It might not have been him. The police told you it appeared to be a robbery gone bad. E was a hustler and anyone could have plotted on him." Essence tried to reason. Something in her gut was telling her that Esco was innocent.

"E didn't have any problems with no one else. Him and Esco were beefing with one another. It had to be him."

"Why would Esco rob him Sinnamon? He has money."

"Well, that doesn't stop someone from wanting more." Sinnamon has her mind made up.

"So what are you going to do?" Essence asked. She wanted to feel Sinnamon out because Sinnamon told her she would kill Esco. She really was hoping her friend wouldn't take it there. But, by the look in Sinnamon's bloodshot eyes, anything was possible.

"I don't know what I want to do." Sinnamon let out a deep breath. She was just waiting for the right time to execute her plan. "Why don't you call him so I can talk to him?"

"I'm not getting involved in that."

Sinnamon gave Essence a look of disbelief. She couldn't believe her friend didn't want to help her.

"What do you mean you're not getting involved? It's not like I'm asking you to do something to him with me. I just want to ask him a few questions. I need to know for myself what happened."

"Essence soaked in Sinnamon's words. She felt bad for her friend and wanted to help. At the same time, she didn't want Sinnamon to try anything weird. Looking at Sinnamon's puppy dog face was really getting the best of her.

"I just need some closure." Sinnamon spoke softly.

"Damn, you get on my nerves." Essence pulled out her cell phone. "What do you want me to tell him?"

Sinnamon cracked a huge smile. She really wanted to talk to Esco. "Just tell him I'm over here and I want to talk to him." Essence dialed the number to Esco's cell phone and let it ring. She was about to hang up just as Esco answered.

"What you doing?" Essence asked as soon as he said hello.

"Chilling. What's good?" He replied.

"Sinnamon's over here and she wants to speak to you."

Esco paused a moment. He was happy to hear that Sinnamon wanted to talk to him, "She aiight? I heard about home boy." Esco said sincerely.

"Yeah, she's cool, just stressing." Essence looked over at Sinnamon, who was staring at her intensely.

"Put her on the phone."

"Hold on." Essence covered the phone with her hand. "Here, he wants to talk to you." Essence passed Sinnamon the phone.

"Hello." Sinnamon spoke softly.

"Everything cool? I'm sorry to hear about E. If you need me, I'm here for you." Esco said sincerely.

"I know you are, that's why I want to speak with you face to face. I'm going through some things right now and I think you can help me," Sinnamon said.

Esco thought about it for a minute and wondered why she wanted to speak with him, when she was over there with her girl. Then it dawned on him, he figured she wanted to ask him if he killed E. With that in mind he was determined to clear his name. He didn't want Sinnamon to think he had anything to do with the murder.

"Well, I have a feeling on what you want to talk about, so I'll be over there in a few. We do need to clear the air on a few things. I'm not too far away anyway."

"Okay then, I'll see you when you get here." Sinnamon hung up with a slight smile. Essence gave her a look of suspicion. She felt Sinnamon looked too pleased to hear from Esco.

"So what he say?" Essence was digging for information.

"He's on his way over here." Sinnamon picked up her pocketbook and headed towards the bathroom.

"I know that much." Essence paused. "And what are you about to do?"

Sinnamon could sense Essence's suspiciousness. She turned around to Essence, who was following her to the bathroom. "Damn, I can't go to the bathroom. Look at my hair." Sinnamon pointed to her frizzy hair.

Essence washed it for her the night before because E's blood was in it.

She didn't do anything to it after that. "I'm going to put it in a ponytail or something. I don't want Esco to see me like this. Now, can you excuse me?" Sinnamon softly shut to bathroom door in

103

Essence's face. Essence stared at the closed door momentarily, then blew Sinnamon off and went back to the front room.

On the other side of the door, Sinnamon sat on the toilet and pulled out a small, silver .380 handgun from her purse. E gave it to her when she moved in with him. He wanted her to have a weapon that she could handle in case someone broke into the house.

Sinnamon sat on the toilet and stared at the piece of metal that was known to end so many lives. She pushed the release button for the clip to come out. It was filled to the top with hollow-tipped bullets that E loaded. Sinnamon took a deep breath, cocked the gun back and then sat it back in her purse. After checking the gun, Sinnamon looked at herself in the mirror. She didn't feel she looked the same. Her hair was all over the place and her eyes were bloodshot red, with bags underneath them. She took a brush from under the sink and brushed her hair back in a ponytail. She stared at herself for another five minutes as if she was in a trance. Her trance was interrupted when she heard Esco enter the house and began to talk to Essence. Sinnamon took a deep breath, grabbed her purse and left the bathroom...on her way to avenge E's death.

When Sinnamon made it to the living room, Esco was standing by the front door with a big smile on his face. He and Essence were just sharing a joke. Seeing the smile on Esco's face made Sinnamon hate him more. She didn't understand how he could be laughing and joking, especially after what he did. Esco's smile quickly faded when Sinnamon pulled the .380 from her purse and aimed it at him. She held the gun with a trembling hand as tears streamed down her face. Essence looked at the expression on Esco's face, and then followed his gaze. She couldn't believe Sinnamon had a gun in her hand.

"Why did you have to kill him?" Sinnamon screamed.

"Put the gun down Sinnamon." Essence said. She was now crying. She didn't want her friend to make a mistake that would ruin her life.

Esco remained quiet. He was contemplating on pulling out his baby nine and sitting Sinnamon down. He stared at her intensely. Her baby face and light brown eyes made it hard for him to draw a gun on her. He loved her too much.

"Shut up Essence! He killed E. Why do you keep defending him?" Sinnamon was now getting mad at Essence. Her sudden focus on Essence gave Esco the opportunity to get a clear shot at Sinnamon, but he couldn't bring himself to do it. He did however manage to get a step closer to the door.

"Don't fucking move!" Sinnamon screamed and shook the gun in Esco's direction. Her shaking hand flinched too much and she pulled the trigger.

"Boom!" The gun shot caused everyone to jump. The bullet struck the wall, about nine feet from Esco.

"Sinnamon, you need to chill the fuck out!" Esco yelled at Sinnamon. In one quick motion, he pulled out his nine and held it steadily pointed at Sinnamon. "I didn't kill that nigga. I wouldn't be standing here if I did."

"Oh, so now you're going to kill me too?" Sinnamon began to cry harder. "Well do it then!" She fired another shot that missed Esco, but it was closer than the last one. Esco looked at the wall where the bullet hit, then looked at Sinnamon.

"I ain't gone let you kill me, now put the fuckin' gun down Sinnamon." Esco's heart was racing. He didn't want to kill Sinnamon, but didn't want to catch nothing hot in him either.

"Please put the gun down." Essence cried. She got off the couch and slowly walked over to Sinnamon.

Sinnamon was staring at Esco with a million thoughts in her head. On one hand, she wanted to believe Esco didn't do it, but her gut was telling her that he did. Then on the other hand, she loved him and didn't want to kill him, just like he didn't want to kill her. They both kept their stances with their guns pointed at each other.

Essence suddenly jumped on Sinnamon and tried to fight the gun away from her. In the mist of the struggle, Sinnamon fired two more shots. Both of the shots struck the wall over top of Esco's head.

"What are you doing? You're supposed to be on my side." Sinnamon managed to say as she struggled with Essence.

"I am on your side. You don't want to do this. It's not worth it." Essence really was looking out for Sinnamon's best interest.

As the women fought for the gun, Esco tucked his and slid out the door. He was relieved because he was seconds away from shooting the woman he loved. If Essence jumped in a few seconds later, he wasn't sure what the outcome would have been. One thing Esco had to admit was that he was digging the fact that Sinnamon was willing to ride for her man. He never expected that from her. As Esco made his escape, Sinnamon and Essence were still tussling over the gun. It took Essence almost five minutes to get Sinnamon to put the gun down. They didn't even notice that Esco had left. When Sinnamon finally dropped the gun, she broke down and cried. Essence just held her tight in her arms. She felt her pain.

"I'm going to kill him." Sinnamon cried.

"Calm down. You have to calm down." Essence rocked Sinnamon lightly and rubbed her back. Sinnamon just cried harder and harder. She was mad at herself for hesitating. Then she thought on how Esco pulled a gun on her. She could've gotten herself killed and she promised herself right there, to never let that happen again. Next time, she was going to hit her target quick and easy. She had to come up with another plan. All she needed was to convince Essence to help her.

Chapter 16

"I don't know what I'ma do about Sinnamon." Esco was talking to Cozy as they cruised down Market Street, headed to downtown Wilmington. They were on their way to Malaoto's, a Japanese restaurant in town. Malaota's is a small hole in the wall type of restaurant that had the best Japanese food in Wilmington.

"I would've shot that bitch. You better than me." Cozy spoke as he drove. He giggled as he thought on the story that Esco told him.

"That shit ain't funny nigga."

"I know, I know. I'm just saying that shit is crazy. She could've killed you on some real shit. So what you going to do?" Cozy looked to Esco.

"That's what I'm stuck on." Esco paused for a moment. His feelings for Sinnamon stood in the way of his normal thinking. Any other time or person, it wouldn't have been an issue. "I'm saying, I'm really digging Sinnamon, but she tripping right now. I think if I don't put her to sleep the next time I see her, she might not miss. And I always said, I ain't letting a bitch hold me down, so I damn sure ain't gonna let one kill me."

The thought of killing Sinnamon cut Esco deep in his gut, but what else could he do. This was a case of do or die.

It Gets Dirtier

"Enough said then nigga. You gotta do what you gotta to do for ya self. I say handle that ASAP, cuz if she don't try to off you, she probably call the police and make you a suspect in that nigga E's murder and you know how they is down here. All they need is simple hearsay to put you away for life. They don't play fair." Cozy spoke seriously. He knew of several men that are doing life in prison in the Delaware system for murders that had no physical evidence at the trial. All the state will have is a weak motive that anyone could've had, and someone saying they saw something. Half the time they only claim they saw something to get the reward money that's offered by the police for tips. It's sad how it goes down, but Delaware does its own thing.

"I was thinking the same thing and I damn sure ain't doing a life bid. I'd rather die."

"You might want to off her girl Essence just to be safe. Ain't no telling how she'll act when Sinnamon's gone." Cozy was thinking of all the possibilities.

"You right. I'ma get on top of that shit asap. I just need a solid plan."

"You know I got you if you need me." Cozy parked the car near the restaurant. He and Esco got out and made their way in. They both were trying to figure a way to get rid of the girls. That's how the game goes sometime. You can go from having love for someone to having thoughts of killing them in the blink of an eye. A friend is not promised today or tomorrow. Neither is your life.

* * * * *

On the day of E's funeral, Sinnamon finally jumped in her Benz and made her way home. It was her first time in E's house since the murder. When she entered, she got an eerie feeling. She felt as if she could feel E's presence. The first place she went was to the murder scene. To her surprise, it was fairly clean. E's mother had a few people clean the house up because she knew Sinnamon would return. His mother would have tried to sell the house because it was in her name, but before his death E told his mother he wanted Sinnamon to keep the house if something were to happen to him. He assured his mother that he would leave Sinnamon enough money to pay the mortgage. If not, he knew his boy Dez would hold his girl down. Dez was the closest thing he had to a brother.

After Sinnamon stared at the very spot where she found E, she made her way up the stairs to the bedroom. She had three hours to get ready for the funeral. The bedroom was just as she left it...even the TV was still on. Sinnamon stripped down and got her things together for her shower. She almost felt as if she was reliving the fatal night. In the shower, Sinnamon broke down once again. Her tears showered down just as hard as the water from the showerhead. Sinnamon sat in the tub with her knees to her chest and her head down she let the water rained down on her head. She flashed back to the day she killed Sam. The sight of her bloody hands never left her mind, even after the therapy session's she and Betty had to attend.

The therapist wrote Sinnamon off as being a normal child, forced to defend herself. Sinnamon did a good job to hide her emotions, but that day still haunted her. Sinnamon finally got herself together and showered. Once she was finished, it was time to get dressed and do something with her hair. Because she was pressed for time, she had to settle for a long curly ponytail, which looked nice on her anyway. In the closet, she found a black Armani suit, perfect for the occasion.

By the time she got dress, Sinnamon only had 20 minutes to get to the funeral. She took a glance at herself in her large mirror before heading out. She was dressed in a black skirt that resembled a business suit. Even though it wasn't tight fitted, it still clung to her womanly curves complimenting her figure. To her, the mirror was like a glimpse in the future, because she planned to dress like that every-day when she became a lawyer. Sinnamon put on some large dark sunglasses and grabbed her small black purse that held her .380 and made her way to the car.

It Gets Dirtier

Lucky for Sinnamon, funerals never started on time because by the time she made it to the funeral site, parking was hard to find. Thefuneral was at Handover Church in Wilmington. It seated a larger crowd so it was ideal for a well-know person like E. With cars parked block to block, Sinnamon was forced to park four blocks away from the church. When she entered the church, she took a seat in the front row with E's family. They welcomed her warmly. E didn't bring Sinnamon around much but his family knew how much she meant to him because he spoke so highly of her.

"If you need me, don't be afraid to call." One of E's aunts whispered in Sinnamon's ear as she hugged her. The entire family basically said the same thing. When the funeral started, it was fairly quiet in the building. The only thing that could be heard was the sniffling and soft cries of the people in the crowd. E had a lot of people that would miss him, especially women. Due to the severity of E's wounds, he had a closed casket and the only visual were the pictures that were placed in front of the church. Everyone slowly walked passed E's casket and paid their respects. Another soldier down.

When everyone was seated, Pastor Shannon from Kingdom Harvest Fellowship began to preach. He didn't know E, but knew his family. It hurt him to see the continuing violence that the black community suffered. So many young lives, that were once full of potential, continue to be taken away, if not to murder, then to the system.

"Another son is taken away from his mother." Pastor Shannon was in the middle of his spill. He wiped the beads of sweat from his forehead. "When is it going to stop? Our young black men are leaving young women alone to raise babies by themselves. We cannot bring E back, but what about you all out there. When will you change? If not for yourself, for your family, kids, wives…somebody. How many of you will it take to get life in prison, or die in these cold streets before you decide to change? Before it hits home?" He paused to let his words sink in.

"Amen, Amen." Some people in the crowd chanted.

"I know some of you are his friends, or his boys. Some of you are mad and want revenge." Pastor Shannon made eye contact with Dez and Spoon, who were sitting a few rows behind the family. Dez wiped the tears that fell from his eyes. "But revenge won't change anything. The only thing it will do is continue this sad cycle." Pastor Shannon continued to preach. By the time he was done, there wasn't a dry eye in the building. He hit some very strong points in his spill. Wilmington's a small city but the crime rate was on the rise and most of the people dying and going to jail were young black males. Fathers leaving their children behind to grow up without them.

After the service, everyone got in their cars and followed the Hearst to the burial site. There, family and friends said their last goodbyes to E. Sinnamon managed to stay strong up to that point. When the words "Ashes to ashes and dust to dust" were spoken and the casket was lowered, she flipped. She tried to jump in the hole as they lowered the casket. Dez had to grab a hold of her. He held her tight as she cried into his chest. He felt her pain and couldn't help but to join her in her tears. He lost a close friend and no matter how hard he prayed, the pain was written on his face.

"It's okay." Essence was behind Sinnamon, rubbing her back as she cried.

"Dez, you have to do something. We gotta get him." Sinnamon cried. She was referring to Esco. Dez just remained silent and rocked Sinnamon back and forth. He didn't know what to say. Essence made eye contact with Dez and tried to read his thoughts. She never saw him cry before, and seeing his sensitive side made her feel some type of way for him. She just wanted to hug him and let him know that everything was going to be all right, but she had to be there for Sinnamon first. Instead of hugging Dez, she surprisingly mouthed the words, "love you" to him. Dez did the same in return as he continued to cry. He was definitely going to need some support for this, his best friend was gone.

Chapter 17

After E's funeral, Essence found herself spending more time with Dez. They spent the nights at Dez's apartment that he once shared with E. He now shared the spot with Spoon. They fixed it up a little more than E and Dez had it, but they were still outgrowing it due to their progress in the game. They were both thinking of moving, especially Dez. He and E had too many memories inside the apartment for him to stay there.

"What are you thinking about?" Essence asked Dez. They were lying in Dez's queen size bed, watching TV. Dez was lying on his back, staring at the ceiling, while Essence rested her head on his chest.

"A bunch of shit." Dez let out a deep breath and continued to stare at the ceiling, he had a lot on his mind.

"Like what. You can talk to me Dez. That's what I'm here for." Essence was trying to be supportive. She knew he was taking the loss of E bad. Not only did he loose a close friend, but Essence also knew Dez lost his weight man, a key figure in his moneymaking plans. E was the plug.

"This shit is just driving me crazy." Dez sat up in the bed. Essence did the same and they made eye contact. "I mean, my boy is gone and I don't really understand why. It's just crazy. I don't even know where I stand right now. I got money and shit but it don't mean nothin'. I'd give my right hand to get my boy back. All the money in the world can't help me deal with this shit." Dez wiped away the few tears that fell from his eyes.

"It's okay Dez. Ya'll were close and it's going to take time for you to get over this, but in due time you will. You just have to stay strong. I've been tellin' Sinnamon the same thing." Essence paused for a moment. She had a question for Dez, but wasn't sure if it was appropriate to ask at the present time. She saw Dez pulling himself together and decided to shoot the question. "So, do you have any idea who killed E?" she stared deep in Dez's eyes as if his eyes would reveal the answer.

"Do it matter?" Dez answered with sudden anger. "E's gone, what difference does it make if I knew who did it?"

Essence didn't like the way Dez responded. To her, it made a big difference whether he knew or not. That could save her friend's life. It wasn't her job to be seeking revenge for E's murder, it was his.

"Yes it makes a fuckin' difference." Essence rolled her neck and eyes. "My fuckin' girl is goin' crazy tryin' to kill the nigga she thinks did this shit, while you sittin' here cryin' like some bitch. Ya'll got ya roles mixed up. I can't tell if it was her pumpin' with him and you fuckin' him or what." Essence's words were sharp like daggers and cut Dez deep and hard.

"Watch ya fuckin' mouth!" Dez shouted. In the blink of an eye, he back smacked Essence. The blow caused her to fall to the floor. When she hit the ground, she touched her lip and saw the blood on her hand.

"Don't hit me. Hit them niggas that killed E, pussy." Essence was shocked that Dez hit her. No man had ever laid a hand on her. She wanted to strike back but Dez was too big and no one else was in the house to stop him if he chose to beat her down.

"What the fuck I tell you?" Dez jumped from the bed and grabbed Essence by the neck. "Didn't I say shut the fuck up Bitch. I ain't for ya shit right now. I will fuckin' kill you in here. You understand?" He squeezed her neck harder and shook it. "Do you fuckin' understand me?" Dez had a look of murder in his eyes as he choked Essence. She tried her best to shake her head yes. When Dez noticed that she was changing colors, he released her neck and pushed her away from him. Essence fell back and hit her head on the floor. She inhaled deeply, trying to breathe the life back into her lungs. She looked up at Dez with fire in her eyes. The tears she released wasn't from pain, they were from anger and frustration. She wanted badly to attack Dez but knew not to. She didn't stand a chance. Knowing she was in a losing situation, she decided to play things cool until she got the opportunity to strike back. Even if she had to catch Dez literally sleeping, she was going to get him back.

* * * * *

"Thank you so much Ms. Jones. I know I have been throwing Shaquan on you a lot lately, but there's so much that has been going on in my life." Sinnamon was finally picking up Shaquan from her old neighbor. Ms. Jones didn't mind keeping Shaquan at all, he kept her company and busy. She did however, worry about Sinnamon and her lifestyle. Especially after what Sinnamon's mother told her a few days ago.

"Don't worry sugar." Ms. Jones spoke in a way only an old woman from the south could. She paused briefly. "You know, your mother stopped by here the other day." She tried to gauge Sinnamon's reaction. Naturally the mention of her mother put a smile on her face. It's been almost six months since she last saw her mother, and even though she knew her mother was deeply stuck into the streets, she still had a burning love for her. "Did Shaquan get to see her?"

Ms. Jones lowered her eyes to the ground. She didn't want to disappoint Sinnamon but she had to tell her the truth. So reluctantly, she answered the question. "She didn't want to see him." Ms. Jones said sadly.

"What do you mean she didn't want to see him. That's her son." Sinnamon was hurt and began to feel bitter.

"I know honey, but you have to understand her condition. She didn't want him to see her the way she is. She knows she not doing good. She only came by because she was concerned about you." Ms. Jones tried her best to help the situation.

"Concerned about me? She needs to be concerned about Shaquan even more. I'm grown. She needs to just come back home. Why is she worried about me anyway? She doesn't care when she's running the streets." Sinnamon tried hard to hold back her tears but allowed one to escape.

"Sinnamon, she's concerned about how you live. She heard about your boyfriend and she was worried."

"Well Ms. Jones, I thank you for the message." Sinnamon wiped her face and grabbed Shaquan's bags that were already packed. "And next time you speak to her, tell her I said don't worry about how I live. She needs to focus on her own life." Sinnamon headed for the door.

"Sinnamon wait." Ms. Jones said before Sinnamon was out the door. "She left you a number. She said call her, and wanted you to know that she's been where you are in life. She also said that she loves you." As Ms. Jones gave Sinnamon the number, she held Sinnamon's hands. "Call her Sinnamon." Ms. Jones spoke softly. She could tell by the look in Sinnamon's light brown eyes that behind the beauty, and expensive clothes, she was still a lost little girl that needed her mother.

Sinnamon took the number from Ms. Jones and stuck it in her purse. "Come on Shaquan. Say bye to Ms. Jones." Shaquan hugged Ms. Jones and kissed her on the cheek. Sinnamon did the same. "Thanks again Ms. Jones." Sinnamon disappeared out the door.

When Sinnamon reached her house, once again, she felt the weight of the world on her shoulders. She held the number that Ms. Jones gave her in her hand. Deep inside, she wanted to call her mother to find out what was going on with her, but she couldn't bring herself to pick up the phone. She questioned why should she call her mother; her mother should be calling her.

Sinnamon also had to worry about how she was going to pay all the bills that she had. E took care of everything and she had no source of income. Looking through the house, she only found a little over five thousand dollars that E had stashed in a drawer. That wouldn't do much being that her mortgage was high and so was the payments on her Benz. Sinnamon knew it would be hard but she wanted to maintain her lifestyle. She refused to go backwards. With that in mind, she knew her first option was to call Dez and Spoon. She was sure they had some of E's money. Sinnamon flipped open her cell phone and found Dez's number. Once she located it, she pressed the send button and the phone rang.

"Hello" a male voice answered. Sinnamon knew it wasn't Dez.

"Is Dez around?" Sinnamon questioned.

"Yeah, why? Who this?"

"Sinnamon".

"Oh, this Spoon, what you want?" His tone was of a frustrated person.

"I want to speak to Dez. That's what I want." Sinnamon replied smartly. She couldn't stand Spoon.

"Hold on." Spoon covered the phone and yelled out to Dez. "This bitch Sinnamon on the phone." Sinnamon could hear Spoon disrespect her and wished E was still living. She would've told him and he would've been cut off.

Dez came into the room and took the phone from Spoon. He didn't like Spoon disrespecting Sinnamon like that. She was good peoples in his eyes. "What's up?" Dez said when he got on the phone.

Being frustrated from Spoon's ignorance, Sinnamon got straight to the point. "Do you and Spoon have any of E's money because I need it? I have bills to pay Dez.

"E's money." Dez hesitantly repeated. Spoon overheard the conversation and snatched the phone from Dez. He didn't have any plans on giving Sinnamon anything. E was dead, and she didn't earn anything in his eyes. He didn't support spoiling a woman.

"E's money?" Spoon spoke with force. "You ain't getting' shit. You ain't do shit for it."

"I have bills Spoon." Sinnamon cut him off.

"I don't give a fuck. You should've been savin' all that money that sucka-for-love ass nigga was givin' you. Sell ya Benz if times are that bad." Spoon laughed.

"Fuck you Spoon." Sinnamon said emotionally.

"Don't fuck me. Fuck that nigga Esco that was beefin' with E Bitch!" Spoon hung the phone up on her.

Sinnamon stared at the dead phone and broke down. Once again the guilt of being cool with Esco took over her. That made her want to kill Esco even more. She had it in her mind that murder was her only option. She had to kill Esco, even if that was the last thing she did.

Chapter 18

After the fight with Dez, Essence kept her distance from him. She wasn't sure what had gotten into him, and wanted to avoid another confrontation for the time being. She knew in time, she would have to make up with him in order to get her revenge and that would be an easy task because he'd been calling her day and night apologizing. So it was only a matter of time before she reeled him in. Other than that, everything else was good on her end. She just needed to get Sinnamon together.

"What's up girl?" Essence was stretched out on her bed talking on her cell phone to Sinnamon.

"Nothing much, just bored." Sinnamon sighed. She had been stuck in the house all day with Shaquan and her misery. She was still mad at Spoon for his smart remarks.

"Let's go to the mall." Essence suggested. She knew the mall always brightened Sinnamon's day. It had been like that since they met.

"I don't have any money." Sinnamon whispered. She was feening to do some shopping, like a dope head feens for his first bag in the morning.

"I know you got some money stashed for a rainy day." Essence was sure Sinnamon had something. She had Esco and E both giving her money, so there was no way Sinnamon was broke. Even she herself had a couple grand put away.

"I wish." Sinnamon was ashamed of herself. "All I found was five thousand dollars in here and that's barely enough for the bills.

"You wasn't savin' anything?"

"No, and you don't have to rub it in."

"Well don't Dez and Spoon owe E some money?" Essence assumed.

"I'm sure they do but Spoon told me I wasn't getting shit."

"Call Dez then, he wouldn't do E dirty like that." Essence gave Dez the benefit of doubt.

"I don't know about that because he was right there when I spoke to Spoon. I don't know what's up with them." Sinnamon huffed. She was beginning to get frustrated again. Hearing the news Sinnamon gave her, Essence really had more of a reason to get at Dez. She didn't understand how he could leave Sinnamon hanging like that. It wasn't like Sinnamon was just some young girl E was fucking, she was wifey. They lived together and spoke about marriage and the whole nine.

"I don't know what I'm going to do. I have no money Essence." Sinnamon began to cry again.

"Don't even worry about it girl. We'll figure something out. Matter of fact, come get me so I can help you search the house. I'm sure E has something stashed in there somewhere." Essence still had the car that Esco gave them, but it was acting up so it was parked out front.

"Alright, I'm on my way." Sinnamon really hoped Essence was right about the money.

When Sinnamon arrived at Essence's house, she was already out front waiting for her to pull up. Essence jumped in the front seat and greeted Sinnamon and Shaquan.

"What's up Sinnamon?" Essence shut the door then turned around to face the backseat where Shaquan was. "What's going on handsome? You miss me?" She hadn't seen Shaquan in a few days.

"Yeah." Shaquan blushed. He was reaching the age where he could tell when a woman looked appealing.

Sinnamon was speeding on I-95 south and they made it to her house in less than fifteen minutes. Essence took a look at the nice three bedroom home when they pulled up. Her memory took her back to the night of E's murder. She could picture the gruesome murder scene in her mind. She shook the thoughts off and entered the house. Once inside, Shaquan shot past Sinnamon and Essence and ran upstairs to his room.

"So where you think we should start?" Essence questioned. "I guess the basement because I searched everywhere else. Besides, that's the spot he would always count his money." Sinnamon answered. She checked the basement partly, but not in detail like she did the bedroom and other places she felt was suspect.

The two of them went into the basement and began the search. They tore the basement apart. They went as far as flipping the couch over and ripping out the bottom. Despite their efforts, they came up with nothing. All they found was an empty safe and empty Timberland boxes.

"Them niggas must have cleaned him out." Essence assumed when she saw the empty safe, and boxes.

"I figured there wasn't anything down here." Sinnamon felt defeated. She grabbed a pool stick and began to shoot the balls around that were on the table. Essence watched the colorful balls roll around and noticed something wasn't right. There was a certain area on the table that made the balls change directions.

"You see that?" Essence came closer to the pool table.

"What are you talking about?" Sinnamon looked at Essence puzzled. She didn't notice what Essence saw.

121

"Watch this." Essence grabbed the 3 ball and rolled it slowly down the middle of the table. When it reached the dead center, the ball shifted its direction slightly to the left. "This table ain't even or somethin." Essence was now like a detective. She felt as if she was on to something. She pushed down on the middle of the table and it sank in. "Somethin's in there." Essence assured Sinnamon.

Sinnamon pushed down on the same spot that Essence did. "I can feel something but how the hell is something in there?" Sinnamon began to frisk the entire table, looking for some type of opening. Essence didn't have the patience for that. She went upstairs to the kitchen, and found a large knife. When she joined Sinnamon back in the basement, Sinnamon was still searching for some type of opening.

"Watch out." Essence moved Sinnamon out of the way and began to dissect the table. "Bingo!" Essence shouted when she saw a white powder break through the green. Essence set the knife down and ripped away the rest of the green material from the pool table. Sinnamon was more than relieved to see stacks of bills in the rubber bands, staring at her. There was also a large amount of cocaine and a forty-caliber handgun.

"Bingo ain't the word." Essence said when she saw everything that was in the table. She and Sinnamon jumped into each other's arms and jumped around in joy. They removed everything from the hiding spot and took it upstairs where they counted the money in Sinnamon's bedroom. It turned out to be One hundred thousand dollars. That was enough for Sinnamon until she found other means of getting money.

"So what are we going to do with the coke?" Sinnamon looked at the powder as if she was scared to touch it.

"Sell it. Esco taught us how to cook coke, so we may as well put our skills to use." Essence wasn't an expert on cocaine but from what she learned from Esco, she knew what she and Sinnamon had was worth a lot of money.

"To who Essence?" Sinnamon really wondered. She didn't have the slightest idea who she would sell drugs to.

"We'll figure something out, but for now, we'll hide it back downstairs. We can keep it for whenever we need it." Essence grabbed the gun that she found. "As for this, I'm taking it with me." She tucked it in her purse. "You don't need any more guns." Essence cracked.

"Whatever." Sinnamon chuckled, and then fell silent. "I'm still going to get him though. Are you going to help me?" She batted her light browns at her friend in a cry for help.

"You still don't know for sure if he did it or not." Essence said. She wanted Sinnamon to squash her beef with Esco. He was their bread winner.

"Essence I understand where you are coming from, but it's not like he's going to admit it to me. I really feel he did it. Your my girl, are you going to help me or what?" Sinnamon was going to go through with her plan against Esco either way it went.

"Yeah Sinnamon, I'll help you." Essence agreed even though it was against her own judgment. She felt she didn't have much of a choice being that Sinnamon was like her sister and she knew she needed her help. By herself, Sinnamon was likely to get killed.

"Thank you." Sinnamon gave Essence a strong hug. She felt a strong connection between her and Essence. Plotting a crime such as murder had a way of bringing people closer together.

Essence looked at her watch and saw it was getting late and wanted to get home. She wasn't ready to stay at Sinnamon's house because of the murder.

"You ready to take me home?"

"I don't feel like it. Shaquan's probably sleep and I'm tired. Just take my car or stay in the guest room."

"Where your keys at?" Essence got off the bed and grabbed her purse.

"In my purse." Sinnamon pointed to her purse that was on the dresser.

Essence dug in the purse to retrieve the keys. Sinnamon's .380 was also in there.

"I see you keep Peggy Sue with you." Essence closed the purse back and stuck the keys in hers. "I'ma call you when I get home."

"Make sure you lock the door behind you." Sinnamon said as Essence walked out of the room. She was going to sleep with a smile on her face now that she had the money she needed.

On the ride home, Essence thought about the promise she made to Sinnamon. How could they kill Esco? She was so close to him. If it wasn't for him, there was no telling where she'd be. But a promise is a promise so she had to go through with it. She just hoped something happen before it went that far. She had to find a way to clear Esco's name.

When Essence reached her house, a surprise was awaiting her. Once inside the small place, it looked as if a tornado hit. The entire apartment was upside down. She looked around in disbelief. Who would do something like this, she thought. Essence checked the door and windows to see if someone broke in. To her surprise, there was no sign of forced entry. She thought a moment, and then it hit her. Esco was the only one with a key, other than Sinnamon and she was just with her so it couldn't have been her. She tried to figure out why he would ransack her house. After thinking for a full ten minutes, she could only come up with one conclusion. Esco must have killed E, and was now back tracking to clean up witnesses. He knew Sinnamon knew he did it, and probably was afraid she was going to tell on him. That was the only thing that made sense. She was just caught in the middle of a messed up situation. She was glad she took the other gun from Sinnamon's. She opened her purse to make sure it was still there. She took it out and cocked it backed. She feared for her life. Sinnamon was right all along. She thought to herself. With the gun in her hand, Essence began to pack a small bag. There was no way she was going to stay in that house with someone trying to kill her. Being that she didn't want to stay at Sinnamon's, she only had one other option. It was time to make up with Dez. She called him to let him know she was on her way.

Chapter 19

"Damn I miss you baby." Dez grabbed Essence by her waist and gave her a tight hug. He loved the way her body felt against his. She was so soft and it was almost like she melted into him. When they broke their embrace, Dez gave Essence a kiss on the lips.

"You still in the doghouse though." Essence did miss Dez a little, but she was still upset.

"So what happened at your spot?" Dez asked as he led Essence to his bedroom.

"I'm not sure. I don't even want to talk about it right now. I just need some security from you. I want you to hold me tonight." Essence stroked Dez's ego a little.

"I'ma do more than hold you tonight. I miss that good loving." Dez grabbed Essence by her waist and kissed her again when they reached the bedroom. Just the softness of Essence's kiss made him erect.

"Mmmm. You miss me that much?" Essence whispered seductively. She rubbed Dez's hardness through his jeans. "Where you wanna put that?"

"Wherever you let me." Dez turned Essence around so that her soft backside was pressed against his manhood. He kissed her softly on her neck, turning her on. Then, he reached under her shirt and massaged both of her breasts with his large hands. He found her nipples and teased them with his pointer fingers and thumbs.

"That pussy wet for me yet?" Dez whispered in Essence's ear. She let out a soft moan.

"It's dripping baby." Essence closed her eyes and enjoyed her breast massage. Her breast was a major sexual spot for her. She began to grind her backside against Dez in a circular motion. He lifted Essence's shirt over her head and tossed it across the room. She was now standing in a pair of jeans and a royal blue satin bra. Essence removed her own bra and Dez stared at her beautiful breast. No matter how many times he saw them, he still got excited when they were out. They were only a B-cup, but to him they were perfect. They sat up just right, even without the bra and her nipples were large, just the way he liked them.

Dez gently pushed Essence back on the bed, and put one of her nipples in his mouth, while massaging the other one. Essence kicked off her shoes and rubbed the back of Dez's neck as he went to work. When her breasts were satisfied, Essence put both of her hands on Dez's head and pushed him down to her love. She wanted some oral pleasure. Dez kissed down to her belly button and at the same time, tugged at her belt. When the belt came loose, he unfastened her jeans and pulled them down. Because they were so tight, Dez had to literally rock her out of them. When her jeans came off, so did her panties. Essence's beautiful body was now fully exposed. Dez looked down at her and admired her nakedness for a moment. Essence maintained her body well. From constant shaves and waxes, her skin was hairless and smooth as a baby's bottom. In between her thick thighs was her perfectly groomed womanhood. She kept her pussy lips bare. The only hair she had was right above her clitoris and she kept it shaped like a heart and cut low. She knew that men loved to see it like that, and she felt it invited them to put their face in it. Being turned on by Dez's foreplay, Essence's clitoris swelled and stuck out toward him. She was dying for him to nibble on it. Dez teased

Essence by kissing her inner thighs and licking around her pussy. Essence licked her fingers, and then pinched her erect nipples. She began to massage her breast the way Dez did as he put his lips and tongue where Essence wanted him to. He grabbed her thighs and held them locked opened, then went to work.

Dez used his free hand to part Essence's lips and licked her soft wet flesh. Her juices were flowing, and found their way into his beard. He began to flick his tongue back and forth across her clitoris, causing her body to tighten up. She naturally tried to close her legs but Dez's tight grip prevented her from doing so.

"Don't run now, this what you wanted right?" Dez came up for air. He had Essence going and knew it. There was nothing like it; for a man to know he's pleasing his woman. The sensation Essence felt caused her to arch her back and lift her butt slightly off the bed. That gave Dez a better angle and room to do a little more. He took Essence's sudden movement as an opportunity to lick the area right between her pussy and asshole.

"Damn, that feels good." Essence moaned. She felt a slight numbness in her legs and chills shot up her spine. Seeing that she liked that, Dez took it a step further and flicked his tongue around and over her asshole. The feeling caused Essence to grab Dez's ears and head. She was going crazy. After teasing her ass for a few minutes, he put the focus on her clitoris once again. Covering his teeth with his lips, Dez nibbled softly on Essence's clitoris. He took his thumb and pushed back the skin that covered the more sensitive part and fluttered his tongue across it. That was the straw that broke the camel's back.

"Ooh shit! I'm coming." Essence screamed. Her entire body released and her legs began to tremble uncontrollably as her liquids oozed on to Dez's beard. He continued to lick and bite. Essence tried everything in her power to run from him. She couldn't take the feeling anymore. With all her might, she pushed down on his head. Dez laughed as he let up. He was satisfied with a job well done.

It Gets Dirtier

"You ain't never make me feel like that." Essence was out of breath and her body continued to shake. Her orgasm drained her. Dez stripped off his clothes and stood before Essence with his manhood rock hard. He got on top of her and began to kiss on her, but didn't get the response he wanted.

"Not right now baby. You sucked the life out of me. Let me lay down for a moment. I need to get myself together." Essence was out of breath. She pushed Dez off of her and rolled over. Her right leg continued to shake. Within seconds, she was sound asleep. Dez looked down at Essence and didn't know how to feel. On one end, he was mad that he wasn't getting any pussy, but then on another note, he was pleased with his work. Like any man, he was swelled with pride because he put Essence to sleep with a smile on her face. He kissed the sleeping beauty on the cheek and left her alone. He had some things to discuss with Spoon anyway.

* * * * *

Around 2 a.m. Essence was awaken from the sounds of two people arguing. She had been asleep for a little over two hours and was still drowsy. "I know this nigga ain't got no bitch over here while I'm sleep."

Essence immediately thought the worse. She jumped out of the bed and put her jeans on without her panties, and found a tee shirt to put on. She started to grab the .40 caliber that was in her purse, but decided Dez wasn't worth it. Instead, she grabbed an old basketball trophy that Dez had on his dresser. Somebody was going to feel her wrath. Essence cracked the door open and stopped in her tracks. She realized Dez wasn't arguing with a woman, it was a man. From the sound of things, they were beefing over money.

"What the fuck you mean you spent some of the money?" Dez was trying to keep his voice down. He didn't want to wake Essence.

"Like I said, I spent some of the money. I got tired of not having a nice whip, nigga. I wanna shine too." Essence could hear the other person saying. She tried to put a face to the voice, because the voice was very familiar.

"Twenty stacks though Spoon." Dez revealed the other person.

"You act like that's a lot. We got that nigga for damn near half a mil. Just take it out of my cut." Spoon blew Dez off.

"That's not the point Spoon. We agreed that we wasn't going to touch the money yet." Dez was tired of Spoon doing his own thing. The tone of Dez's voice made Spoon defensive. He felt Dez was challenging him and knew Dez didn't have the heart he did. He stared deep into his cousin's eyes and stepped closer in his face.

"Listen here nigga. You ain't trill, so don't try to play a role you can't. It was my idea to rob E nigga, not yours. You was scared." Spoon spoke in a harsh tone.

"That don't matter. Without me, you wouldn't have got shit. You moved too fast. You killed him before you even found the safe or got the code. It just so happened, I knew the shit nigga." Dez wasn't backing down. He returned Spoon's cold stare.

Oh shit! They killed E. Essence said to herself. She was shocked. They were the last two people that she would expect. Spoon maybe, but not Dez. He and E were too tight for something like that, in her opinion. She thought about Sinnamon and wondered if she would believe her or not. Essence was relieved that Esco wasn't the killer. She undressed again and climbed back into the bed, as if nothing happened.

In the living room, Dez and Spoon's argument died down. They were family and didn't want to take things too far, so they agreed to split the money in the next few days, and Spoon agreed to relocate somewhere else. They were on two different levels. Dez was laid-back and thinking about leaving the game with the money they took from E.

Spoon however, was just getting started. He planned to take his share of the money and buy enough coke to lock a spot or two down. He wanted to be that man in the game that had it all. He never stopped to think about E's outcome. E was once the man, and that didn't get him anything but an early grave. Spoon was blinded to the lesson that was right in his face. He couldn't see past the money. Greed does that to people.

Chapter 20

Early the next morning, Essence went straight to Sinnamon's house to deliver the news. On her way there, she began to devise a plan to get E's money back and kill Spoon and Dez at the same time. She then thought about Esco and the beef that she and Sinnamon now had with him. She needed to settle that problem ASAP. In due time, Esco would come in handy with the plans she had in mind.

"Esco didn't kill E?" these were the first words Essence spoke when Sinnamon opened the front door. It was only 7:30 a.m. and the sound of Essence ringing the doorbell woke her up. She still had her nightclothes on underneath a large robe.

"Girl, what are you talking about this early in the morning?" Sinnamon shut the front door and let out a soft yawn. She followed Essence into the living room and took a seat next to her on the couch.

"Last night, I stayed at Dez's house." Essence started.

I thought you were mad at him?"

"I am, but when I went home, the crib was a mess. Somebody broke in and tore it apart. I was thinkin' it was Esco because he's the only one with a key, besides you. I figured he was tryin' to get rid of me and you because he really did kill E." Essence was talking real fast.

"Hold on a minute. You need to slow down because you're confusing me. I thought you just said Esco didn't kill E."

"He didn't, you just have to let me explain." Essence took a deep breath and did her best to talk slower.

"I stayed at Dez's last night because someone broke into my spot. Well, last night when I was sleepin', I heard two people arguin' and woke up. I was about to snap because I thought Dez had a bitch in the front room. So I was on my way out there, but heard it was a nigga he was talking to. He and Spoon were arguin' over the money that they took from E". Essence explained. She waited for Sinnamon's response.

"You sure they weren't talking about the money E left behind?" Sinnamon couldn't picture Dez doing anything to E.

"Sinnamon, I heard them with my own ears say that they robbed E and killed him. Spoon had the idea and Dez was with it." Essence really wanted Sinnamon to believe her.

Sinnamon thought on things for a minute. She could see Spoon doing some slimy shit, but Dez was iffy. Then she thought on how Dez was acting funny towards her. Anything was possible.

"You know I wouldn't lie to you." Essence was still waiting for Sinnamon to respond.

"I know you wouldn't. I just can't believe this." Tears began to stream down her face. "I don't understand why Dez would do something like that." Sinnamon wiped her face with her forearm

"People will do anything for money." Essence said.

"So, who do you think broke in the apartment?" Sinnamon remembered what Essence said in the beginning.

"I think Esco did that shit. He's the only one with a key."

"Why do you think he did that?"

"I'm not sure. Only thing I can think of is because of that shit that happened with you. Maybe he thinks you're going to go to the police." That was the only logical explanation she could think of.

"We need to call him." Sinnamon wanted to apologize.

"I am. I'ma tell him to meet us at the mall or something because I know he ain't gonna come to my house again. Plus, it's just safer to be in a public place. I don't know what's on his mind." Essence said.

"Well call him." Sinnamon was anxious to get things out in the open.

Essence pulled out her cell phone and called Esco. She let it ring, but she got no answer. The answer machine picked up.

"Call again." Sinnamon insisted. Essence called again, and this time got an answer.

"What." Esco answered.

"We need to talk." Essence said.

"For what? Last time I agreed to talk to ya girl, I almost got shot." Esco was still hot about that. But deep down inside, he wanted to fix things.

"That's what we need to talk about. We wanna squash the beef. We found out who really did the thing." Essence didn't want to say too much over the phone. That sparked Esco's interest because he too wanted to know who did it. Then he thought that the girls were trying to set him up. He wasn't falling into a trap.

"I ain't fuckin with ya'll. You bitches crazy." Esco hung up. Essence stared at the dead phone. She couldn't believe Esco just called them bitches. He never disrespected them in any way before. But she did understand where he was coming from. Sinnamon tried to kill him.

"What did he say?" Sinnamon was waiting for Essence to say something. "He said he ain't fuckin with us and hung up." Essence simply said. She turned to Sinnamon. "So what do we do now?"

"Give me your phone. I'm going to call him myself." Sinnamon snatched the phone and redialed Esco's number.

"What?" He answered in a frustrated tone.

"Esco, this is Sinnamon. We need to talk. I'm so sorry for the way I acted last time I saw you. I really am. You just have to understand what I was going through." You could hear the sincerity in Sinnamon's voice.

"How I know I can trust ya'll?" Esco's feelings always softened up when it came to Sinnamon. He wanted to settle things with her so he could finally have her to himself. He just wasn't sure if she could be trusted.

"We can meet anywhere you choose." Sinnamon was willing to go anywhere. "That way we're wherever you want to be." Esco thought a moment. The evil in him wanted to tell her to meet him somewhere low key so he could knock the girls off. He knew of a few quiet areas around Wilmington. The girls were making things too easy. After a few seconds of thinking, the perfect spot came to mind. He explained to Sinnamon of a spot in Chester where they could meet. He figured if the police were involved in anyway, the Wilmington PD wouldn't be able to cross state lines. Only thing he had to think about now was what he wanted to do with the girls.

* * * * *

"So what's up?" Esco was sitting alone on a bench at a small park when Essence and Sinnamon approached. He held his 9mm in his hand and rested it on his lap where it was visible. This time, if Sinnamon even looked as if she was going to pull out something, he was going to put her down. No if's ands or buts on this one!

Sinnamon locked eyes with Esco and felt butterflies in her stomach. Something in Esco always touched a special spot in her. He made her feel like a little schoolgirl with a crush.

"Can we sit down?" Essence watched Esco's gun closely. She didn't like the idea of meeting at a park. She wanted to be somewhere that had a lot of witnesses. She wasn't ready to die.

"I ain't stoppin' you." Esco motioned toward the empty space on the bench. "Let's get down to business. I got shit to do."

The girls took a seat at the bench. Essence observed the park, looking for different ways to get away if things went bad. She and

Sinnamon also had firepower with them. Esco just had the jump on them because his gun was already drawn.

"Can you please put your gun away? That shit makes me uncomfortable." Essence still had her eyes on the gun.

Esco cracked a smile. "That's what it's supposed to do. Now speak ya peace because as I said before, I got shit to do." He was beginning to get impatient.

"Okay." Sinnamon started. "I apologize for the other day."

"We already established that." Esco said plainly. Sinnamon took a deep breath and blew Esco's attitude off. "Well I did what I did because I really thought you killed E. I had to ride for my baby Esco." Sinnamon looked deep into Esco's eyes. "I would've done the same for you."

"So what cleared my name?" Esco showed no emotion on his face, even though he was feeling what Sinnamon said. She was a true rider in his opinion, the perfect wife for a thug.

"We found out his boys did it." Sinnamon told him.

"Dez?" Esco was surprised.

"Yeah, him and that black fucker, Spoon." Essence joined in.

"So what are ya'll going to do now?" Esco was concerned. He didn't want the girls to jump off the deep end with the situation and get themselves into something they couldn't handle.

"We're not here to talk about that. We just wanted to make sure things were straight between us." Essence answered.

"I hear that gansta." Esco cracked another smile. He felt he taught his girls well. He stood up, tucked his gun in his waistband and extended his hand to Essence. She took it and he pulled her in for a hug. "Ya'll still my peoples." He did the same with Sinnamon, but he held her a little tighter and a little longer. They enjoyed the hug, equally. It was a while since their last embrace.

"My number ain't change. If ya'll need me, call. I got ya'll." Esco turned and walked away. He was relieved to have things settled with the girls. It felt as if a ton of bricks were lifted from his shoulders.

Chapter 21

"So, we got one problem out of the way. Now all we have to do is figure out how to handle Spoon and Dez." Essence said in between a mouth-full of snickers ice cream. She and Sinnamon were in Sinnamon's living room a few hours after meeting Esco.

"We know where they live so it shouldn't be too hard to get at them." Sinnamon responded.

"It's more to it than killing them Sinnamon. We gotta get that money too." Essence was determined to get the money that Spoon and Dez were arguing about. There was too much of it not to want it.

"So what do you think we should do?"

Essence put her bowl of ice cream down on the coffee table. "Here's the plan. We go out there together and push up on them. Use our looks."

Sinnamon shook her head no. "Hell no! There's no way I'm pushing up on Spoon's black ass. I can't stand him and he knows it."

"You don't gotta give the nigga no pussy, just seduce him. Get him talkin' and take it from there." Essence knew her plan would work.

She saw how Spoon always looks at Sinnamon. And Dez was a no brainer. She already had him open. "Are you with it?"

"I'm with it." Sinnamon sighed. Essence and Sinnamon talked over their plans for a while. Their goal was to get Dez and Spoon drunk and see if they could get them to brag about the money. If they did, then they would get them to show it to them. If that didn't work, they would have to go with plan B. Sinnamon preferred plan B anyway, so she hoped the first plan didn't go well.

"Well, it's getting' late. I'ma come back out here tomorrow, so we can put things into action." Essence got her things together to leave. She still didn't feel comfortable in Sinnamon's house.

"Just call me tomorrow when you wake up." Sinnamon walked Essence to the door and gave her a hug. She watched Essence walk to the driveway and get into her car.

After Essence left, Sinnamon went into her bedroom and laid on her bed. She had a lot of things on her mind. She wondered if revenge was worth the consequences. If she got caught, a murder charge was a hard pill to swallow. She couldn't see herself doing life in a prison. At the same time, being exposed to all the money and finer things in life had Sinnamon feening for the money that was involved. She thought about how Spoon and Dez left E dead in their house. They didn't have to do him the way they did, and Sinnamon felt they needed to be dealt with. She knew deep down inside, E would ride for her. He and Esco were the only men she ever had in her life. That's why her feelings for them were so strong.

Sinnamon was also thinking about her mother and all they been through. Every day that went by, she worried about her mother even more. It's been months since she and her brother have seen their mother, and that wasn't like her. Sinnamon grabbed her purse and began to look through it. She was trying to find the number that Ms. Jones gave her. Once the number was in her hand, she just stared at it. Picking up the phone and dialing the number was harder than she expected. What would she say, would she be able to handle what her mother might tell her. These were a couple of things she thought about as she stared at the number.

It Gets Dirtier

After a few minutes went by, Sinnamon decided to go through with the call. She grabbed her cell phone, took a deep breath and dialed the number. On the third ring, she got an answer.

"Hello, can I speak to Betty please." Sinnamon spoke with perfect manners. Her heart fluttered as she waited for a response.

"Hold on a minute." The voice on the other end spoke with an attitude. "Betty, pick up the phone and don't take long. I'm waiting for somebody to call me back."

Seconds later Betty picked up the phone. She had just started drinking, so she felt a little tipsy, but she wasn't her normal drunken self.

"Hello. Who this?" Betty's voice was a little rough.

"It's Sinnamon mom."

"Hey baby, I didn't think you'd call. How have you been?" Betty was excited. She truly believed Sinnamon would never call her. Sinnamon's nervousness quickly turned into anger. How could her mother ask how have she been doing, when she hadn't made an attempt to see her. Sinnamon sat up in her bed. She had a mouthful to say to her mother.

"You would know how I've been if you would come by or something. Where the fuck you been mom?" Sinnamon's voice was shaky. You could hear the hurt.

Betty was caught off guard. This was the first time Sinnamon ever cursed, or raised her voice at her. She was speechless for a brief second and all she could do was stare at the phone. This wasn't the conversation she thought she was going to have with her daughter.

"Sinnamon, I'm sorry." Betty managed to get out. She could feel her daughter's pain. When she was younger, her parents abandoned her as well. So she knew how Sinnamon was feeling.

"Don't say sorry. Please don't say that. Why do you have to put us through this? You left me and Shaquan for dead." Sinnamon snapped.

It Gets Dirtier

"No I didn't. You're well taking care of from what I hear." That was Betty's only defense. "You had that nigga takin' care of you. You didn't need me."

"What do you mean I didn't need you? You're my mother. And what about Shaquan? He calls me mom. What type of shit is that? You don't know all the shit we've been going through. You're never there mom. You're never there." Sinnamon's voice began to break up. Tears started to build in her eyes as she let her anger out.

"Sinnamon, I'm a dope head. I can't help it." Betty began to cry.

Sinnamon was facing reality again. The material things that Essence, Esco, and E bought into Sinnamon's life took her away from all the misery. Now, she was forced to remember all the pain. Tying the rope around her mother's arm so she could shoot up, sleeping in front of the stove during harsh winter nights, having no lights, the roaches and mice, the lack of food and clothes, killing her mom's dope head boyfriend. Everything ran through her mind.

"Why did you have to put me through all of this mom?" Sinnamon's anger built more and more. "I didn't even have a fucking childhood!"

"Sinnamon, I'm sorry baby. You just don't understand. This thing is so strong, and I can't help it. I'm trapped. I'm sorry." Heroin had Betty in a tight grip that she couldn't escape. Nothing came before her high.

"Don't be sorry. I'm sorry I even made this call." Sinnamon paused. "But then again, it's okay. Hearing from your sorry ass just makes me want to succeed so much more. I'll never be like you. I'm going to make something of myself. I don't care what I have to do." Sinnamon hung up the phone and threw it across the room. She laid back in her bed with her arms folded, in deep thought. All of the thoughts Sinnamon had about not robbing and killing Dez and Spoon went down the drain. She felt she had to do it now. There was no way she would end up like her mother.

Chapter 22

The next day, everything was in motion. Thanks to Essence, she and Sinnamon were scheduled to see Dez and Spoon that night. They were anxious to get things done and over with so they could put the situation behind them. The suspense of waiting for the time to meet Dez and Spoon were killing them. Time seemed to move in slow motion.

"Eight o'clock ain't never gonna get here." Essence huffed. She looked at the clock that read 5:42 pm. She and Sinnamon were at her house, already dressed for the night. The girls kept things somewhat simple. They both had on tight seven jeans that would get any man's attention and button down oxford shirts. Sinnamon had her hair in the long ponytail that she grew accustomed to wearing. The ponytail gave her the Lora Craft look from Tomb Raider. Essence on the other hand, wore her hair out looking like a black Barbie. The women were still stunning with little effort.

"I know." Sinnamon stood up from the couch and paced the small living room. "I'm about to take a nap or something until it's time to go. I need to calm my nerves." Sinnamon was a little nervous about the deeds they had planned.

"I might as well do the same thing." Essence agreed. She knew sleep would pass the time by. They already went over their plan numerous times, so they didn't have anything else to do. Essence made her way to her room, and Sinnamon laid out on the couch. Both girls had a lot on their minds, mainly money and murder.

Essence always fantasized about having a large sum of money. She wanted to be like the hustlers that she was often involved with. They had all the money, power, and respect, and she wanted in. She could care less about avenging E's death, she was about the money. Sinnamon, on the other hand was thinking about the hard life she lived. Thinking about how far she had come in one year, still amazed her. One thing Sinnamon would never do was move backwards. Everything had to be about moving forward. Ending up like her mother was out of the question, so she was willing to do anything. The robbery wasn't even about E, the more she thought about it. It was about her and her needs. E's death just provided an opportunity of a lifetime.

In the mist of their many thoughts, the girls found themselves in dreamland. Even in their sleep, they could smell the money they would soon have. In one night, they would have more money than some people would have in a lifetime. Before they knew it, it was a quarter to eight. Essence's phone woke them up when it rang.

"Hello." Essence yawned. She stretched her arms out and arched her back. She looked as if she was reaching out to God.

"Damn baby, ya'll ain't forget about us did you?" Dez said on the other end of the phone. Just hearing Essence's voice was enough to get his dick hard. He couldn't wait to get another piece of her.

"No baby, we still comin'. Actually, we're about to leave now." Essence spoke in a soft sexual tone.

"Alright baby. I'll see you when you get here." Dez hung up. Essence got off her bed and went in the front room to wake Sinnamon, but she was already up and ready to go. Essence's loud phone ringer woke her up as well. "I see you ready." Essence observed Sinnamon patiently waiting with her purse in her lap. She knew Sinnamon had her gun in her bag.

It Gets Dirtier

"I've been ready, let's go." Sinnamon stood up and grabbed her keys off the coffee table.

"Let me go comb my hair again to make sure I'm picture perfect." Essence made her way to the bathroom.

"Alright, I'm about to go next door and kiss Shaquan good night then I'll be in the car." Sinnamon left out the front door, and walked next door to knock on Ms. Jone's door. Seconds later, the older woman answered the door and greeted Sinnamon with a hug.

"I thought you and your friend were going out?" Ms. Jones asked as she broke their embrace.

"We are. I just wanted to give Shaquan a kiss good night. What are you cooking? It smells good in here." Sinnamon could smell the food coming from the kitchen.

"I got a slow start with my roast. It's about done now. I'll save you and Essence a plate if you want." Ms. Jones always made enough food to feed extra people.

"Yes please save us a couple of plates. I love your cooking so much." Sinnamon said with a huge smile.

"Okay honey, your brother's in the back room watching that movie you sent over." Sinnamon found Shaquan with his eyes glued to the TV. He was watching "Finding Nemo" for the hundredth time.

"You're not tired of that movie yet boy?" Sinnamon startled him. Seeing his sister, Shaquan jumped up and gave her a big hug. "Well, I love you too." Sinnamon laughed and held on tight to her brother. "If I don't see you tomorrow, know that I love you and will always love you forever." Sinnamon knew there was a chance she wouldn't return. There was no telling how things would go.

"I love you too." Shaquan spoke with the innocents of a child. He was unaware of the thoughts in his sister's head.

"Sinnamon spoke with Shaquan a few seconds longer, and then made her way to the door.

It Gets Dirtier

"See you later Ms. Jones." Sinnamon yelled as she walked out the door. Just as she walked out of Ms. Jones house, Essence came out as well.

"Perfect timing." Essence said with a smile.

Chapter 23

"What's up baby?" Dez spoke with excitement when Essence and Sinnamon walked through the door. He was excited to see Essence. Essence returned Dez's smile and kissed him softly on the lips.

"You miss me?" She asked in her bedroom voice. She looked around for Spoon. "Where's ya cousin at?" Essence began to worry because the plan wouldn't work without having them both there.

"He in his room." Dez took Sinnamon and Essence coats. "So you really ready to move past E?" Dez asked.

The question caught Sinnamon off guard, and she didn't know how she wanted to respond. She wanted to answer the question without disrespecting E in the least bit.

"Well." She hesitated. "I mean, it hurts. It hurts a lot but this is the only way to move past this."

"I can understand that." Dez wanted to say more but decided against it. Inside, he wondered why Sinnamon would want to talk to Spoon out of all people. He decided she was just going through something. "I'm 'bout to let Spoon know ya'll here." Dez disappeared in the back and found Spoon in his room smoking a blunt, and playing John Madden on his Playstation2.

"Yo, the girls here and they look good cuzin." Dez boasted.

It Gets Dirtier

Spoon got up and turned the game off, then looked at himself in the mirror. He stood looking into his chunky eyes as he blew out the weed smoke. He was wearing a black and gray Coogie pull over shirt; he also had on a pair of black Coogie jeans, with some black Air Ones. He topped it off with a Raiders fitted cap that he pulled just above his eyes. With his fresh gear on, a blunt in his system and close to ten grand in his pocket Spoon felt really good about himself.

"Damn nigga, you still ugly, lookin' in the mirror ain't gonna change shit." Dez joked.

"Fuck you nigga." Spoon adjusted his hat one last time, and then left the room still smoking the blunt that he had. When Spoon and Dez reached the living room, the girls were seated on the couch watching videos. They were trying to relax a little. They were getting more nervous with each minute that passed.

"What do ya'll have to drink?" Essence asked before Dez could take a seat. Spoon had quickly found a spot next to Sinnamon. She gave him a quick look over and had to admit, he didn't look as bad as normal. She thought on how money could improve a person's appearance. In this case, it was her man's money doing the improvements.

"Somethin' to drink? Like what?" Dez wasn't sure if Essence was talking about regular soda, juice or alcohol.

"You got some liquor?"

"I think so." Dez disappeared into the kitchen. He opened his refrigerator and pulled out bottles of Hypnotic and Remy. He and Spoon kept more alcoholic beverages in their refrigerator than they did food. The refrigerator was filled with different Cognacs, Heinekens, Moet, Alize and Hypnotic. It looked like a mini bar inside. After getting the bottles, Dez grabbed some glasses and returned to the living room.

"Ya'll smoking?" Dez sat next to Essence and pulled out a vanilla dutch and a bag of weed. He tore the plastic off the cigar and began to split it open.

"Naw, I'm straight on that." Essence didn't want her mind to be clouded. The liquor would be enough to settle her nerves.

"You?" Dez looked at Sinnamon.

"Never again, you remember what happened last time." Sinnamon reminded Dez.

"That's cuz you was dealing with that lame ass nigga E and he slipped you that shit." Spoon interrupted without thinking. Everyone fell silent, even him. He didn't want to come out disrespectful that time, but he couldn't help but speak his mind. Essence kept a watch on Sinnamon's response. She knew Sinnamon didn't like that comment by the way her nostrils flared up. It took everything Sinnamon had not to act out. She grabbed her handbag that held her .380 a little closer. She couldn't wait to put it to use. Spoon had no remorse for what he did to E and she would be sure to show no remorse on him when his time came.

"Turn the music on." Essence broke the uncomfortable silence.

The eye contact she gave Sinnamon said "girl, calm down." Sinnamon let out another breath of air through her nose and closed her eyes. Dez finished rolling his blunt, lit it, then got up and turned the stereo on.

'Summer in Miami' by Jim Jones blew through his speakers. The smooth melody of the song eased the mood a little and everyone found themselves bobbing their heads to the beat.

"This my shit." Dez spoke. He turned the stereo up a little more, then took his seat back on the couch. He took three deep pulls from his blunt and blew out the smoke as he passed the blunt to Spoon. The room was silent other than the music that filled the air. Everyone seemed to be in their own world. As Lloyd sang about having bottles in the air and living without a care, the group all thought about their own hood dreams of living ghetto fabulous and being hood rich. Money filled all their minds.

"Those niggas are really balling." Sinnamon broke the silence. She took a sip of Hypnotic and thought of a plan that she knew Spoon and Dez would fall for.

"They're talking about popping bottles of Crystal, Don-P, and shit like that, while we're sipping on this bullshit." She turned her nose up at her cup and sat it down. Essence immediately caught on to what Sinnamon was trying to do. The bait was out there, now it was time to reel in the big fish.

"I know right. I would love to hang with some ballin' ass niggas like them one day." Essence added. She watched as Dez seemed to squirm in his seat. She could tell he was getting agitated.

"That's why I miss my baby so much. No one in Delaware was balling like him." Sinnamon rested her eyes on Spoon and waited for his response. Just like she guessed, he took the bait.

"What the fuck you mean, wasn't nobody ballin' like E?" Spoon jumped to his feet. "This the shit I be talkin' bout Dez. Bitches don't never recognize the real niggas." He took a deep pull of the blunt and held in the smoke. He passed the blunt back to Dez, blowing out the smoke as he began to speak again. "See, we was the ones getting' money." Smoke blew out with each syllable, "We was the ones ballin', that's why we still ballin'."

"I can't tell." Sinnamon crossed her legs and rolled her eyes.

"Where's the money at then? Because E was living it up." Her eyes were glued to Spoon and her arms were folded over her chest. Her body language said, "Stop bullshitting and prove it me."

"And that's why that nigga ain't breathin' no more. He wanted to be flashy and all that bullshit. That's why he got robbed and murdered."

Dez jumped in. Everything he said was true. All the material things E had caused envy in his circle.

"Exactly, we got cash money. Fuck the cars, the jewels and shit. That shit don't mean nothin. This is what it's all about." Spoon dug in

148

both of his pockets at the same time and pulled out two large knots of $20's, $50's and $100's.

Sinnamon smiled seductively at Spoon. She knew she had him where she wanted him. All she had to do now was dig a little deeper. Spoon's ego was going to get the best of him and Sinnamon knew it.

"That's probably your pack money. E use to give me knots like that to go shopping. How are you going to handle a woman like me if that's all you're working with?" Sinnamon stood up in Spoons face. Her face was so close to his that he could smell the Hypno on her breath and feel the softness of her breast on his chest. Although she was pissing him off, Spoon found it hard to get mad at Sinnamon because she moved with a sex appeal that was hard to ignore.

Sinnamon looked into Spoons eyes and saw lust. She always saw that look when she saw him. He wanted her bad and she knew it. She got closer to him then bought her lips to his ear. The closeness sent chills down his spine and made his dick hard.

"Do you think you can handle all of me?" Her tone was so sexy, Spoon felt as if he could explode in his pants. Before Spoon could respond, Sinnamon turned her back against him, brushing the softness of her round backside against him. Looking at how her back naturally arched and the roundness of Sinnamon's butt, the only thing Spoon could do was think of how good it would feel to enter Sinnamon from the back. He grabbed her by her waist as she walked away. His hands squeezed into her soft flesh. He pulled her back to him, wrapped his arms around her, and kissed her neck.

Sinnamon only let him enjoy the softness of her body for a few seconds. She broke free from his grasp and turned to face him again. She knew she had him open.

"Naw, you're not ready yet baby."

"That's what I'm talkin' 'bout girl." Essence exclaimed. She was impressed by Sinnamon's bold moves and decided it was her turn to join in the fun.

"Yeah Dez, I'm feelin' like my girl. I need a ballin' ass nigga that's gonna spoil me. If you can't handle that, I may have to fall back from you. You gonna miss this good ass pussy too, ain't you?" Essence spoke in a teasing voice.

Dez threw back a shot of Remy and gave Essence the evil eye. At times he always thought she was only about money when it came to him, but he was into her. He looked her over and a million thoughts floated through his mind. One part of him wanted to call her a bitch, and tell her and Sinnamon to get their gold-digging asses out of his crib. The other half of him wanted to give her any and everything she wanted, so he could keep her forever and a day. He ran across many women in his lifetime, but there weren't many that were on her level.

"So is that all it's about?" Dez asked in a voice that was almost too calm. He knocked the ashes from his blunt, then took a deep pull from it. He blew out a ring of smoke and looked at Essence and waited for her response. "Is it?" He said when she didn't respond.

"It's not all about that, but yes I do feel that I deserve more than what you give me. I shouldn't have to ask you for anything, you should just look out for me as much as you like to fuck." She said matter-of-factly.

"So you sayin' I gotta pay for the pussy now?"

"No! What I'm sayin' is, if you're ballin' so much, I should get more than you give me. You don't have to ask me for no pussy. I put it down every time it pops up, and that's every time I come over here, or when I'm with you period. I give it to you anytime, anywhere, way, however your ass want it. So why can't I get the same from you? I'm supposed to be ya girl."

Dez nodded his head and poured himself another shot of Remy. He felt where Essence was coming from and truth be told, he did have plans on giving her more, especially now that he had more. He put the other shot down before speaking. "You know what, you right." Dez dug in his pocket and pulled out a knot. He began to peel off fifties and hundreds. He passed Essence a thousand dollars, thinking he was doing something.

"That's it?" Essence wrinkled up her face and looked at the money with disgust. She thought he would have come better than that. "I can get this kind of money myself boosting clothes. You gotta come better than this." Essence rubbed her middle and index fingers against her thumb, signaling for more money.

"Show us some real money if ya'll got it like that." Sinnamon jumped in. "E used to show us thousands on top of thousands when we were with him. So where's the money at?" Sinnamon paused as another plan came across her mind. "How about we make this interesting." She smiled at Dez and Spoon.

"We listenin." Spoon eyed Sinnamon down.

"The more you show us." Sinnamon spoke slow and sexy. She unbuttoned the top three buttons of her shirt, exposing her cleavage, "the more we show you."

Dez and Spoon looked at one another. They weren't sure what to do. The girls were coming on strong and they wanted them bad, but they didn't want to show them their stash.

"Come on ya'll. This will be a fun game." Essence joined in. She seductively unbuckled her belt and unbuttoned her pants.

"Aiight, fuck it." Dez pulled out more money from his pocket and threw it on the coffee table. "What's that gonna get us?"
Essence tugged at her pants and wiggled her smooth brown skin out of them. She stood before Dez and Spoon in a red lacey pair of boy shorts. Dez and Spoon both got hard, just looking at Essence pose in her panties. The way the panties fit her you would've thought they were made especially for her. Where her womanhood was, you could see the shape of her fat pussy lips because the material was wedged between them, and the way her thick legs were shaped, made a large gap that looked as if you could shoot arrow straight through it.

"Ya'll like this?" Essence turned around so they could see her back side. The lacey material cramped in between her butt cheeks and then came out covering just the top half of her butt cheeks. Her ass was so phat that the panties looked too small for her.

"You know I love that shit. Let's go in the room." Dez didn't like Spoon seeing Essence half naked. He wanted her for himself.

"Don't leave yet. You might miss the show." Sinnamon said smoothly. She unbuttoned the remaining buttons of her shirt and took it off. She wore an expensive green bra that held her breast perfectly. Seeing Sinnamon in the bra, Dez took a seat on the couch and decided to let things flow in whatever direction it was going.

"Shit. I need to see more." Spoon threw all his money on the coffee table. Essence now removed her shirt and Sinnamon removed her jeans. They stood in front of the men in their lingerie, looking like super models. Spoon and Dez knew they were in for a night of fun. They laid back on the couch with large smiles on their faces. Life couldn't get any better from where they stood. They had two beautiful women half naked in their front room with close to twenty grand on the coffee table and hundreds of thousands more in their rooms.

"So what are ya'll going to show us to see more?" Essence walked over to Dez and sat on his lap. "You do want to see more right?"

"Damn right I wanna see more."

"Well, show us the money." Sinnamon spoke up. She wanted to see if they had more money in the house. "Ya'll are balling right?"

"Damn right we ballin'." Spoon hopped to his feet and headed towards his bedroom. He returned a minute later with a bag of money and dumped it on the table. It was close to one hundred grand of wrapped twenty's and fifties.

"Mmm. So ya'll are balling." Sinnamon said seductively. "I'm sorry I doubted your handle." She unfastened her bra and threw it directly at the men.

"Come let me put dat thong in my mouth." Spoon said.

"Hold on girl." Essence stopped the action suddenly. "Before we get naked, I need to see some skin." Without hesitation, both Dez and

Spoon stripped down to their boxers. They watched in amazement as Sinnamon and Essence took off their remaining clothes. They were now totally nude, and there wasn't a flaw on their bodies. They were the definition of perfection. Their womanhoods were freshly waxed and so were their legs. They used baby oil to moisten their bodies, so their skin was soft and shinny. Dez and Spoon sat on the couch hard as steel. Their eyes darted back and forth from both women and all over their bodies. It was hard to focus on just one of them.

"Damn ya'll look good." Dez said as he admired them.

"Do we?" Sinnamon gave Dez a seductive smile. She then sashayed over to her handbag, bent over in a sexy pose and grabbed it. Essence saw Sinnamon's moves and followed suit.

"Come over here and let me feel that soft ass of yours." Spoon spoke lustfully. He bit down on his bottom lip as he thought on how good Sinnamon would feel on top of him. He grabbed his dick and rubbed it.

"You want me to do that for you?" Sinnamon sashayed her way back over to Spoon, carrying her bag. She grabbed a handful of Spoon's dick. "You like that?" She whispered in his ear. She placed the bag safely behind Spoon on the couch. She then rubbed her small hands all over Spoon's lower body, getting him aroused. Essence waited patiently for Sinnamon to make her move as she entertained Dez with a sexy dance.

"You ready for this?" Sinnamon was straddling on top of Spoon, staring into his eyes with her arms wrapped around his neck. They looked as if they were about to share a passionate kiss.

"I been ready." Spoon looked deep into Sinnamon's eyes, but failed to see the hate in them. He just sat there, with a hard dick and hands full of ass. She had him hypnotized.

Sinnamon sat up just enough to reach behind Spoon and unzipped her bag. Spoon didn't see what she was doing because he took her sudden move as a sign that she was ready for penetration.

He took his dick out of his boxers and lined it up with Sinnamon's womanhood.

"Crack;" Sinnamon's gun hit Spoon right above his left eye. He grabbed his face as he fell over on the couch.

"You didn't think it was going to be that easy did you?" Sinnamon stood over top of Spoon in her birthday suit pointing the gun in his face.

"I'ma kill you bitch." Spoon tried to shake the blow off. He gave Sinnamon a look of death.

"What the fuck is up yo?" Dez stared at Sinnamon. When he turned back to Essence, he was staring down the barrel of a 40 cal. He couldn't believe what was going on.

"Just make this easy and tell us where the money at?" Essence said. She had a huge smile on her face.

"I ain't givin' you bitches shit. You gonna have to kill me." Spoon spoke, through clenched teeth. His pride wouldn't allow him to cooperate.

"So you want to make this hard?" Sinnamon asked.

"Fuck you." Spoon was still playing the tough guy role.

"Grab the tape." Sinnamon told Essence. Essence grabbed her bag and pulled out the duct tape. "Now go over there and sit in that chair."

Sinnamon used her gun to direct Spoon to a chair that was at the dining room table.

"I ain't doin' shit bitch."

"You think I'm fucking playing don't you?" Sinnamon rolled her eyes in frustration. She placed the barrel of the gun on Spoon's kneecap and pulled the trigger without flinching. Blood splattered on her face from the impact.

"Awww, Awww." Spoon screamed out in pain. He fell off the couch and rolled around on the floor.

"Not so tough now?" Essence laughed at Spoon then focused back on Dez. "So are you gonna make this easy, or do you have to end up screaming like some bitch like your cousin?" Dez just looked at Essence confused. He was scared out of his mind and didn't know what to do. He looked like a deer caught in the headlights.

"Go sit in the chair dumb ass!" Essence screamed when Dez didn't move fast enough. Dez quickly made his way over to the chair. He looked at Spoon on the floor and didn't want any parts of the pain he was feeling. Essence followed Dez to the chair. "Take ya boxers off." Essence pointed the gun at Dez's dick when she spoke.

"Come on baby. Don't point the gun down there."

"Shut the fuck up!" Sinnamon spoke up. When Dez was naked, Sinnamon began to duct tape him to the chair. She taped his leg, arm and mid section to the chair very tight. When she was done, she took a step back and looked at her work. Once again, a devilish smile came across her face. With Dez in his proper place, it was time to get Spoon into his.

"So, are you ready to cooperate now tough guy?" Sinnamon spoke as if she was talking to a baby. She let out a wicked laugh.

"Fuck you." Spoon struggled to talk. His knee was throbbing.

"Shoot yourself. I tried to help you." Sinnamon took the heel of her shoe and jammed it into Spoon's Wounded Knee.

"Awww shit." Spoon screamed out in pain, before passing out.

"Help me with this nigga." Sinnamon told Essence. Essence taped Spoon's ankles together.

"Get them M-80's." Essence told Sinnamon as she finished taping Spoon's ankles together. Sinnamon retrieved the M-80's from her bag. Spoon began to come back to and tried to break free.

"How are we going to do this? He's not cooperating?" Sinnamon asked.

"Look at how small he is. Just sit on him." Essence said.

"You sit on him. You weigh more."

155

"Fuck you." Essence laughed. She hovered over Spoon's face before sitting on him. "Ain't this what you wanted?" Essence looked down on Spoon, and then sat on his neck so he couldn't move. The pain he felt in his leg and loss of blood made it hard for him to put up much of a fight.

Sinnamon grabbed Spoon's left hand and taped it to his right one. She started with his wrist and worked her way up to his hands. She left enough of his hands exposed to stick one of the M-80's in the pouch that she created. She then taped it shut, leaving the wick of the M-80 exposed so it could be lit.

When Sinnamon was done, she and Essence quickly put their clothes on. They were ready to finish executing their plan so they could make their escape. Essence grabbed a trash bag from underneath the sink and loaded the money that was on the coffee table.

"Where's the safe?" Sinnamon questioned.

"Find it ya self, bitch." Spoon spat through the pain. Beads of sweat covered his forehead. The hat that he had on was now on the floor next to him.

"Go check his room." Essence suggested. Sinnamon went into Spoon's room and found his safe in no time. She then searched Dez's room and found his. Now all she need was the combinations.

"What's your code Dez?" Sinnamon asked calmly. She was staring face to face with him.

"Why you doing all this?" Dez asked.

"What do you mean why am I doing this? Nigga, you killed my man."

Dez's eyes popped open wide. He didn't know that Sinnamon knew. He figured she was just doing bad and was looking for some money. He also knew she was mad that he didn't give the money to her, when she asked for it. He thought the robbery was all a get back plan.

"Who told you that shit?"

156

It Gets Dirtier

"Save the bullshit Dez. I already know. Now what's the code?"

"Don't tell that bitch shit." Spoon screamed. Essence walked over to Spoon and smacked him in the mouth with her .40 cal. The blow knocked out his front teeth and blood began to pour from his mouth. "Shut the fuck up!" Essence said harshly.

Sinnamon enjoyed watching Spoon go through pain, but she focused her attention back on Dez. "Make this easy for yourself." She still had a calm voice. She wasn't nervous anymore and was ready to end things.

"Just take the money that's on the table. It's probably over a hundred grand." Dez didn't want to give them everything.

"No, I want it all. It's not even your money, its E's." Sinnamon told him.

"Fuck all this dialogue." Essence grabbed a lighter from the coffee table and walked over to Spoon. She stared deep into Dez's eyes as she flicked the lighter releasing the flame. "This is what's going to happen to ya dick if you don't act right." Staring at Dez she lit the wick to the M-80 that was in Spoon's hand.

"Boom!" the explosion sounded like a gun going off and pieces of Spoon's fingers blew across the room. The small blast caused his right pinky, and a few of the tips of his finger to fall off. The pain was so unbearable that he began to go in and out of consciousness again.

"Now." Essence began to speak. She grabbed Dez's limp dick and held it next to a M-80 as Sinnamon taped the two of them together.

"You see what happened to your friend for playing tough. You do want to keep ya precious piece of flesh, don't you?" Essence waited for Dez to respond.

Dez could hear Spoon moaning in pain and pictured his dick in pieces. He quickly shook his head yes.

"Well you better start screaming out some numbers." Essence said plainly. She still held her .40 caliber in her hand.

"Okay, okay." Dez started. "23-0-12"

157

"What's Spoon's?" Sinnamon questioned.

"I don't know." Dez answered.

"Bullshit." Sinnamon grabbed the lighter that Essence had and lit it. She waved the flame in Dez's face. "If you wanna play games, we can play. Fuck with me if you want."

"Don't tell her." Spoon whispered with bloody lips. He was lying in a puddle of blood that leaked from his mouth, hands, and right knee. He felt he was near death. Sinnamon walked over to Spoon and raised her gun. She was tired of his mouth and knew they didn't have any use for him anymore. Spoon looked her in the face and waited for the shot. He was determined to die like a soldier.

"Fuck Y..."

"Boom" The bullet silenced Spoon before he could finish his statement. Sinnamon shot him directly in his temple, immediately ending his life.

"Now, back to you." Sinnamon said when she returned to where Dez and Essence were. They were both surprised to see Sinnamon kill without hesitation. Dez began to think he might not survive either. He silently prayed to himself. He was looking for a miracle. "What's the code?" Sinnamon dropped the hand that held the gun, lit the lighter and waved it in Dez's face.

"17-7-12" Dez said quickly. Sinnamon and Essence repeated the combinations to themselves. Once she knew she had the combination lock in her head, a wicked smile came across Sinnamon's face.

"Thank you." Sinnamon said. She patted Dez on the head then flicked the lighter once again. She lit the M-80 in one quick motion.

"Boom!" Dez's screams were loud to the point that Sinnamon and Essence feared someone would hear him. Essence quickly put an end to the yells with one shot to his forehead. Dez's head snapped back from the impact, then his chin dropped down to his chest and his head tilted slightly to the left.

"We gotta hurry up." Sinnamon grabbed Essence by the arm and pulled her in the direction of the bedroom. Sinnamon held the trash bag with the money tightly in her grasp.

Essence was star struck for a moment. The scene was more brutal than she expected. Dez's dick and pieces of his brain were splattered all over the place. Some of it even colored her clothes.

"Snap out of it." Sinnamon told Essence, and dragged her into Dez's room. Sinnamon quickly began to open Dez's safe. The sight of money quickly bought Essence back to reality. She put the cash into the bag as Sinnamon held it open. The girls quickly did the same with Spoon's safe and began to make their exit.

"I told you I was going to get them." Sinnamon said in a low tone before walking out the door. She looked back at her victims for a brief second, and then shut the door. With the bag loaded safely in the back seat, the girls slowly pulled off from the scene as if nothing happened.

Chapter 24

"Look at all this money!" Sinnamon said in disbelief. She and Essence were at Sinnamon's house in her bedroom. They were in from the robbery feeling like new women. They were now murderers with a large sum of money. Looking at all the cold hard cash on the bed made the girls feel like everything was worth it. If given another chance, they would do it again.

"I never thought in a million years, that I would have all this cash. How much do you think it is?" Essence grabbed two stacks of the rubber band-wrapped money and smelled it.

"I'm guessing a few hundred thousand. We have to count it." Sinnamon began to take the rubber bands off the stacks of bills. The two of them sat and counted the money until almost four o'clock in the morning. They walked away with 357 thousand dollars. They couldn't believe it.

"This what I'm talkin about." Essence said. She was smiling from ear to ear. She waited for an opportunity like this all her life. There were so many days and nights she only dreamed of having that much money at her disposal. The feeling was intoxicating. She grabbed some of the money and hugged it

It Gets Dirtier

"Girl you are crazy." Sinnamon laughed. "I feel you though. Look how far we came. We can never go backwards from here." Sinnamon spoke seriously; and she was right. There was no turning back.

"Ain't no way I'm goin' backwards. You see how easy that shit was. Killing them niggas wasn't even as hard as I thought it would be." Essence said.

"It was easy." Sinnamon sighed. She wasn't satisfied.

"What's wrong?" Essence was concerned about Sinnamon's sudden change of mood.

"I think we could do better." Sinnamon answered seriously. Essence looked at Sinnamon puzzled. "How much better could we have done?" She thought to herself.

"What do you mean do better? We got 357 thousand. Essence pointed to the money on the bed. "How much more do you want?"

"I know they took more than that from E. You saw the kind of money E use to show us. And what about the drugs? I know them niggas had coke somewhere.

"Sinnamon, what would we have done with all that coke? I mean seriously, where would we sell all that shit." Essence didn't know where Sinnamon was going with the conversation.

"I don't know, we can ask Esco." Sinnamon figured he would've helped them. "That's what I was going to do with the coke we found in the pool table."

"I hear that, but it's too late now. They dead." Essence shrugged her shoulders. She was satisfied with the money she had.

"Well, let's get somebody else." Sinnamon's eyes were filled with greed. The taste of money had her yearning for more.

"Are you serious?" Essence looked at Sinnamon as if she was crazy.

"Yes I'm serious Essence. This is our chance to make millions. Look how easy that was. We made over 300 grand, and had fun doing it. Three or four more hits like that and we'll be millionaires." Sinnamon had dollar signs in her eyes.

Essence thought for a moment. She felt Sinnamon had a point, but still thought the idea was crazy. She began to think of something to make Sinnamon change her mind.

"   There's nobody else in Delaware with that kind of money that E and them had." Essence spoke truthfully.

"Who said anything about being in Delaware? Staying here would be dumb anyway." Sinnamon waited for Essence's next excuse.

"Well, what about Shaquan? What will he do if something happens to us? " Essence struck a nerve with that one.

"Why are you thinking so negative? If you're scared, just say it, shit. I'm trying to get what everybody dreams of and you're playing. If something happens to us, Shaquan will be straight. We'll leave some money where Ms. Jones can find it. I know she'll take care of him." Sinnamon already had things mapped out. Essence couldn't believe the monster that was created. She could see the flames in Sinnamon's eyes as she spoke. Her girl was officially sucked into the black hold of greed. Essence had a love for money too but she didn't feel how Sinnamon did.

"Well, look, I'm going to do it whether you chose to come along or not." Sinnamon said when Essence remained silent.

"Okay, okay. I'm with you. A few more times Sinnamon. Once we get a million dollars, we done right?" Essence looked to Sinnamon for the answer.

"A million dollars apiece and we're done." Sinnamon said. A wicked smile crept on her beautiful face.

"So where do we start?"

Chapter 25

"More money, more murder, more homicide. You catch that body nigga, betta have that alibi." Az rapped the chorus of his and Nas' song.

Sinnamon an Essence had their stereo blasting as they rode down I-95 south, headed to Virginia. The song they were listening to could've been the sound track to their life. After their first robbery, money and murder was all that the girls thought of. With some of the money they got from Dez and Spoon, the girls brought themselves a '96 Cadillac Deville to get around in. They both agreed that the Benz Sinnamon had would draw too much attention to drive on a daily basis. The Caddy they drove was stylish but not too fancy. It had 20" chrome rims, a light tint, and a banging system. It was a regular hood car.

"So what do you think it'll be like down there?" Sinnamon asked. She was seated in the passenger seat, looking out the window while Essence drove. Sinnamon loved looking out at the country fields as they rode by. When she got the chance, she planned to buy some property out there somewhere.

"I really don't know." Essence held the steering wheel with two hands as she drove. She didn't really know anything about the south. She just heard that the people down there were doing good in the drug game.

"I'm guessing all niggas are the same. We'll be able to pick out the ballers from the broke niggas. The way niggas be droolin' over pretty women, somebody will make things easy for us. We got everything we need."

In the trunk of the Caddy, they had some clothes, ten grand, two .357 snub nose handguns. One was silver with a mahogany wood handle and the other was silver with an all black gorilla grip rubber handle. They also had two black plastic baby nine's that held 10 shots, along with handcuffs, blindfolds, duct tape and rope. With all that, their best weapons were still themselves. Their sex appeal could leave the hardest man defenseless, and they knew it.

"We definitely have everything we need. I just hope we can run into the right guys." Sinnamon said. She was still staring out the window.

"We'll be the new faces in town. I guarantee you we will run into a few victims in no time." Essence assured Sinnamon.

A few hours later, Essence and Sinnamon reached their destination, Hampton. It was close to 5 p.m. and the sun was starting to go down. The temperature was still warm so they observed people walking the streets with shorts, and short sleeve shirts on. The scenery was a lot different from Wilmington. Almost every other car was a supped up older model car with big rims. By the looks of things, Essence's source didn't fail her at all. A lot of niggas in Hampton were doing their thing.

"Look at that Caprice girl. That shit is hot." Essence exclaimed. She pointed to a fire engine red Caprice, sitting on 23" rims. The dark tint prevented them from seeing the occupants inside.

"That is nice. I wonder whose driving." Sinnamon admired the car briefly. She would have much rather seen the man that owned the vehicle. She could smell money. After another few minutes of driving, Essence pulled into a nice hotel and parked in the lot. The girls were tired and needed some rest. They had a lot of ground to cover the next day. They had plans on going shopping and club hopping.

It Gets Dirtier

"These rooms should be nice." Essence spoke as she opened the trunk of the Caddy. She grabbed her new Louis Vuitton suitcase and matching duffel bag. Sinnamon did the same and slammed the trunk shut.

"I love when the trunk does that." Sinnamon said with a smile.

"What are you talking 'bout?" Essence looked at Sinnamon puzzled.

"You didn't notice how when you shut the trunk, it doesn't close all the way at first. Then it just seals shut on its own." Sinnamon said matter-of-factly. The women began to walk towards the hotel's entrance.

"Whatever you say. I don't pay that shit no mind. I like how it drives though." Essence continued to walk. She pushed the hotel door open with her large suitcase and shoulder when she reached it.

"Let me help with that sexy." A man came from behind Sinnamon and Essence. He held the door open for the girls and stared at their asses as they walked by. Essence quickly sized the man up, and took inventory on his appearance. His mouth was iced out, as well as his wrist and neck. He wore a large style link chain that was filled with diamonds. Essence wasn't sure if the chain was white gold or platinum. It didn't matter though because it was filled with diamonds. His clothes were no different than the men she saw in Wilmington. He had on a designer pair of jeans, white long sleeve tee shirt and fresh butter Timberlands.

"Thank you so much." Essence said sweetly. She gave the man a flirtatious smile.

"No, thank you." The man answered back, just as flirtatious. He licked his lips and thought of something to say. He didn't want to let Essence pass by without asking for her number. Taking a deep breath to ease his nerves, he cracked on Essence.

"So what brings you to the hotel? Are you on vacation or some-thin'?" He asked shyly.

165

"I guess you can say that." Essence turned all her attention to the man. For her, he was possibly the first victim. Sinnamon checked them into their room as Essence spoke to the unknown man.

"So what's your name?"

Essence paused briefly. She didn't want to give the man her real name. "Jasmine." She finally answered. "My name is Jasmine."

"I'm Javar." He stuck his hand out and shook Essence's hand softly. "So where are you from?" He asked as he let her hand go.

"How do you know I'm not from here?" Essence was trying to buy time. She and Sinnamon didn't talk about where they would say they were from.

"I can tell from your accent. You sound like one of them up North women." Javar cracked a smile.

"I figured that's what you'd say, but you are right. I'm from up North. I live in Lancaster, PA.

"Well since you from out of town, do you think I can show you and your friend around? How long ya'll stayin'?"

"I'm not really sure how long we're gonna stay, but sure you can show us around. I would really like that." Essence kept her voice sweet as she spun her web.

"Well here's my number." Javar pulled out a colorful business card. He passed it to Essence and watched as she placed it in her purse.

"I see you're prepared." Essence laughed. "I'll give you a call tonight."

"I hope you do that Jasmine. I guess I'll talk to you tonight then." Javar tried hard not to smile too much. He didn't want Essence to see exactly how excited he was. She was one of the finest women he had the chance to meet. When he got the chance to hook up with Sinnamon and Essence, he wasn't going to spare any expenses. His pockets were deeper than one could imagine. He was what you call a heavy hitter in the drug game. In his mind he viewed Essence as the

166

average woman with her eye on the wallet. So with that in mind, tonight she would know she was dealing with a "baller".

"So what's good with your friend?" Sinnamon asked Essence when she joined her at the hotel counter.

"From the looks of it, we're fishing in the right pond but we'll see what's up tonight. He wants us to meet up with him so he can show us around." Essence answered.

"Sounds good to me." Sinnamon was thinking about dollar signs and plans to get them.

Chapter 26

"Hello." Esco answered his phone in a groggy voice. He was still in the bed with a slight hangover from partying the night before at Pharaoh's nightclub. On a Saturday night, women from all over the tri-state area made their way in.

"You have a collect from Gage, an inmate at the state correctional facility." The automated system continued its normal spill. Esco was waiting to hear from his boy for a while now. It has been at least two months since the last time they spoke. Esco sat up, stretched, and got out of the bed. He briefly admired the cocoa complexion woman that was lying naked in his bed. He smiled as he thought about the fun they had last night. He knew once he was done on the phone, he was going to get another taste of her.

"What's good my nigga?" Esco said when the call finally went through.

"Alhumduallah. Just striving in the way of Allah. Staying strong at a time of weakness." Gage had a lot on his mind over the last few years. He was serving a 56-year prison term in the state pen for something he had nothing to do with. In his mind, he knew that if he kept his faith in Allah, he'd get an appeal. Even though the first one was denied, his lawyer told him there were other angles to approach.

It Gets Dirtier

"You have to stay strong. So what's been good? I ain't hear from you in like two months, then when I tried to make a visit and they said you couldn't have any."

"I know, I got into a fight with some dude." Gage said plainly. Esco was shocked because Gage did a lot of changing since being back in prison. All he did was talk about living by the Qur'an and doing things right. He was looking for another chance.

"What that nigga do to you to bring the old Gage out?" Esco knew the man must have really done something to Gage.

"The old Gage will never come out." Gage answered sharply. He hated his past. "The man gave me no choice. I caught him in my room. Now if he would've been diggin' through my commissary, I would've just gave him some. Instead, this guy was goin' through my paper work. I don't want no one in here knowin' about my case. I'm still workin' on an appeal."

"Keep it real though, you gave him the business didn't you? I know you beat the shit out of him." Esco was laughing.

Gage cracked a slight chuckle of his own. "I'm not even gonna get into that." Gage wasn't into bragging about that kind of stuff anymore.

"I hear that. So how's everything been coming along?"

"Arrissa hired another lawyer to help with my case, but only time will tell. I've been in the law library tryin' to find a loophole, but all in all, the only thing I can do is look to Allah." Gage answered.

"That's what's up. Arrissa's still holdin' you down." Esco admired Arrissa's loyalty. The average woman would've been left Gage.

"Yeah man, she's really been a blessing.... You hear from Mills and Flip lately?" Gage asked. "I called earlier but didn't get an answer from either of them. I'm trying to make sure everything's good."

"I spoke with them yesterday and they asked if I heard from you. You had niggas worried. You can probably catch up with them later on. They had some business to handle today from what they told me."

It Gets Dirtier

Esco and Gage talked for the remainder of the time they had available. Gage encouraged Esco to leave the game alone before it was too late. He didn't want to see Esco end up like him. Esco told him he'd think about it, but wasn't sure what he'd do when he was done. He went from nickel and diming to pushing bricks. He didn't know anything else.

After hanging up the phone, Esco made his way back into his bedroom. The cocoa woman was still asleep, lying on her stomach. The covers only covered her butt and one of her thighs, which left her back and one leg exposed. Just by the little bit of her body being exposed, it was still easy to tell she had a nice shape.

The night before was slightly blurry to Esco. With all the alcohol he consumed, all he could remember was bits and pieces of meeting the woman that laid in his bed. He wasn't even sure of her name. One thing he did remember was the banging sex they had. Esco thought about how she pushed him on his couch as soon as they walked in the door and sucked his dick for a good ten to fifteen minutes. Just the thought of her oral pleasure gave him a hard one. Esco climbed back in the bed and softly removed the hair from his mystery woman's face. Another winner, he thought to himself. When his sleeping beauty began to stir awake, Esco grabbed a condom from the pack that laid on his nightstand. It was a pack of three Trojan dual pleasure condoms and lucky for him, there was one left. After putting the condom on, Esco pulled the blanket off the woman. The sudden cool air made goose bumps appear on her soft skin. Esco kissed the back of her neck as he reached under her and began to play with her clit. She was fully awake now that Esco was playing with her favorite spot. She reached behind herself and spread her thick butt cheeks apart, exposing her pink flesh.

"Stick it in." She moaned. Esco began to move the tip of his penis around in her wetness playing with her. She was getting wetter by the minute.

It Gets Dirtier

Once he knew she was as wet as she was going to get, Esco slid himself all the way in. She stuck out her butt and arched her back so he could get even deeper.

"Is it wet enough?" She moaned. In a zone, Esco ignored her question. He just began to pound her harder and harder. He yanked her by her hair, forcing her off her stomach and on to her knees. As he pushed in, she pushed back just as hard. The collision of their flesh caused a loud clapping sound. Twenty minutes later, they both collapsed after having an orgasm. They laid in the bed breathing hard and sweating. Esco looked over to his mystery lady and cracked a smile.

"That was good." He told her.

"Who you telling, I ain't get it in like that in a minute." She spoke in between breaths. The room went quiet again. Esco was thinking of a way to find out her name without asking. He didn't want to piss her off by not remembering. After thinking a moment, he just went for the kill. He already fucked her so what did he have to lose.

"What's ya name?" Esco asked. She looked at him for a minute, stunned. She couldn't believe he didn't know her name. She figured he was drunk and let it slide.

"Brandy."

Chapter 27

"Can I speak to Javar?" Essence asked softly.

"Who's this?" Javar had been waiting for Essence to call since he gave her his number the day before. It was close to 11 p.m.

"This is Jasmine. You met me yesterday, do you remember?" Essence said sweetly. Javar sat up on his bed and got an instant hard on just thinking about the beauty he met.

"How could I forget such a beautiful face?"

"Ahh. You're so sweet."

"So how's everything at your room?"

"It's nice, the bed is so comfortable and it reminds me of the King size we have at home."

"We?" Javar was hoping he ran into some freaks.

"Yeah, me and my girl Lovey. After we hit the shower earlier, we fell asleep. That's why I'm just now calling." Essence's voice was very convincing.

"So ya'll live together?" Javar was still trying to figure out if they were freaks. He'd have no problem paying them anything.

"Yeah, me and Lovey been together almost three years now." Essence knew she had Javar wrapped around her fingers at this point.

"Together?" Javar couldn't hide his excitement.

"Oh, I'm sorry. I never told you. That's my lover?"

"So ya'll gay?" Javar's smile grew wider.

"No we're bi."

Javar couldn't believe his luck. Hearing the ladies we're bi was music to his ears. He tried to maintain his composure and played things cool. He didn't want to sound pressed or seem like a lame. Javar covered the phone as he thanked God for the gift. Being that they were calling quarter to eleven, he figured it was a booty call.

"You still there?" Essence thought the phone went dead.

"Yeah, Yeah, I'm here." Javar said quickly. "So what's ya'll plans for the night?"

"We haven't the slightest idea. Lovey told me to call you so you can give us some ideas." Essence knew that would put the nail in the coffin. With Javar thinking her lover was asking about him, she knew it was a wrap.

"What do ya'll want to do?" Javar began to get dressed. He didn't want to waste any time if they wanted him to pick them up.

"Do you know any bars we can go to? We want to have a few drinks and chill for a while. Our treat."

"Ya'll treat huh? Well, I don't know how them up north niggas do, but we don't do it like that round here. We old fashioned so the men be doin' the treating. Besides, you must not know the caliber dude you dealin' with. I almost feel insulted." Javar spoke arrogantly, trying to boost himself up. By then, he already had on a fresh pair of jeans and a spanking new pair of butter Timberlands. He put his phone on speaker so he could brush and grease his hair. He then took out a burgundy and tan button up shirt.

"So you a balla huh?" Essence said. She knew the routine and was tired of it. She hated when a dude bragged about his status. That was a turnoff in her eyes. She felt any real nigga would hide his hand. Not display it for all to see. She knew he was going to be an easy target.

"Something like that. I guess you can say I'm above average." Javar spoke proudly. He finished getting dressed by throwing on a burgundy and tan fitted and then applied some Kush oil. He took a look in his full-length mirror and admired himself. He was satisfied.

"So am I coming to pick ya'll up?" He was confident now.

"How long will it take you? I still have to put my clothes on." Essence began to look through her bag for the perfect outfit.

"Can I help?" Javar was testing the waters.

"No boy. You crazy?" Essence laughed. "But who knows, if you're the balla you say you are, you might can help me take them off."

Javar smiled from ear to ear at the thought of undressing this girl named Jasmine. His smile grew wider when he thought of her friend. Never in his life did he have a threesome, so this was going to be interesting. He went to his closet and removed two large stacks of money that were wrapped with rubber bands out of one of his shoe boxes. He kept several five thousand dollars stacks in Timberland boxes in his closet. In his mind, he was going to ball like Fat Joe and Lil Wayne and make it rain. Wasn't no shame in his game. It wasn't tricking if you got it and that he did. He had six boxes filled to the top with money, so the ten grand he took out didn't put a dent in his stash.

"So when do you want me to come?" Javar questioned. He put his ice on, and was really ready now.

"We'll be ready by twelve." Essence informed him.

"Cool. I'll be there. I'll just call this number when I'm out front." Javar was referring to the number Essence called from.

"We'll be ready." Essence hung up.

"Girl, this nigga dumb." Essence spoke half irritated. "Niggas trip me out. Got a little paper and think they the shit and can get any bitch they want. I bet we got more money than that lame."

"If not, we will by the time we're done with him." Sinnamon appeared from the bathroom. She slid the full clip to her 9mm in its

174

proper place and cocked the gun back. "He's not going to do anything but trick his money off anyway.

Sinnamon and Essence finished getting dressed and were ready to play the game that needed to be played. As they got dressed, they played their new theme song on the little boom box that was in the room.

"More money, more murder, more homicides...." That got them in their zone. You could smell murder in the air.

* * * * *

Javar arrived at the girls' hotel at exactly twelve o'clock. He couldn't wait to see the ladies. He flipped his phone out and scrolled his recent calls. Once he located the number, he pressed send.

"I'm out front." He told Essence when she answered.

"Okay, we'll be out in a second." Essence hung up her phone.

"That was him. You ready?" Essence asked Sinnamon.

"Yeah, I'm ready." Sinnamon was in the mirror applying her lipgloss. The girls both gave themselves one more look before leaving the room. With their guns safely hidden in their purses, they were ready.

As the girls approached Javar's black on black Range Rover, all he could do was stare. "Damn," he said out loud. The girls were even flyer than he remembered. Essence was dressed in a pair of denim high-waist Rock & Republic shorts that hugged every part of her lower figure. Javar couldn't help but notice the gap in between her legs. It was wide enough to see straight through. Her top was a multi-color form fitting sleeveless ruffle Moschino blouse that exposed her slender shoulders. Her hair was out and flowing. She finished the outfit with a green leather pair of peek toe Emporio Armani pumps, and matching purse. Sinnamon chose to expose more skin. She was laced in some black Bebe shorts, a black and white Arthur Maurice blazer jacket, and a black satin Marc Jacobs push up bra. Her belly button sported a real platinum and diamond belly ring that E brought for her. Her hair was in a tight neat ponytail that went down her back,

175

with a full Chinese cut bang. She finished her outfit with a pair of black Stella McCartney sandals with silver rhinestones. She too had a matching purse. Coming out of his trance, Javar quickly exited his Range Rover before the ladies got to the door. He opened the door for them one by one. Sinnamon slid in the back, while Essence took shotgun.

"So where are we going?" Essence quizzed as Javar pulled off.

"To a nice spot called McFadden's. They serve food, the drinks are good, and it's a mixed crowd." Javar answered.

"Do you go there a lot?" Sinnamon asked

"Actually naw, last week was the first time I went. I normally go to Norfolk somewhere."

"So what made you go here?" Essence wondered.

"I don't know. Just wanted to try something different, plus, I was half drunk and didn't want to drive too far." He answered.

"So you live close by?" Essence asked.

"Bout five minutes away."

"Cool". Sinnamon thought to herself. The closer to his house, she figured, the easier it would be to get him there.

"So balla, do you live in a big house?" Sinnamon asked in a teasing tone. Javar looked in his mirror at Sinnamon and flashed his smile. Sinnamon had to admit, he was kinda cute.

"No I don't live in a big house." Javar mocked Sinnamon. "Naw, I live in a condo. I don't need a house just yet cuz it's only me." Javar explained. Their conversation was cut short when they got into McFadden's parking lot. From the outside, you could tell it was big for a bar.

"Damn this a big bar?" Essence said. She got out of the car and looked at the building.

"This is a sports bar, club and restaurant type place. It got a deck in the back to get ya party on and everything."

The trio entered the building and went straight to the bar. As they sat, Sinnamon and Essence looked around at the place. It was semi crowded and Javar wasn't lying about it being a mixed crowd. This was really Sinnamon's speed. She hated ghetto spots. Essence, on the other hand, wasn't sure how she felt. To her, it seemed a little too less 'ethnic' but the music was jumping.

"Let's dance." Sinnamon swallowed the rest of her drink, got up and pulled Javar to the back, where she spotted everyone dancing. Essence followed closely behind. The trio was having a good time as Kelly told everyone she was "gonna bump like this." They really snapped when Beyonce told everyone to drop and hit the floor with it. The girls couldn't help but laugh when Javar did his old school dance. He broke out the MC Hammer on that one. Before they knew it, the party was over and it was time to clear the building.

"Damn. I forgot this place closed at two." Javar was hot. He knew he was showing the ladies a good time. They were partying hard. He was a little upset they only had one drink a piece. By having them drunk, Javar felt he had a better shot at getting them in the bed.

"This shit just like Delaware." Essence sucked her teeth, not realizing her mistake. She was really mad about the party ending.

"Dela what?" Javar asked. He never even heard of the small state.

"It's a small club in Lancaster." Sinnamon cut in. She shot Essence the evil eye.

"So, what are we gonna do for the rest of the night? I need another drink." Essence said.

"I don't even know. Everything round here is pretty much closed. What are ya'll trying to do? The only thing we gonna get to drink this time of night is beer." Javar informed the girls.

"I don't do beer. You live close by right? You don't have anything at your house?" Sinnamon gave Javar a puppy dog look. Being in his line of work, Javar rarely took women to his house. You had to be special for that. He knew women could line you up to get robbed in a flash. That's why he didn't trust them.

"My spot?" Javar was contemplating on an answer.

"Yeah, your spot." Essence jumped in.

"Oh what, we're not good enough to take home?" Sinnamon said tartly when Javar didn't respond.

"Naw, it ain't like that. I was just trying to think if my house was clean enough." He lied.

"Whatever." Sinnamon rolled her eyes.

"So what are we doing?" Essence asked impatiently.

"My spot it is." Javar wasn't going to let this opportunity slide.

The trio pulled up to Javar's condo in no time. He had a nice spot by the water with his own entrance. The ladies were impressed when they entered the condo. They could tell right away that Javar was dealing with money. His two bedroom condo was decked out with the best and it looked like it had been decorated by a professional.

"Your place is laid. Who did the decorating?" Essence asked as she looked around. A smile came across Javar's face.

"Would you believe me if I told you I did."

"Yeah, if you had your shirt in a knot, a perm, and a pair of tight jeans." Essence cracked.

"How you doin'?" Sinnamon sounded like a gay man.

"Damn. Ya'll got jokes huh." Javar couldn't help but laugh. "Naw though, on some real shit, I picked out most of this shit. My mom put it together for me though, and gave it that homely touch. Ya'll like it?

"Ya this is nice." Essence admitted.

'Too bad you won't be enjoying it too much longer. I wonder if his mom will have enough sense to come get his stuff.' Sinnamon thought to herself. A slight giggle escaped her.

"What's so funny?" Javar turned to Sinnamon with a smile that matched hers.

"Nothing. Just thinking about you and those tight jeans." Sinnamon told him.

"How yooouu doooin'?" Essence cracked.

"Comedians huh? So what ya'll want to drink? Dark or white?" Javar held up a bottle of Remy VSOP and a bottle of Grey Goose.

"It doesn't matter. Whatever you want." Essence told him. She figured, why not give him the choice. It was his last drink anyway.

"Dark it is."

"Where's your bathroom?" Sinnamon questioned.

"Second door to your left." Javar pointed down the narrow hallway. "You coming?" Sinnamon took Essence by the hand and gave Javar a devilish look. Blood immediately rushed to his lower area. He returned Sinnamon's look with a smirk.

Once at the bathroom door, Essence used her shirt to turn the knob. She was sure not to leave fingerprints. When they got inside, they took gloves out of their bags and slid them on. They also removed their weapons. Sinnamon had her nine, while Essence carried a .357. Sinnamon and Essence exited the bathroom and found their way to Javar's master bedroom. They looked around and once again, were impressed by his taste. He had a chocolate and tan color scheme going on.

"Javar, your bedroom is so nice." Sinnamon yelled out in her sexiest voice.

"I know, and your bed is so soft." Essence added; hook, line, and sinker. Javar threw back the drink that he poured and raced to this bedroom, only to find himself staring down the barrels of two guns. He was caught in the web.

"Damn. I should've known this was too good to be true." Javar put his hands up in defeat. "Who put ya'll on me?"

"So you think this was a set up huh?" Essence said.

"I know it is."

"Actually, ya arrogance put us on you. I don't know why you niggas think it's cool to be flashy. Running around showing ya cash, and bragging for the bitches. Ya'll make it too easy. Now, empty ya pockets and take off ya jewelry." Essence spoke with authority. Javar did as he was told.

"Now drop that shit on the floor." Essence locked eyes with Javar, showing no emotion. Sinnamon quickly grabbed Javar's jewelry and money from the floor. She put everything in a footlocker bag she found.

"See, look at this shit. Why would you bring all that cash out late at night, just to go out with some bitches you don't even know?" Essence spoke with force. She was schooling Javar on a few things. He made a vow to himself to never slip like that again. He put his head down in shame.

"Now strip and lay face down." Sinnamon spoke up. She wanted a piece of the action. Javar quickly removed his clothes and then laid down on his carpet.

"Where's the stash?"

Javar paused, debating whether or not he wanted to tell them where his money was. He knew he had well over a quarter million in his closet. That was just a fraction of what he had though. He had money in a few other spots as well. He wasn't all the way dumb. He even had money in a safety deposit box, which was in his sister's name.

"What chu think this a game?" Essence spoke boldly. She hovered over Javar, and then let off a shot in his right butt cheek.

"Boom." The large revolver smoked a little after the shot was fired.

"Aww shit!" Javar screamed in agony.

"Where's the money Javar?" Essence jammed the gun in the back of Javar's head. She pulled the hammer back to let him know she wasn't playing. "Don't let me ask you again. Next time, it's a wrap and we'll just find the shit ourselves." Essence spoke coldly.

"Ok, Ok, ok. Just don't shoot me again. It's in the closet." Javar pointed to his large walk-in closet where his shoeboxes full of money were. "It's in the Timberland boxes."

"Boom." Essence pulled the trigger a second time. The last shot sent Javar to his death. The .357 magnum bullet entered the back of his head and exited his face, just under his right eye, which caused it to fall out of the socket.

"Thank you." Essence said coldly. She watched as Javar took his last breath. Sinnamon and Essence quickly filled shopping bags that Javar had around with his money. They stepped over top of his body and headed for the front door. Before exiting, Sinnamon grabbed the keys to Javar's Range Rover, and then left. Once in the truck, Sinnamon pulled off smoothly, headed to the hotel to pick up their things and the Caddy. It was check out time.

Sinnamon and Essence continued their tour of Virginia. They hit two spots in Norfolk and three in Richmond. When it was all said and done, they left Virginia with a little over nine hundred grand, seventeen keys of coke and at least a half million in jewelry. They also left behind a trail of bodies, including Javar's there was a total of eight people dead and one man that was turned into a vegetable. He was never going to come out of his coma. Virginia didn't know what hit them. The girl's next stop was Atlanta.

Chapter 28

"Hey baby, what's up?" Esco answered the phone. Looking at his screen, he knew it was Sinnamon calling. Almost two weeks have passed since the last time they spoke, and he was worried about her.

"Where you been?" Esco asked.

"Out of town, needed to take a little vacation;" Sinnamon was lying across the bed in her hotel room.

"I hear that. When you coming back? I need to talk to you." Esco was at Sinnamon's old apartment, cooking his powder to the oils. His coke was a guaranteed nine on the scale out of ten, at the minimum.

"About what?" She questioned.

"You'll see when you come back. It ain't nothing crazy. You good out there though?" Esco spoke with concern.

"Actually, I'm great."

"Where you at?"

"ATL."

"I hear that playgirl. Ya should've brought me. I'm tryin' to make it down to Strokers one of these days." Esco was referring to a popular strip club.

A little jealousy ran through Sinnamon's veins. "I, I guess you want to see some raunchy girls. I heard it's musty in those places."

"Stop hating." Esco laughed.

It Gets Dirtier

"Not hating, just keeping it real. Anyway, I need you to give me a few addresses. I need to mail you something." Sinnamon got to the point.

"What you picking up souvenirs and shit?" Esco cracked.

"Something like that. You'll see when you get it."

"Aiight." Esco gave Sinnamon four different addresses. He had a feeling Sinnamon was up to something, probably another one of Essence's schemes. He would've never thought she was sending him 17 bricks of raw powder.

"Do I need to send somebody else to pick up the packages, or should I do it myself?" Esco asked before hanging up.

"Send one of your chicken-heads. I'm sending them overnight delivery, so they should be there tomorrow before noon.

"So when you coming back?" Esco couldn't wait to see her. He would never tell her over the phone, but he really missed her.

"Next week." Sinnamon answered. She too was looking forward to seeing him. She hoped he liked the gift she was sending.

"Aiight. I'ma holla at you tomorrow to let you know the mail came through."

"Alright." There was a slight pause. "Be safe." Sinnamon said.

"You too." They hung up.

* * * * *

The next day all four of Esco's packages arrived on time. He had one of his young girls go to each address to pick up the boxes. She met Esco at one of his friend's house around three o'clock that afternoon. When she arrived, Esco removed the boxes and slid the girl a hundred dollars for doing as she was told.

"Can I stay here with you?" The young girl looked at Esco with puppy dog eyes. The way she was rocking her Seven jeans almost made Esco tell her yeah. She was very petite but had a nice round ass.

"Maybe later on." Esco walked her to her car and opened the door for her. She got in and rolled her window down.

183

"What time? I really wanna see you." She whined. Esco loved to see them beg.

"You want some of this don't you?" Esco grabbed between his legs and flashed the girl his smile.

"You know I do, so why you playin' with me?"

"I ain't playin', I told you later. I got shit to do right now. I'ma call you." Esco gave her a kiss on the cheek and made his way back to the house. The young girl was a nice look, but he wanted to know what was in those boxes. She watched Esco disappear into the house. She was disappointed because she knew he wasn't going to call her.

Once inside the house, Esco locked the doors and grabbed the boxes. "Gator." Esco screamed for his favorite smoker. She was up stairs testing his latest batch of work. When Gator finally made it down the steps, Esco couldn't help but to laugh. It felt good for him to see firsthand that his work was the shit. Gator's eyes were wide open and she had what everyone calls lock jaw. That's when the crack's so good the feens can hardly talk. They just move their mouths around like they're chewing on their tongues.

"Ain't nothing down there." Esco laughed when Gator began to look for shit on the ground. She was really geeking. "Calm down Gate." Esco still had a smile across his face. "Help me open these boxes." They were sealed extra tight and Esco didn't feel like going through the hassle. Why should I, he thought to himself. He had already given Gator a whole gram to smoke just for trying his shit, and sweeping up the block.

Gator got herself together, and then quickly opened the boxes. She dumped out four tightly sealed plastic bags filled with white powder from each box, except one. That one had five. Esco was shocked.

He cracked one bag open.

"Taste that shit Gate. Tell me if ya mouth gets numb." Esco demanded.

"Yeah, that's it right there S." Gator said. She took her finger and rubbed it all around her mouth.

This girl done sent me coke in the mail. "She's fucking crazy." Esco said out loud to himself. Just looking at the bags, he knew they held a kilo a piece. He pulled out his phone to call Sinnamon.

"What the hell are ya'll doing down there?" Esco asked as soon as Sinnamon picked up the phone. He was worried about them. He would hate for something to happen to them. Sinnamon was stretched out on the bed, exhausted from the night before. She and Essence had struck again. This time it was only for a little over fifty grand and one and a half bricks of coke. That made them go back out and look for a new target, and they did just that. They ran into a pair of dudes they knew they would have to do their homework on because they seemed low key. The only thing that gave them up was the fact that Sinnamon saw them tipping heavy at the club. They were at Strokers, the spot Esco mentioned. One of them also had on a big iced out chain that read "Dirty South". As they conversed with the two men, they learned two things: One, they both had guns on them, and two, their names were Mills and Flip.

"Boy, what are you talking about?" Sinnamon was slightly agitated. She was still sleepy.

"You know what I'm talkin' bout. That shit you sent me. You crazy as hell." Esco told her.

"Did you like it?" Sinnamon was smiling.

"Where you get this shit from?" You could still hear the concern in Esco's voice. He had an idea where she got it. He just couldn't picture it. Not his Sinnamon.

"Do you tell me where you get your shit from?" She challenged.

Hearing Esco's concern gave her that feeling of love once again. The same feeling he always gave her, security and affection. This made her miss him more.

"You never ask." He wanted to win the debate.

"I never will either." Sinnamon won.

"We'll talk 'bout that shit when you come home." The line went silent for a moment. "Ya'll safe though?"

"We're cool. We'll be home sometime next week."

"I heard that, so what I owe?"

"170"

"That's what's up. Esco was pleased with the price. It was lower then he normally paid. "I'll have that for ya'll soon as ya'll get back."

"That's what's up." Sinnamon said.

"Aiight. Be safe."

"We will. You make sure you be safe too."

"Yo, Sinnamon." Esco caught her right before she hung up.

"Yes." Sinnamon was expecting him to tell her to stop what she was doing.

"I love you." Esco said seriously. Sinnamon was shocked, but she loved what she heard.

"I love you too." Sinnamon hung up with a smile.

"Who was that?" Essence caught the tail end of the conversation. She had just gotten out of the shower.

"Esco." Sinnamon answered while blushing.

"Look at you, all goofy in the face. I knew that nigga was on you." Essence teased.

"Whatever. So what are we going to do with the guys from last night?" Sinnamon changed the subject.

"Who? Mills and Flip?"

"Yeah."

"The same thing we always do."

"I don't know girl. They both had guns with them in the club. Maybe they always carry them." Sinnamon was uncertain about trying to rob them.

"You saying it like we don't have guns. Besides, we gonna catch them with their pants down, just like the rest of them. Ain't nothing changed. Sex is the deadliest weapon." Essence was confident.

Sinnamon grew quiet. She had a bad feeling about this one.

None of their other victims ever carried guns. They pulled most of them from clubs, so they couldn't carry any weapons. She knew Mills and Flip must have been heavy hitters to have guns in Strokers. The security was tight.

"Damn Sin. This was ya idea, not mine. Don't tell me you backing down now." Essence stared at Sinnamon like she could read her thoughts.

"Oh, I get it. Now that Esco said he loves you, everything's different. What, you gonna let him carry you like E did? We got our own money now girl. We don't need no niggas to treat us like we can't do shit." Essence was slightly jealous over Sinnamon's luck with men. She too wanted to feel love. "Are you with me or what?" Essence looked at Sinnamon with pleading eyes.

"You know I'm with you girl. We came too far to turn back now. We're going to pull this last caper and roll. With the money we have now, what we have at home, plus Esco owes us 170, then what we get from Mills and Flip, we should be good." Sinnamon really wanted to tell Essence to quit while they were ahead.

"Cool. I'm with that, as long as we hit our target. Anything less, I'ma still get mine. You with me?" Essence was hyped.

"I'm with you."

Chapter 29

"So where do ya'll want go today?" Mills questioned the girls. Flip, Mills, Sinnamon, and Essence all were riding in a pearl white Escalade with Flip at the wheel. This was the third day the four of them hung out. Sinnamon and Essence were trying to get as much information on Mills and Flip as possible. So far, they didn't find out much, but they felt they were starting to build their trust.

"I don't know really. I don't feel like doing much. I just want to lay back." Essence replied.

You just wanna lay back huh?" Flip said. He was getting a little frustrated hanging out with the girls, and not having sex with them yet. Not that they didn't have fun together, he was just used to getting what he wanted, when he wanted it, especially when it came to women, but these two were different. He could tell they had their own money.

"Chill where though?" Mills asked.

"This is your town. We don't know where to go." Sinnamon spoke up.

Flip knew where he wanted to go. He began to drive to a small house that he and Mills shared together. It was in a secluded area, just outside of Atlanta where they took women every now and then. They never took women to their real homes because they both shared houses with their girls. Their little honeycomb hideout was decked out though. This was also where they went when they were beefing at home.

"What chu goin to the spot?" Mills questioned. He noticed the direction Flip was driving. A slight smile came across Flip's face. He was hoping to score this round. He and Mills made eye contact.

"Yeah. We might as well. I ain't for this riding around with no destination."

"I'm with him." Essence quickly added. She was happy to finally be getting somewhere. For a moment, she thought they were going to have to switch their plans. Twenty minutes later, they reached the small two-story house. It sat on a small piece of land that sat by itself. The neighbors were about twenty yards away on both sides. The small house looked pretty much dead. The only thing visible was the Crown Victoria sitting on 22" rims that Mills bought when he first came home. He stepped it up since then but couldn't get rid of his baby. He kept it just as clean as his Benz.

"This is where you guys live?" Sinnamon quizzed. She expected something a little bigger.

"Something like that." Flip said as they all made their way to the door. Flip let everyone in and then Mills led them straight to the basement.

The girls were fooled by the somewhat raggedy exterior of the house. The basement was laid with the finest technology that money could buy. On one wall sat a huge flat screen TV that was set up like a movie screen. Actually, that whole section of the basement was setup like a small movie theater. It had reclining leather movie seats with cup holders and everything. Of course, there was surround sound throughout the entire basement. Sinnamon's favorite thing in the room was the all white pool table. She could tell it cost a pretty penny.

It looked as if it was carved out of Ivory. The face of the pool table, which is normally green, was pure white and had a silkier look.

Even the balls were different. Some were crystal clear with a colored stripe that was somewhat see through. The others were colored but clear. It was quite impressive.

"I love this pool table." Sinnamon commented.

"I see you have taste." Mills responded. "I picked it out myself."

Essence made her way to the bar area to check out what drinks they had to offer. She noticed a small stage with what appeared to be a stripper pole in the middle. Essence hopped on the stage and swung on the pole for fun.

"Ya'll some freaks." Essence teased.

'If you only knew.' Flip said to himself. He watched Essence do a little dance. She was a natural.

"You dance?" Flip couldn't help but ask.

"Yeah right. I wouldn't be caught dead stripping." Essence replied. "I can move though." She locked eyes with Flip and gave him a look of seduction. Flip laughed and then turned the radio on. He immediately heard T-Pain talking about buying a woman a drink.

"Ya'll want something to drink?" Flip asked. He was at the bar pouring himself a shot of Remy.

"Sure, why not." Sinnamon replied. She didn't mind a little drink. She knew they weren't going to make a move that night. This was just a warm up. The next time they were there, it would be on.

The four of them had drinks, shot pool and watched movies until around two in the morning. They really enjoyed each other's company. In the mist of them hanging out, Sinnamon finally saw what she was looking for; A safe, it wasn't the biggest she'd seen, but she knew it could hold a pretty penny inside. They were going to strike soon.

* * * * *

"Fuck them bitches' dawg." Flip said the moment he dropped Sinnamon and Essence off at their hotel room.

It Gets Dirtier

"You gotta learn to be patient. You can't always fuck within a few days." Mills said smoothly. He watched as the ladies disappeared into the building. He got a kick out of them holding out.

"Fuck that patient shit. I'm Flip." he said arrogantly.

"I hear that player. Flip the pimp huh?"

"Fuck you man." Flip smiled. "On some real shit though, dawg, I ain't playing games with these whores."

"I don't know about you, but I don't always want no fast ass bitch. Every now and then, it feels good to run into a babe with some morals." Mills was serious. That pissed Flip off even more. He wasn't mad at Mills because he understood where he was coming from, but it was too late in the game for that.

"I'ma break it down to you like this cuz." Flip put the radio on mute before continuing. He wanted Mills to hear his every word.

"Mills, bitches like them is a threat to your household."

"Any bitch you trick with is a threat. What makes them any different?"

"Hear me out. For one, look at them, they bad as shit." Flip tried to continue but was cut off.

"And I seen, and had better."

"Are you gone listen or what? I'm trying to put you down on some real shit. Just listen to ya boy."

"Aiight." Mills decided to listen. He could tell Flip was really serious.

"On some real shit, we both got good women, and don't have no business tricking in the first place. So if you gonna do it, do it respectfully. I say those bitches are a threat cuz they the type that'll have you spending too much time with them. Getting to know them, and all that bullshit. We ain't got time for that. Think about it, we getting' to know these whores and the whole nine. That's a violation. Next thing you know, we'll have an emotional attachment. Then, when shit ain't right at home, we'll be running to them and all that bullshit. That's why when I do trick, I do just that...trick! I'd rather pay for the pussy or hit something the first night and never speak to them again. That way, I ain't gotta deal with the extra shit. You dig me?" Flip glanced over at Mills to see if he was listening. He could tell his boy was feeling him. He could also tell Sinnamon was getting under Mills' skin. "I know that bitch bad dawg, but don't let her make you fuck up a good thing. I can tell by the way you look at her, that you dig her. Don't do it to ya self. I almost fucked up like that before. I got caught up and everything. Wifey kicked me out and shit, and guess what? I went to go chill with home girl and come to find out, this bitch ain't even have her own spot. She was living with some nigga."

Flip let out a laugh.

"Talk about hot. I was steaming. Lucky for me, I got my baby back."

Mills soaked in every word that Flip was saying. Everything he told him, he already knew was true. He did feel himself falling for Sinnamon in a way that he knew he wasn't supposed to. There was no way he was trying to lose his girl. She was his everything. Not only that, but everything they had, they got it together. They had built something solid. Mills had to admit, Sinnamon was really more of a threat than he thought. The more he thought on it, the more he felt what Flip was saying. It even made him appreciate his girl even more. He refused to lose her.

"You right cuz. I really needed to hear that. I can't even front, home girl got my attention. I gotta say fuck that bitch." Mills said seriously.

"I would say fuck em right now, but since we told them we'll holla at them tomorrow, I'm with that. And I'm telling you, I'm goin hard. After an hour of chillin', if they don't seem to be with it, I'ma offer a few dollars and if they ain't with that, I'ma put em out. Fuck em. They ain't as bad as they think."

"Aiight. That's all it is then."

Chapter 30

"Tonight should be the night." Sinnamon told Essence. They were having breakfast at a Waffle House near their hotel room.

"I sure hope so. I'm trying to get that money. You said you saw a safe right?" Essence shoved a forkful of food into her mouth.

"Yeah, it's right in the basement too. I can't wait to get this shit over with. I'm trying to get home. I really miss Shaquan." Sinnamon said picking over her food. She was doing a lot of thinking. She only spoke to her brother every other day, and really did miss him. The last time they spoke, he asked her when she was coming back. This was the longest they've ever been apart.

"That's not the only person you missin'. You tryin to see that nigga." Essence rolled her eyes. Once again, she couldn't help but let her jealousy show. "That nigga just better have that money. I know that for sure."

"Girl you're crazy. You know he has the money. Why are you acting funny with him all of a sudden?" Sinnamon questioned.

Essence remained silent. She was embarrassed that her feelings were showing. She wasn't even sure why she felt the way she did. She loved seeing Sinnamon happy. Esco was a cool person in her eyes and she knew he was good for her friend. She was just jealous for no good reason.

It Gets Dirtier

"I'm not acting funny." Essence said defensively.

"Whatever you say." Sinnamon could sense the attitude.

"Well anyway, this shit will be over and done with soon, and we can go back home. I'm a little home sick myself. Besides, I'm tryin' to spend some of this money. I'ma get a new spot and everything. I'm thinkin' about moving in one of them new apartments across from Al's. I heard they're nice." Essence switched the subject.

"Let me buy you a drink" T-Pain came through on Sinnamon's phone. That was one of her many ring tones. She looked at her screen and saw that it was Mills.

"I was just thinking about you." Sinnamon answered.

"I'm on ya mind like that?" Mills said.

"Ever since we met." Sinnamon said sweetly.

"I hear that." Mills was smiling from ear to ear. He loved how Sinnamon made him feel. Just her voice alone was refreshing. He had to shake her off. "I was callin' to let you know that I'ma be coming a little late tonight. Flip still gonna pick ya'll up around ten like we said, but I got a few things to do. If you want, you can wait at ya room till I'm done, and then we can go." Mills informed Sinnamon.

"No, it's cool. I don't mind hanging with Essence and your friend until you come." Sinnamon told him.

"Okay cool. I'll let him know."

"See you tonight then." Sinnamon hung up.

"So Mills not gonna be there?" Essence questioned.

"He's coming, he's just going to be late." Sinnamon told her.

"That's good. By the time he comes, we'd be done took care of Flip, took the money and rolled." Essence was loving the idea.

"I don't know about that." Sinnamon had a bad feeling. "I mean, it does sound a lot easier if it's just Flip but you have to think about it...Mills will know it was us."

"So what, he don't know us. They think we from Lancaster." Essence assured Sinnamon.

194

"I just don't want to leave any witnesses. What if he goes to the police? He does know what hotel we stay at."

"No, he knows what hotel Jasmine and Lovey stay at. Besides, that nigga ain't goin to the police. If anything, he'll try to come back at us but by then it'll be too late. We'll be long gone. We're gonna hit the highway soon as we're done. Matter of fact, I'ma call Flip and let him know he doesn't have to pick us up. We can drive our car."

Essence had it all figured out. Essence pulled out her phone, dialed Flip's number and told him the change of plans, and he was cool with it. He gave them the directions and told them to meet him there at ten. Flip was actually glad he didn't have to pick them up. Sinnamon and Essence finished their food and then left the waffle house. When they reached their hotel room, they packed all of their belongings and gave the room a real good cleaning to make sure they didn't leave too much of themselves behind. They wanted to disappear without a trace. Once they were packed, they just sat and waited until it was show time.

Before the girls knew it, they were in the Caddy blasting their theme song on their way to see Flip. Sinnamon tried talking Essence out of the plan, but she wouldn't go for it. She had already made up her mind. Sinnamon had a bad feeling about the whole thing. She felt they were better off heading home or picking a new target.

"So you sure you want to do this?" Sinnamon asked as she pulled up behind Flip's truck.

"How 'bout this...You drop me off and I do this shit myself. I don't have time for you second guessing shit. You either with it or you're not." Essence was staring Sinnamon in the face. Seeing that Essence wasn't going to listen to her' Sinnamon felt like she had no choice but to be with the plan. There was no way she was going to leave Essence by herself. No telling what would happen then.

"Don't talk to me like that." Sinnamon said in a calm aggressive tone. "I just don't have a good feeling about this. But if you want to do it, you know I'm going to do it with you. I would never leave you by yourself."

"Well come on then. It's on my lead this time." Essence got out the car and headed for the front door. Sinnamon followed. Before they could knock, Flip opened the door.

"Hey Flip." Essence spoke energetically. She gave Flip a tight hug and a kiss on the cheek. Essence was a natural actress. No one would've ever imagined what she was up to.

"I see you're happy to see me tonight." Flip gave Essence a smile. He led the ladies down to the basement. They all took seats in the movie chairs and began to make small talk for a while.

"I have to go to the bathroom." Sinnamon said suddenly and got up to go. She made her way to the bathroom, but had to pass where the safe was. When she looked, it was still in the same spot as yesterday. She wanted to make sure it wasn't moved. She knew people tend to move their stuff around. Sinnamon sat on the toilet and pulled out her new .38 Taurus snub nose from her purse. She double-checked to make sure it was fully loaded. She had butterflies in her stomach. Something didn't feel right. Sinnamon closed her eyes and said a short prayer before going back to join Essence and Flip.

When Sinnamon came back into the room, she gave Essence a slight nod to let her know that the safe was in the same spot. Taking a seat, she waited for Essence to make her move. They had only been in the house for forty-five minutes or so. Not sure when Mills was coming, they planned to get the robbery out the way ASAP.

Essence got up from her seat, carrying her small bag. For some reason, she wasn't the least bit nervous. She eyed Flip as he sat watching "Belly" on the large TV. In one quick motion, Essence pulled out a chrome .45 ACP handgun and cocked it back. Hearing the familiar sound of the metal, Flip automatically reached for the gun he had on his hip.

"Don't even think about it." Sinnamon told him forcefully. She pressed the barrel of her gun to his temple. She now felt in charge and her butterflies quickly left her.

"Ain't this a bitch." Flip said.

"Yeah it be like that sometimes. What's the combo Flip?" Essence spoke calmly.

"You can't expect me to just give ya'll the combo that easy." Flip looked at Essence without an ounce of fear. He was more mad than afraid.

"You would if you want to live. I have no problem pulling the trigger. You can try me if you want." Essence told Flip.

The look in her eyes let Flip know she was serious. He thought on how much money was in the safe. He guessed it to be a little over 200 grand. He laughed to himself; that was nothing to him. Especially not enough to die for.

"Somethin' funny?" Essence asked.

"Naw, I just can't believe this shit is happening. Ya'll got me. Iwould've never guessed. I could've used some gansta bitches like ya'll on my team."

"We good with the team we have. Now stop wastin' our time and give us the combination. We don't have all night." Essence said smartly.

Sinnamon walked over to Essence after removing Flip's gun. "I like this. What kind of gun is this?" Sinnamon asked, looking at the large gun.

"357." Flip answered.

"Never knew they made automatics. So what's the code?" Sinnamon asked. She couldn't believe how cool Flip was being about the situation. Right then and there, she knew he had major money and what they were robbing him for didn't hold any weight.

"17-32-10" Flip said smoothly.

Sinnamon walked over to the safe and opened it. She quickly removed the nicely stacked bills and put them in a plastic bag that she got from her purse.

"I got it all." Sinnamon told Essence.

"Sorry Flip. See you when I get there." Essence flashed a wicked smile at Flip. That's when the fear finally hit him. He knew he was dead.

"Boom, Boom, Boom!!!" All three shots hit Flip in his chest.

Essence tucked her gun back in her purse, and she and Sinnamon quickly left the house. They jumped in the Caddy, played their theme song and jumped on I-95 North. It was time to go back home

Chapter 31

"Parker, you have a visit." The CO informed Gage. Gage was surprised by the visit because it was Wednesday, the middle of the week. Due to her work schedule, his wife Arrissa only came on the weekends. As he made his way to the visiting room, Gage wondered who was here to see him. He hoped it was his mother, because it's been years since he last seen her. She'd just pray for his release. Mrs. Parker couldn't stand to see her son locked up in a cage.

As Gage entered the room, he searched the booths for a familiar face. After a good minute, he didn't recognize any one until his eyes settled on an older woman carrying a little boy in her arms. She motioned for him to come over.

"Hey Anthony," The woman spoke cheerfully. She and Gage shared a hug, and then sat down. The woman could see the confused look on his face.

"Hey Mrs. Carter, what are you doing here?" Gage was speaking to Mrs. Carter, but was staring at the little boy. He appeared to be around three.

"I know you're surprised to see me, but my daughter forced me to come. She would've came herself, but figured you wouldn't want to see her, plus she's sick." Mrs. Carter sighed. It pained her to think of her daughter's condition.

"Your daughter?" Gage was surprised. He thought her daughter killed herself a few years back. "Shantel? I thought she was dead."

"Everyone did. And I let them believe what they wanted. I know what happened between ya'll and I didn't want anything else to happen to my baby. It's a shame what you and your friends did to her. AIDS Gage! Do you know what type of torture she's going through?" Mrs. Carter was visibly angry. For the last few years she watched her daughter try to battle the disease.

"I don't know what you're talking about." Gage spoke without looking Mrs. Carter in the eye.

"I'm not even going to go there with you Anthony. My baby is fighting a losing battle and you know why? Sometimes when I look at her now, I almost wish I would've let her bleed to death in that tub." Mrs. Carter wiped a tear from her eye. "That's right, it was me that found her...just in time too. I saved my baby's life that day." A slight smile broke across her face.

"Listen Mrs. Carter. I'm sorry about your daughter's condition but I'm not the one responsible. For every action, there's a reaction." Gage didn't feel much remorse for Shantel. She tried to have him killed and he knew deep down inside, she was responsible for him being in jail now.

"Let's not discuss that matter anymore. That's not why I came here." Mrs. Carter was beginning to get upset. She took a deep breath, "Listen Anthony. As I told you, the only reason I'm here is because Shantel sent me. She may not see many more days. She's very ill, but last week she told me that she wanted to let you know that she forgives you and she wants you to take care of ya'll's son."

Gage was at a loss for words. He looked at the sleeping little boy in shock. The little boy was his complexion but Gage couldn't see himself in him. The boy looked a lot like Shantel. Gage refused to believe it.

"No disrespect to you Mrs. Carter, but that's not my son. Ain't no way." Gage spoke calmly.

It Gets Dirtier

"Shantel figured you'd say that and she's not mad. She said ya'll only had sex one time and until she was at the hospital after cutting her wrist, she didn't even know she was pregnant. She calculated the time and knew it was yours. She even eliminated the other possibilities. She was never going to say anything to you about it, because for the longest time she hated you. It wasn't until recently; she finally let go of the hate and moved on. More importantly, she knew it wouldn't be fair to Hakeem." Mrs. Carter looked Gage in his eyes and waited for him to speak.

"What do you want from me?" Gage questioned. This was too much for him to take in. "I can't take care of that boy. I'm in here. And, and, ain't he sick? What do you want me to do?"

"Let me tell you something Anthony Parker." Mrs. Carter spoke in a angry mother's tone. "I'm not too happy about this either. If it was up to me, you'll sit and rot in this place just like you deserve. I'm just honoring my daughter's request. And no, she did not pass it on to him." Mrs. Carter said sharply.

"I still don't understand. What you want from me? I'm here. They gave me 56 years, and I really don't think he's mine." Gage spoke as calm as he could.

"You may not be sitting in here as long as you think. Shantel has hired a lawyer and came clean about framing you. They even have the maintenance man's signed confession about letting her in your apartment. They just need your permission to speak with your lawyer. Shantel didn't want to do it without asking you." Mrs. Carter said reluctantly. She didn't care if Gage did 100 years.

"So what about Hakeem Mrs. Carter? I can't say that boy is mine." Gage looked at Hakeem once again. He was a cute kid but Gage just couldn't see him being his son. He only had sex with Shantel that one time.

"Don't worry about that. My daughter said she's 100 percent sure he's yours. The subpoena for DNA has already been issued. Shantel said you're a good man at heart and that once you to learn the truth about Hakeem, you'll do right by him." Mrs. Carter said.

Gage thought on things for a moment. He didn't have anything to loose and Shantel was right, if Hakeem was his he would take care of him without a doubt. The thought of coming home put a smile on Gage's face.

"So when do ya'll plan on speaking to my lawyer?"

"As soon as you let us know who he is."

Gage gave Mrs. Carter all of his lawyers' information. After that, they made small talk for the remainder of the visit. They mostly spoke on Shantel's condition, the case and Hakeem. When Hakeem woke up, Gage even spoke with him. Being a sucker for kids, it didn't take long for Hakeem to win Gage over. Gage made a promise to himself and Mrs. Carter that no matter what the results come back as, he would be there for Hakeem. He felt that was the least he could do, being that Shantel forgave him and was going to get him home. He even hoped secretly that Hakeem was his. The only thing he was afraid of was how Arrissa was going to take things.

Chapter 32

"It feels so good to be home." Sinnamon said out loud to herself. Essence had just dropped her off at home. They took turns driving nonstop to Delaware from Atlanta, and Sinnamon was exhausted. She didn't realize the trip would take that long. Going the speed limit, it almost took them a whole day.

Sinnamon made her way to the kitchen to grab herself something to eat. She paused at the door and pictured E's lifeless body in front of the refrigerator. She quickly shook the image out of her head. After making a sandwich, Sinnamon ran upstairs to her room. Selling her house was now an option for her. Picturing E's body was not something she planned on doing every day.

The girls were so tired, they didn't even want to count their money yet. They both just wanted to get into their own beds and go to sleep. They agreed to meet up the next morning at Sinnamon's. She kept the large bag of money at her house. She tried getting Essence to stay with her but Essence wanted to go home.

After eating, Sinnamon stripped down and ran herself a hot shower. It was time for her to relax. The last month had been a rollercoaster ride from hell. Before jumping in the shower, Sinnamon sat at the foot of her bed and dialed Ms. Jones. She knew Ms. Jones and

Shaquan were sleep but she felt it was necessary to call and let her know she made it home safely.

"Sorry to bother you this late, but I wanted to let you know I made it home." Sinnamon spoke into the phone.

"Oh child, you're not bothering me. Don't think cuz I'm old, I'm always sleeping." Ms. Jones let out a light chuckle. She was up watching TV.

"Still have the young spirit in you huh?" Sinnamon was smiling from ear to ear. She loved to see how Ms. Jones seemed to stay with so much energy. "Is my little knucklehead up?"

"That little rug rat done ran himself tired. He's knocked out." Ms. Jones answered.

"I figured he was. I miss my little knucklehead. Essence is going to pick him up from you tomorrow morning and bring him to me.

"Okay. What time honey?"

"I'm not really sure, probably around ten. I know she's tired because she had the last driving shift. Hold on, this is her now." Sinnamon's phone clicked and she saw it was Essence.

"You don't have to keep me on hold. Go ahead and talk to your friend. I'm sure I'll see you sometime tomorrow." Ms. Jones said sweetly.

"Okay Ms. Jones." She clicked over."What's up?"

"Nothing, just letting you know I'm home. I'm about to take my ass to sleep." Essence said.

"You and me both."

"Your man was leaving outta here when I was coming in." Essence teased.

"That's not my man." Sinnamon was cheesing.

"That's what you say now. He said that's messed up you ain't call him and tell him you was home. He's going to bring that money in the morning too."

"Damn. I was supposed to call him. I guess I'll call him when I get out of the shower.

"You guess you will? No bitch, you know you will. Stop frontin'." Essence was laughing.

"Ha Ha Ha." Sinnamon was all smiles.

"Just call me when you get up in the morning.

"Okay."

They both hung up. Sinnamon grabbed her towel and made her way into the bathroom. She jumped into the steaming shower and let the water soak her hair. It instantly began to wave and curl up. The warm water felt so good to her skin that Sinnamon ended up standing in the shower until the hot water became luke warm. Before stepping out, Sinnamon grabbed her towel and began to dry off. She hated to let the water from her body soak the floor. That was one of her pet peeves. Once dry, she wrapped her towel around her body and grabbed another one for her wet hair. Inside her room, she replaced her towel with her thick robe and moisturized her body with Vaseline and lotion. Before she was done, the phone rang.

"You wasn't gonna to call?" She heard Esco say when she picked up.

"Well hello to you too. And yes, I was going to call. I just got out of the shower. I was going to call you in a few. I'm just getting settled." Sinnamon continued to lotion her legs.

Esco wanted to say something slick about her being fresh out the shower, but caught himself. He wasn't sure how far he could take it with her just yet. He knew she was feeling him but it wasn't official.

"So what are ya plans for tomorrow?" Esco questioned.

"I have a few things I need to handle in the morning. After that, I may take my brother to Chuck E. Cheese or something. I need to spend some time with him."

"Am I invited? Cuz I wanna spend some time with you too. Little man can't have all the fun, plus, I really want to talk to you."

"Yes, you're invited if you want to come." Sinnamon said sweetly. She was glad Esco couldn't see her blushing.

"What time?"

"I'm not sure yet. I'll call you tomorrow and let you know."

"Make sure you do that."

"I will."

"Okay babe." He paused. "Love you baby girl." Esco tried to make his words sound more friendly than affectionate.

"I love you too Esco." Sinnamon responded. She couldn't hide her emotions.

It Gets Dirtier

Chapter 33

Mills paced back and forth in the hospital lobby. He, Sharon, and Flip's girl Monica were waiting to get an update on Flip's condition. He was having his second surgery and things didn't look good. The doctors had to bring him back three times already. The bullets collapsed one of his lungs, and nicked his heart. If Mills didn't make it to the house when he did, Flip would've died. The only thing the doctors had to say so far was that Flip was a fighter.

Mills replayed the events in his head over and over. When he made it to the basement, he found Flip on the floor, gasping for air. In his hand was his blood covered cell phone with the 911 operator still on the line. She kept Mills on the phone until the paramedics arrived. The operator walked Mills through taking Flip's pulse and trying to keep him alert. Mills could picture the blood coming out of Flip's nose and mouth. And his eyes rolling to the back of his head. Mills thought he had lost him. Last thing he remembered was Flip saying was 'kill them bitches.' So Mills knew what happened.

"Everything's going to be okay." Sharon followed behind Mills and patted him on his back to calm him down.

"I should've been there." Mills said out loud. "I should've fuckin' been there." This time he yelled. His voice made others in the area jump.

It Gets Dirtier

Mills was covered in blood and crying. He couldn't believe they were set up. It really pissed him off when he thought on how he actually was feeling one of the girls. He could hear Flip now telling him not to let the girl get to him. His thoughts shifted to Sharon. What if I was there and we both would've got hit. Then what? He wondered. They would be dead. Dead over some women they had no business being with in the first place. We got beautiful women by our sides. Why be so greedy, he thought. Is this karma? He wondered. The lying, cheating, killing, living a thug lifestyle.

One thing he knew for sure was that this was an eye opener. He just prayed that his boy made it to see another day. Mills was so caught up in his own thoughts that he almost forgot that Monica was there. He could only imagine how she was feeling. She and Flip came a long way together. She rode with him through it all. She almost lost her own life behind Flip's street dealings. After she was beat and put in the hospital, she begged Flip to make a change and to move them out of Philly. He managed to make half of that happen by moving to Atlanta. The other half was always put on hold. He always told her just one more flip and he'll be done, or another couple hundred thousand and he'd walk away. Greed consumed him.

"What happened to my baby?" Monica cried as Mills held her. Mills didn't know what to say. "I don't know Monica. I don't know." Was the only thing Mills could come up with. The truth was out of the question and he prayed the truth would never be revealed. After sitting and praying for another hour, the doctor finally came out. The look on his face wasn't very promising. You could see bloodstains on his scrubs. He made his way over to Monica to break the news.

"So far the surgery was a success." The doctor got straight to the point. "It's a touch and go situation right now. I…"

"Is he going to make it?" Monica cut the doctor off. Her voice was almost a whisper. She looked up at the doctor with watery eyes. She was in pain.

It Gets Dirtier

"Right now, I can't say. We did all we could. He lost a lot of blood and one of his lungs. It's very touchy. All I can say is pray." The doctor hated breaking the news to patients' loved ones.

"Can we see him?" Monica asked.

"Yes, but only one at a time and only briefly. He needs to rest." The doctor informed everyone.

"Okay." Monica spoke weakly.

One by one, they all went to see Flip, Mills went last. Just seeing his friend hooked up to all the machines made him cry. He squeezed Flip's hand tight to let him know he was there.

"I love you my nigga. You gotta make it through this. You can't give up. We got so many things to do dawg. I was thinkin' bout what you said earlier, 'bout trickin' and all that." Mills talked as if Flip was up and well. "You made a valid point cuz. Word, you did. But I was thinkin', when I was watchin' ya girl cry her heart out, I was like, this shit is fucked up. Fuck bitches. I'ma stick to my girl cause she loves me too much. You feel me? On some real shit dawg, I'm like fuck this shit altogether. I can't do it no more. I'm on the run. The police was questioning me all crazy. Luckily my baby got me a fake I.D. They wanted to lock my ass up at first, thinkin' I did somethin' to you. I told them you were my brother and luckily one of the neighbors said they just saw me pull up." Mills let out a sigh.

"Flip, if you make it, we gotta leave this shit alone. Look at Gage, that nigga got 56 years...56 years! Niggas don't even live for 56 years." Mills paused and wiped his face. "I know you gonna want revenge, but fuck it dawg. We gotta let this shit go cuz, it's not worth it. We millionaires, let's just get fat and move to Miami. We gangstas and we ain't got shit to prove no more. We put in work, and we need to get right on that Deen and try to make things right with Allah. You know, ask for forgiveness, so we can make it to paradise. I ain't tryin' to see that fire. You feel me?" Mills paused, as if he was waiting for Flip to respond. "Listen my nigga. I'ma let you get ya rest and we'll talk when you wake up. Just stay strong and pull through. I love you dawg." Mills let go of Flip's hand and headed to the door. Just as he exited, he heard the machine flat line.

"Flip, you gotta hold on dawg, you gotta hold on. Monica needs you Flip. Hold on!" Mills quickly went back to Flip's bedside. The tears began to flood his face…once again Flip's life was slipping away.

"Sir, you have to leave sir." A nurse said politely.

"I ain't leaving, that's my brother." Mills yelled. "That's my brother." He broke free from the small woman's hold.

"I understand, but you can't be in here. We're going to do all we can. You have to calm down." The nurse tried to sooth Mills. As the nurse guided him out, Mills looked behind and saw the doctors going to work on Flip. He silently prayed for a miracle.

Outside in the lobby, Monica and Sharon greeted Mills. They heard the code blue call over the loud speaker and saw the doctors rushing toward Flip's room. When they saw Mills' face, it said it all.

"Nooo!" Monica cried out. "Not now. Please God not now. Why?" Mills took Monica in his arms. He was trying to be strong, but he couldn't stop his tears. He and Flip had gotten close while living in Atlanta. They became like brothers. Besides their girls, all they had was each other. They made it their business not to make any new friends down south. To them, niggas couldn't be trusted, now they were seeing bitches couldn't either.

Mills finally got Monica to calm down and Sharon held her in her arms. All Mills could do was return to pacing back and forth. A few minutes later, the doctor came out again.

"We were able to stabilize him again. As I said before, he's a fighter. All we can do is pray." The doctor spoke his peace and left. That was music to their ears. Flip was holding on. Mills made his way to the bathroom to get himself together. He washed his face and then performed Wudu (ablution/washing before prayer), so he could offer salat (meaning prayer) and make duaa (personal prayer to God asking for something) for Flip. He knew only Allah could help his friend.

Chapter 34

"Hey knuckle head." Sinnamon greeted Shaquan with a smile and hug when he came rushing into the house. "I missed you so much."

"I missed you too. Where you been?" Shaquan questioned.

"I had to go on a trip." Sinnamon answered.

"Can I go next time?"

"Maybe. So what do you want to do today?" Sinnamon walked Shaquan to the front room. "I don't know." Shaquan answered.

"Do you want go to Chuck E. Cheese? Uncle Esco's going to be there."

"Yeah, I wanna go to Chuck E. Cheese, and Uncle Esco's fun. When you were gone, he took me to the barber shop, the mall, and the park. He said I'm his little homie." Shaquan was excited. Hearing Shaquan speak highly of Esco gave Sinnamon a warm feeling in her heart. She didn't even know Esco did all of that while she was gone. He never mentioned it. She had to remember to thank him.

"Where's everything?" Essence asked when she made it in the house. She was carrying a small gym bag.

"Over there, still in the bags. Take one of them down stairs." Sinnamon pointed to two suitcases that sat in the living room.

"Shaquan go up to your room, and put on a movie while me and auntie Essence clean up.

It Gets Dirtier

"Okay." Shaquan quickly ran up the steps. He was full of energy.

"I hope this doesn't take long." Sinnamon said when she made it down to the basement. She carried the other suitcase with her. Essence had already emptied the other one onto the floor.

"I never seen so much money in my life." Essence admired the money that was spread across the floor. "It shouldn't take too long though, being that we already have most of it in stacks of ten thousand. All we really have to do is count the money we got from the last hit and what Esco just gave me."

"That's good. I want to be out the door by two. That way I can chill with Shaquan for awhile. What are you doing today?" Sinnamon emptied the suitcase she had and sat next to Essence. The one she had held the money they got from Mills and Flip, all the jewelry and the brick and a half of coke.

"I'ma check out some apartments, see about a car, and do some shoppin'." Essence said. She took a pile of money and began to count it.

They started with the money they had already counted out in ten thousand. "Just make piles of a hundred thousand."

"So what kind of car do you plan on getting?" Sinnamon asked.

"A 645 BMW, pearl white with butter guts. I saw it before we left." Essence knew exactly what she wanted.

"And how are you going to get that with no job?"

"My credit is good, and my boy gonna make up some pay stubs. You ain't know, I'ma manager at Bucko's rim shop. I make almost a stack a week." Essence was siked. Her plans were all working out.

"Bucko? Isn't that one of the guy's Esco be with?" Sinnamon asked.

"Yeah, they rap together. He's been trying to get this pussy for a while now. He come through with them pay stubs, I might fuck the shit outta his tall lanky ass. I heard he was a freak. I need it too. This pussy ain't been tampered with in almost a month." Essence went on.

212

"You're crazy." Sinnamon said. She had thoughts of her own, but kept them to herself. She too was thinking about putting the fire out between her legs.

The girls talked over their plans as they counted up their money. They came up with a few business plans, as well as shopping plans. If they invested their money right they would be set for life. When it was all said and done, the girls walked away with over $1.6 million in straight cash.

"I'm pissed." Essence fumed.

"Pissed?" Sinnamon couldn't believe her ears. How could anyone that just counted over 1.6 million dollars be mad? "Pissed about what?"

"That we didn't hit our goal. I hate falling short." Essence explained. She was a perfectionist.

"We came close enough. Plus we still got the coke and jewelry." Sinnamon was content.

"Yeah, but at best, that's only gonna bring in a quarter mil. We'll still be short, and think about it, who we gonna sell that jewelry to?"

"We'll find someone. I'm sure about that."

"Well, I'm sure we'll find someone else to rob too. I'm not for all that extra shit. We fuck around and get caught tryin' to get rid of those jewels." Essence made a valid point.

"So you're trying to hit the road again?" Sinnamon couldn't believe it.

"Naw, we can find someone around here, or maybe Philly." Essence said sharply.

Sinnamon shook her head no. "You're crazy. We need to stop while we're ahead."

"So now you want to stop. But when I wanted to stop before, you didn't." Essence had an attitude.

"That was then, and we have over a million dollars more than last time."

"Are you with me or what Sin?" Essence cut her off. She wasn't trying to hear it. She had her mind made up. "I went with you when I didn't want to. I'm just asking you to do one more with me. Then I'll quit, no matter the outcome."

Sinnamon hated the situation she was in. Essence pulled the guilt trip on her. She knew with that in the air, she couldn't say no. How could she? Essence was right. It was her that wanted to go on after Dez and Spoon. She had no choice.

"So are you with me Sin?"

"I'm with you."

After Sinnamon and Essence split the money, they parted ways to go about their day. Sinnamon was holding on to the jewelry until they found a buyer and Essence's half of the money for safekeeping. She also kept the automatic .357 she got from Flip, and was going to sell the coke to Esco.

Sinnamon put the money away then got herself and Shaquan ready for the day. She dressed Shaquan in a pair of True Religion jeans, a black tee shirt and a pair of black Timberland field boots. He looked like a little man. Sinnamon kept it basic. She had on a pair of skinny light blue True Religion jeans, brown Gucci loafers and a tight brown shirt. From wetting it the night before, Sinnamon's hair was wavy like she just took out braids. When she was satisfied with her appearance, she picked up her phone and called Esco.

"Hey baby." Esco said when he picked up.

"Are you still coming with me and Quan?" Sinnamon asked.

"Yeah, why? You ready."

"Yep, I just finished getting dressed."

"Aiight, well come get me. I'm on Concord Ave by the barbershop. Dee-Dee out here washing my car." Esco told her.

"Okay, I'm about to leave my house now." Sinnamon hung up. Sinnamon grabbed her purse, her Gucci shades, some money, and the keys to her Benz. "Come on Quan." Sinnamon yelled. He came flying down the steps. "Boy you're going to hurt yourself running around here like that. Slow down." Sinnamon laughed. They left out the house and entered Sinnamon's car. She started it up, and felt the power behind the wheel. She couldn't believe how much she missed her car. It felt good to be behind the wheel. She pulled off, headed towards Concord Ave.

* * * * *

Once at Chuck E. Cheese, Sinnamon let Shaquan run wild. He was armed with two pockets full of tokens, thanks to Esco. They ordered pizza and drinks and then took a seat at a booth.

"You need to get your hair done. I can't believe you came out here looking like that." Sinnamon was sitting across from Esco. He only had half of his hair braided.

"I was getting it done when I was around the way. I had to stop when you said you were coming." Esco told her.

"I see you must have been real comfortable too. You even got slippers on." Sinnamon pointed at Esco's feet. She couldn't help but laugh. Esco had on a pair of navy blue slippers, a baggy pair of Antik Denim jeans, a new white tee shirt and a long diamond filled chain that read "Concord Ave Movement".

"It's a thug thing baby. It's a thug thing." Esco flashed his smile. He enjoyed being around Sinnamon. "Naw though, I'm in chill mode right now. You feel me?"

"I hear that Pretty Thugger." Sinnamon teased, calling Esco by his rap name. He flashed Sinnamon his smile again.

"Naw, I'm Esco to you baby."

"Well Esco, what did you want to talk to me about?" Sinnamon put Esco on the spot.

"You get right to the point don't you?" Esco laughed, and then became quiet. He wasn't sure what he wanted to tell her. He decided to go with the truth. "Us." He said simply.

"Okay, what about us?" Sinnamon was all ears.

"Sinnamon, I always had my eyes on you, even before you stepped ya game up and all that. I seen something in you that I ain't never

215

seen in these bitches around here. You're pure." He paused and took a sip of his drink. "When we got to know each other, I was amazed. Your personality exceeds your beauty. I was diggin' that shit and that's why I wanted you under my wing. I was hot when you started fuckin' with E. I ain't have nothing against him or anything, I just felt you were supposed to be with me."

"Ahhh, you were jealous." Sinnamon said.

"Naw, not jealous. I was never a hater in the least bit. He just grabbed you while I was sleepin'. Then when you pulled the hammer out on me after he passed, you really had me. I was like damn, she's gansta too. I couldn't ask for more. I seen you was a rider." Esco looked Sinnamon in the eyes as they talked.

"I would've done the same for you. I have a lot of love for you."

"I know you would've and I know how you feel towards me. I can tell you even felt some type way when you were with E, but your loyalty was with him and I respected that."

"But you were the first man that showered me with love. My father wasn't around and I didn't have anyone else. You took care of me and made me feel safe. I will always love you for that." Sinnamon explained.

"I know and I'ma always love you but it runs deeper. I hate to keep bringin' up E, but when you was with him, I felt I lost you. Really, I almost did and I can't afford to let that happen again." Esco began to dig in his pockets. He pulled out a small box and sat it on the table. "Listen. I'm not really into all the traditional shit, but what I'm sayin' is I want you to love me forever. I wanna marry you." He opened up the box and staring at Sinnamon was the most gorgeous seven-carat flawless ring Sinnamon had ever seen. She couldn't believe her eyes. Sinnamon was shocked that Esco had just proposed to her. She knew her answer, but was at a loss for words. All she could do was cry and cover her face. She took a deep breath to get herself together. People at the surrounding tables looked at them and wondered what had Sinnamon crying. Most spotted the huge ring and knew what was going on. Everyone was waiting for Sinnamon's answer.

"Yes. I'll marry you." Sinnamon reached over the table and wrapped her arms around Esco and kissed him.

"You had me worried for a minute. I thought you was going to say no." Esco joked. He took Sinnamon's hand and placed the ring on her finger. "I love you."

"I love you too." Sinnamon said as Shaquan joined in on the hug.

There were applauses from the spectators at the surrounding tables. They were happy for the young couple.

Chapter 35

After spending the day with Shaquan, Sinnamon and Esco found themselves at Sinnamon's house, packing some of her and Shaquan's things. Esco suggested that Sinnamon sell the house to Essence or let Ms. Jones take it. He explained that under no circumstance was his fiancé going to spend another night in a home that another man purchased.

"So where are we going?" Sinnamon asked as she packed her clothes.

"Don't worry, I got you." Esco said smoothly. The smirk on his face made Sinnamon sense that Esco had something up his sleeve.

"You love me right?" Esco asked.

"I'm about to marry you, so that answers that."

"So it shouldn't matter if I'm taking you to a one bedroom shack, as long as we're together that's all that counts right?" Esco kept a straight face.

"I love you but a shack? I don't know babe." Sinnamon laughed as she zipped up her suitcase. Esco picked up the suitcase and headed for the door. Sinnamon followed behind.

"I'm sayin' it's laid out though. The roaches ain't even that big." Esco told her. You could hear the laughter in his voice.

"Boy, you need to stop playing." Sinnamon pushed Esco lightly.

"Aiight, you keep thinking it's a game. You'll see. I got a pet rat name Chuck too, so be nice to him." Esco said.

"Whatever. Come on Shaquan." Sinnamon yelled for her brother. As always, he came running. Everything they packed for him was already in Sinnamon's car, except his "Finding Nemo" DVD that he kept in his hand. Outside, Esco stuffed one of Sinnamon's suitcases in the trunk. The other one had to go in the back with Shaquan. There wasn't a lot of room in the car.

"So what am I going to do with the rest of my things?" Sinnamon questioned. Seeing Esco go to the driver's side, Sinnamon got in on the passenger side.

"How much stuff do you think you can fit in a one bedroom shack girl? I don't know why you think I'm playin'. Just sit back and ride." Esco said smoothly as he backed out of the driveway. "This car's nice, but you know you gotta give it up right?"

Sinnamon sucked her teeth. She really loved her car but understood why Esco wanted her to get rid of it. She figured it was a man's thing.

"I knew you were going to say that. So what am I supposed to do with it?" Sinnamon had a slight attitude.

"You look so sexy when you're mad." Esco chuckled. Sinnamon couldn't help but smile. "If you don't mind, I was gonna give it to my sister Stacy."

"Geeker?" Sinnamon asked.

"Yeah." Esco looked over to gauge Sinnamon's reaction.

"I don't mind. Geeker's cool. But what am I going to drive until I get something else?"

"You got the Caddy right?"

"Yeah, but it's not just mine."

"As much as you and Essence be together, ya'll only need one car." Esco said seriously.

This time, Sinnamon couldn't tell if he was playing or not. She was pissed. She began to make calculations in her head and made up her mind. When Essence went to the dealership, she would be right with her. Trying to hide her attitude, Sinnamon talked to Esco about her goals and dreams; mainly about going back to school. Esco was happy to hear that. Most of the women he knew got sucked in the games that women play and lost focus on their goals. The only goal they saw was dollar signs.

After being on I-95 north for a while, Esco got off at the Concord Pike exit. He made the first left by Kreston's liquor store and followed Miller road to an area Sinnamon rarely went to. It was in the cut. She never even met anyone that lived back there. Minutes later, Esco pulled up to a beautiful two-story home. It was an all brick house with a two-door garage. Esco got out of the car, opened the door for Sinnamon and then handed her two sets of keys.

"What is this for?" Sinnamon asked.

"One is the key to your house." Esco pushed the button to open the garage door. "The other key is for your car."

When the garage door opened, Sinnamon spotted a pearl white two door Bentley GT. It was the most beautiful car Sinnamon had ever seen.

"You like it?" Esco asked after a moment. He stared at Sinnamon with a huge smile on his face. He knew she was excited.

"I don't know what to say. This is too much." Tears of joy began to roll down her face. It wasn't what Esco brought her because she had enough money to buy the house and car herself, it was the fact that he went out of his way to surprise and provide for her. Sinnamon gave Esco a big hug. "I love you so much baby." She then made her way to the Bentley and got in. She started the engine and rolled the window down.

"Can you move the Benz please? I need to take a ride." Sinnamon said excitedly.

"Damn, you just gonna leave me and Shaquan out here like that? You 'bout to leave with the house keys and everything." Esco was proud to make his woman happy.

"I'm coming right back. I just want to see how it drives." Sinnamon told Esco.

"Well, give me the house key."

Sinnamon tossed Esco the key. He moved the Benz and watched as Sinnamon pulled off in her new toy. The joy Esco saw in her face made him finally see that his patience in the game paid off. He was never flashy, even though he had it. He always kept it basic, even though he had bricks, you could still catch him on the Ave grinding hand to hand.

Most of the time, he broke it down so his young boys could eat. Being conservative let him save more money than one would think. He even had money in stocks...he was set. Not to mention with the help of his Uncle he was able to invest in some foreign real estate, he was only 24 and already owned half of one the most successful resorts in Jamaica.

Esco grabbed Sinnamon's suitcase and let Shaquan out of the car, and made his way into the house. He began to think about the days ahead, focusing on his rapping and giving up the game. He felt that his boy Gage made a good point about leaving the game before it was too late. Being another statistic was something he wanted to avoid.

After putting the bags away, Esco went down stairs to wait for Sinnamon. She arrived minutes later, wearing a grin that could light up the world. When she came into the house, she looked around. Everything was perfect. The house was completely furnished from top to bottom. Mahogany tables and chairs, leather sofas, flat screen TV's hanging on the walls and beautiful black art. Sinnamon was impressed.

"So do you like it?" Esco asked, already knowing the answer.

"I love it baby. It's gorgeous." Sinnamon gave Esco a tight hug and passionate kiss. "I love you she whispered."

"Ill! Gross." Shaquan shouted. He ran in between Sinnamon and Esco. Sinnamon scooped Shaquan up into her arms.

"Ill! To you too." She teased. "It's almost time for you to go to bed."

"Already, we just got here." Shaquan whined.

"I know babe, but bedtime is bedtime. Come on, time to get into the shower." Sinnamon began to walk up the steps with Shaquan still in her arms, and Esco behind them.

"You need to put him down, you gonna make him soft."

"No I'm not."

"I know you ain't cuz I ain't gonna let you."

"Whatever. Which room is Shaquan's?" Sinnamon put Shaquan down.

"That one." Esco pointed to a door. When Sinnamon entered the room, she saw that it was filled with all types of toys and games. She knew Shaquan would play in there all day without a problem. There were more than enough things in the room to keep him busy. Sinnamon gave Shaquan everything he needed to get into the tub. She ran his water for him and left him alone to do his thing. After handling Shaquan, Sinnamon made her way to the master bedroom with Esco.

"This is one helluva shack." Sinnamon joined Esco on the king-sized California bed.

"You really like it?" Esco questioned.

"It's perfect baby. You didn't have to do all this. I would've stayed in a shack with you." Sinnamon snuggled in Esco's arms.

"Yeah! Not the way you looked at me when I said it." Esco grinned.

"Whatever."

"Naw, you had ya nose all turned up and shit." Esco mimicked Sinnamon's face, she shoved him lightly.

"Go check out ya closet. It's the one over there."

Sinnamon made her way over to the closet. When she opened it, she was amazed at its size. It was the size of a small bedroom and filled with nothing but the best designers and latest fashion. Once again, Sinnamon ran over to hug Esco. This time she knocked him over and fell on top of him. As she laid on top of Esco, she looked him in the eyes and gave him another long kiss.

"I love you." She told him.

"I love you too."

"I'm about to get Shaquan dressed for bed and then I'm going to get in the shower." Sinnamon lifted herself up and walked to the bathroom. Shaquan was already out and in his room. When Sinnamon entered Shaquan's room, he was in his pajamas, playing with a few toys. Sinnamon somehow managed to get him into bed and tucked in. They said a short prayer and then Sinnamon kissed him good night.

"I love you." She told him.

"Love you too." Shaquan yawned, after all the running around he was tired and ready to go to sleep.

After putting Shaquan to bed, Sinnamon got in the shower. She shaved her legs and her womanhood, leaving everything silky smooth. Once out of the shower, she wrapped her towel around her body and went back into the room with Esco. He had fell asleep watching a Martin re-run.

"Get up babe." Sinnamon nudged him. Esco woke up wide-eyed. He didn't even notice that he had fallen asleep. He stretched and let out a loud yawn. "Go ahead and get in the shower."

When Esco left, Sinnamon oiled herself with her Vaseline and scented lotion. She dug into her suitcase and pulled out a pink and black thong she had gotten from Victoria Secrets. It came with a sheer teddy that fit Sinnamon to a tee. Leaving her hair out, she looked like a model doing a shoot for a Victoria Secret catalogue. She was drop dead gorgeous.

After showering, Esco entered the room, wearing only his boxers. He was caught off guard seeing Sinnamon in her lingerie. Without touching her, he enjoyed her physically. With his eyes he took in

223

every curve as she did an array of poses. Right then and there, he knew he picked the right one.

"Come here." Sinnamon purred. She was finally ready to put out the fire between her legs.

Esco joined Sinnamon on the large bed and softly pushed her on to her back.

"Just relax." Esco spoke smoothly. He picked up the remote to the TV and turned to the music channel. They caught the beginning of Trey Song's 'Super Woman.' A flash of the girl in the video crossed Esco's head. He smiled when he looked at Sinnamon and saw that his superwoman had Trey Song's girl beat. Esco knew he was about to change Sinnamon's life.

Esco took Sinnamon into his arms and gently place his lips on hers. He sucked a little at her bottom lip, and then gave her a little tongue. They kissed passionately for a moment before he let his lips and tongue wonder to Sinnamon's neck and ear. She let out soft moans that fueled Esco's fire.

"You ready for me?" Esco said in a whisper. From their conversations he knew Sinnamon was a virgin.

"Yes." She moaned as another kiss sent chills throughout her body.

Esco gently sat Sinnamon up and helped her lift the teddy over top of her head, exposing her soft breasts. He grabbed a handful of her breast and massaged them. While still kissing on her, he played with her nipples. Sinnamon felt herself becoming even wetter.

"I want you." She moaned softly. She returned Esco's kisses as she grabbed on to his manhood. She slowly began to jerk him. Esco gently removed her hand. He wasn't ready for her to take charge just yet. The ball was in his court. He laid her back down on the bed and let his kisses slide down to her breast. He teased and sucked each nipple passionately. Sinnamon whined in pleasure. Her sweet moans turned Esco on more. Kissing down to her stomach in one smooth motion, Esco managed to slide her thong off without his mouth ever leaving her skin. Esco took his middle and index finger and rubbed Sinnamon's clit lightly. Sinnamon naturally began to grind up against his hand.

"I want more." She begged.

Kissing down further, Esco grabbed hold to Sinnamon's legs and pushed them back. That caused her tight hole to open slightly. Before diving head first, Esco took a look at what made Sinnamon a woman. Her womanhood was glazed with moisture. Esco began to lick her womb like a cat drinking warm milk. This drove Sinnamon crazy.

"Oh my God." Sinnamon let out. She never experienced such pleasure. As Esco teased her flesh, he massaged her breast at the same time. Making sure he caressed each nipple softly. He licked his fingers to give them a feel like his tongue. Sinnamon rocked slightly back and forth against Esco's mouth. She moved to the beat with the late Luther.

Sinnamon felt as if she had died and gone to heaven. She rubbed her fingers through Esco's hair. As the sensation began to increase, Sinnamon found herself grinding a little faster on Esco's tongue. She grabbed a hold of the side of Esco's hair that was out and began to call out for God.

Seeing that Sinnamon was reaching her climax, Esco took her to another level by focusing on her clit. He took his thumb and pulled back the skin that covered the little piece of erect flesh. Esco went to work by flicking his tongue rapidly against her exposed clit. Sinnamon went wild.

"Oh my God Esco, Please! Hold on... stop.... It feels, it feels so... Oooh shit!" Sinnamon exploded. Her legs began to tremble in Esco's hands. This only made him go harder. He was on a mission. Sinnamon tried to lock her legs shut, but Esco's strength forced her to keep them open. He sucked her clit into his mouth and flicked his tongue around and around. Sinnamon literally began to cry from the pleasure, and Esco loved every minute of it.

It Gets Dirtier

Sinnamon's second orgasm made her feel as if she lost thefeeling in her legs. She never imagined such an experience. She couldn't stop shaking. She tried with all her might to push Esco's tongue away because she couldn't take anymore. Finally satisfied with his foreplay, Esco decided it was time to enter inside of her. He quickly removed his boxers without breaking the flow. He rubbed the tip of his stiff shaft around Sinnamon's flooded area.

She was ready.

"Sssss." Sinnamon moaned when the tip of Esco's head broke the threshold.

"Relax baby." Esco said soothingly. Sinnamon wrapped her arms tight around Esco and closed her eyes. She was trying to prepare herself for the ride.

Esco slowly and smoothly worked his way, inch by inch, into Sinnamon. He held her tight in his arms and kissed her as they became one. She felt perfect in his arms. This was a definite love thing. Esco never felt for a woman the way he did for Sinnamon. This made everything feel more pleasurable. He was actually making love for the first time. When Esco saw that Sinnamon's pain began to turn into pleasure, he began to stroke a little deeper and faster. He took one arm and let it wrap around Sinnamon, while holding her shoulder so she couldn't get away. He used his free hand to push back on her thigh, causing her legs to spread. He stroked deep in a circular motion, filling her walls. When she caught his beat, Sinnamon rocked with him. By now, Ronald Isley was asking his lover what was her fantasy. Between the sheets was playing softly in the background.

"Esco, I love you." Sinnamon moaned. She had her fingers gripping tight on Esco's shoulders.

"I love you too." Esco grunted. Looking down, Esco could see Sinnamon's cream covering his manhood as it went in and out of her soft area. Esco stroked harder and harder. Sweat began to drop from his chin. He was putting in work. As his climax approached, Esco's man began to get harder and harder and he went deeper and deeper.

Sinnamon began to grind with him. Faster and faster, she too began to feel her climax.

"Yes baby, yes!" Sinnamon was almost screaming. Esco and Sinnamon were in perfect rhythm. They stroked harder and harder until finally they exploded at the same time. They both held on tight to one another as Esco's life fluids pumped into Sinnamon. Still holding each other, they kissed passionately.

"I love you." Esco was still on top of Sinnamon. He looked into her eyes, and then kissed her on the forehead.

"I love you too." Sinnamon managed to say. She was exhausted. The moment Esco rolled off of her, she made herself comfortable in his arms and went out like a light. Esco held Sinnamon as she laid on his chest. Esco stared up at the ceiling as Lyfe sung him to sleep. It must be nice was the last thing he heard.

Chapter 36

"Damn Bitch! That's how we doin' it now? You could've told me you were goin' car shoppin'." Essence said as she admired Sinnamon's new Bentley.

Sinnamon was just coming to pick Essence up to take her to the BMW dealership on Pennsylvania Ave. It was just reaching noon, the sun was out, and the weather was nice for it to be the end of September. Sinnamon had her windows down with her hair out and blowing in the wind. With her Dolce and Gabbana shades on, Sinnamon was looking movie star perfect. Everything about her outfit matched her car. She was living a dream.

"I didn't buy this, are you crazy? My fiancé put me in this." Sinnamon stuck her left hand out the window, displaying her ring. Catching the sun's rays, the ring shined brighter than the North Star.

"Fiancé, nu uh, when? Who? Oooh Esco?" Essence excitedly shot question after question, not giving Sinnamon a chance to answer. Essence jumped into the Bentley. "So what happened? Why didn't you call me?"

"Everything happened so fast. We were at Chuck E. Cheese with Shaquan, talking, and the next thing I knew, he pulled out the ring." Sinnamon pulled off.

"Did he get on one knee?" Essence couldn't picture Esco getting on one knee.

"No. He said he's not really the traditional type, but I don't care. I'm just happy. Speaking of the devil-" Sinnamon's phone rang, cutting them off. "Hey babe, what's up?"

"Where you at?" Esco asked. He was on the side street off of Concord Ave., in front of the barbershop, shooting dice.

"Picking Essence up, we're about to go to the BMW dealership on Pennsylvania Ave." Sinnamon said.

"Congratulations brother." Essence yelled in the background. A smile broke across Esco's face. "Come through here real quick. I need you to take my money home before I go broke." Esco told her. He sat watching his childhood friend Reef rake up a big pile of money after rolling his point.

"I'm going shoppin' on ya'll tonight." Reef said with a smile.

"Okay, I'll be there in a minute. I'm turning up Vandever now.

"Aiight."

They hung up.

Moments later, Sinnamon pulled up to the block, and pulled up right in front of the group of men gambling. The sight of her Bentley caught everyone's attention. In Wilmington, it wasn't an everyday thing to see such an extravagant car, and all eyes were locked on it. You could hear the crowd asking who that was driving. Esco kept quiet and waited for Sinnamon to step out.

"God damn that bitch phat as a motha-fucka." One of the men blurted out.

Esco cut him an evil look. He tapped his pockets, checking for his blade. No way was a dude going to disrespect his future wife. Esco was already upset because the man won a few grand from him and he wasn't even from around the way. He was visiting his boy Ran, who worked in the barbershop.

"You got ya thing on you?" Esco whispered to Reef, who was deep in the game. His luck was beginning to change for the worst.

"Yeah, why? What's up?" That caught Reef's attention. He lived for drama.

"Just making sure," Esco said not wanting to reveal his plan. He just wanted to make sure he had a little back up in case the disrespectful man's boys wanted to get involved.

"Hey baby." Sinnamon planted a soft kiss on Esco's lips, killing everyone's hopes of maybe getting her number. Esco returned the kiss. He dug into all four of his pockets, pulling out huge stacks of money. The other hustlers looked on with envy. Esco peeled a few hundred off for himself and gave Sinnamon the rest. She quickly put the money in her purse.

"Tell Essence to get out of the car." Esco told Sinnamon. Sinnamon quickly waved for Essence to get out of the car. She only stayed in because she was on the phone and didn't feel like dealing with the men out there. Once she swung the door open, just as she expected, all eyes were on her.

"You wasn't going to get out and speak, that's crazy." Esco teased.

"Naw, it ain't like that. You know you my peoples. I just didn't want to deal with the vultures." Essence made sure to stress the word "vultures". That caused the men to get back into their game...all but one. Essence and Reef made deep eye contact. Something about him made her smile, and that was his queue. Reef quickly made his way over to Esco. "Yo dawg, you gonna introduce ya peoples to ya peoples?" Reef pointed to himself in an animated way, causing the four of them to laugh. "Nevermind. Niggas are rude." Reef pretended to be upset. "How are you gorgeous? I'm Reef," as he stuck out his hand.

"Essence." she replied and stuck out her hand, blushing. She looked Reef up and down and took inventory as she always did. He was wearing an all black tee shirt, black Phillies fitted, loose fitting LRG jeans, and a black pair of Bugs Bunny Jordan's. What Essence liked most was his beard. He wore it thick and long, letting the world know he was Muslim.

"Damn, you do know you look like you came out of that magazine right?" Reef spoke in a joking manner, causing Essence to blush even more.

"I guess I can take that as a compliment?" Essence laughed.

"A compliment it was." Reef said smoothly. "I'm saying though, I gotta get back over to the dice, to see if I can take some more of these nigga's money, but I was trying to see if I can get ya number?" Reef quickly pulled out his cell phone. "So should I spell ya name like the magazine or do you spell it different?" Reef spoke with confidence.

"Like the magazine." Essence was digging Reef's style. She ran down her number.

"Now, I'm a call you soon. Make sure you got time for me." Reef stared at the number, and then went back to the game. Essence watched as Reef took control of the dice. As he bent down to pick up the dice, Essence noticed the chrome from his .45 on his waistband. That turned her on even more.

"What time you going home?" Sinnamon asked Esco.

"I don't know. Just call me when you're done handling whatever you need to handle." Esco said, walking Sinnamon to her car. Essence already took her seat back on the passenger side.

"Okay baby." Sinnamon allowed Esco to open the door for her. She slid in and he shut the door behind her. Sticking his head in the window, he gave her one last kiss before she pulled off. Esco knew he was in love because normally, he didn't show much public affection. He watched as Sinnamon made a right on Washington and disappeared. Now it was time for him to check the disrespectful dude.

In a few short steps, Esco was standing beside the man, sizing him up. He was a little taller than Esco but not too much heavier in weight. When Esco made eye contact with Reef, he smirked. Seeing the smirk, Reef knew Esco was up to something, he just didn't know what. No one else seemed to notice anything. Not even the man.

"Crack-" Esco's fist crashed into the man's jaw with force, causing him to fall to the ground asleep.

"What the fuck." One of the dude's friends stepped towards Esco. In a blink of an eye, Esco pulled his blade out, and Reef had his .45 gleaming in the sunlight.

"You better back the fuck up." Reef spoke loudly. "Matter fact, get the fuck on the ground." Reef looked around. "Matter fact, if ya'll not from up here, get the fuck on the ground. Think I'm playing if you want, I will air this whole shit out." Reef wasn't sure why Esco knocked the guy out, but he was going to ride. Reef caught the attention of one of Concord Ave's young boys that was laughing as he leaned against the wall. "Yo, Malc run them niggas shit." Reef said with force. He gripped his .45 tight in his hand, itching to pull the trigger. Malc quickly did as he was told. He took money and jewelry. Esco kneeled down next to the sleeping man and began to smack him. It took three hard slaps to wake him. When he awoke, Esco began to speak.

"Do you know what just happened?" Esco asked him. The man looked at Esco with confusion. He was still seeing stars and didn't have a clue as to what was going on. All he knew was that his jaw was throbbing.

"You disrespected my wife nigga." The man's memory began to come back. Esco pressed his blade against the man's cheek. The pressure caused the blade to penetrate and blood began to spill. "Next time, think before you comment. You on another nigga's block. You don't know who that was getting out the car. I tell you one thing though, next time, I'ma cut ya fucking tongue out nigga." With one quick flip of the wrist, Esco's knife opened the man's face from his cheek to his chin. He was marked for life.

"Awww shit." The man screamed as he held his face.

"Now get the fuck from around here." Esco stood up, still holding his knife in his hand. He gave Reef a head nod, letting him know it was cool to ease up.

"You heard him. All you niggas get the fuck outta here." Reef held his aim at the crowd, waiting for someone to move wrong. The men got up heatedly. Most of them mumbled to themselves about getting revenge and what not. They felt violated, especially the man that would have to get close to fifty stitches to sow his face back up.

Chapter 37

"How you feeling today cuz?" Mills asked Flip as he took a seat next to Flip's bed. After being in a coma for a week, Flip had finally woke up a few days ago. He was still in a lot of pain, but living. After two surgeries, he was hooked up to life support and given a slim chance of survival. On assumptions, the doctor's told Monica that if Flip did wake up, he would never be the same. Lucky for Flip, they were wrong.

"I'm good. Hungry as a motha fuck though. I can't wait 'til I can eat some real food." Flip spoke in a low tone. The doctor had Flip on a clear liquid diet for the next week. One of the bullets tore through a piece of his intestines and the doctor wanted to make sure it healed. Due to the lack of food, Flip lost close to twenty pounds already.

"You'll be eating steak and potatoes in no time my nigga." Mills got quiet. This was the first time it was just him and Flip left alone to talk. When Flip first woke up, the police were constantly harassing him and Monica was there 24-7.

"So what happened?" Mills finally asked.

"I don't even know dawg. I ain't even gonna hold you. I ain't see that shit coming. We was chilling and the next thing I knew, Jasmine pulled out on me. I went to grab my piece, and Lovey pulled out. I was stuck. Them some sneaky ass bitches, I can't believe that shit

234

happened." Flip explained. He told Mills the rest of the story. The room fell quiet again.

Flip was replaying the incident in his head over and over. He could feel the burning in his chest as he thought on getting shot. He silently thanked Allah that he was still alive.

"Word on everything though, if I ever run into them bitches again, I'ma kill 'em." Flip said seriously. "That shit they pulled wasn't even necessary. I gave them bitches everything in the safe with no problem. If I would've known they was gonna try to off me, I wouldn't have gave 'em shit. I would've tried my luck.

"I hear that." Mills said. He thought a moment and decided to let Flip know how he felt. The situation with Flip really had him thinking a lot lately. "Yo man, I know you feel some type of way, but I think you should just forget 'bout that shit. I mean, you should just count ya blessings and move on."

Flip looked at Mills as if he was crazy. He couldn't believe his ears. He almost got murdered, and his boy was like, leave it alone. Flip began to lose some respect for Mills. If it was the other way around, he would've been out looking for them bitches the same night. Mills saw the look on Flip's face and tried to explain. "You gotta feel me. I-"

Flip cut him off, "I ain't gotta feel shit. You talking crazy. I'm sitting here in this bed, can't even eat. I almost died and you talking this bullshit. What's really good with you Mills? When them niggas up the way hit you, and it was only ya hand, what happened?" Flip waited for Mills to respond He didn't. He just put his head down. "Exactly nigga. You ain't oppose to that. You got the game fucked up my nigga if you think I'ma take this shit on the chin." Flip fumed.

"You right. I feel where you comin from and if we get the drop on them bitches, it's on. I'ma ride." Mills paused. "But Flip, this game we playin' is getting old. We need to quit while we ahead."

"You know what Mills, I ain't even gonna have this conversation with you. No disrespect, but you sound like my girl. I ain't tryin' to hear that shit right now. I'ma do me. What you chose to do is on you. Three shots ain't gonna scare me away from all this paper." Flip had his mind set.

Silence filled the room as both men sat and thought. Mills felt that Flip should listen to him. Then he began to second-guess himself. He didn't want to seem like a sucker, but he was getting tired of the nonsense that came with the game. He was already facing jail time, Gage got football numbers. Then the murders, he was tired.

Flip, on the other hand had a mind full of crazy thoughts. He knew Mills was making sense about quitting, but not at a time like that. He felt Mills was bitching. Looking in Mills' eyes, he just didn't see the real nigga he used to see. For a moment, the thought of Mills having something to do with the situation even came across his mind. He did know for a fact, Mills was feeling the girl Lovey. He quickly dismissed the thought. Mills didn't have nothing to gain by killing him, he thought to himself...or did he. A second voice whispered.

* * * * *

"I'm so glad to finally be moving. I tell you money talk's cuz at first they were saying I couldn't move for a month or so." Essence explained to Sinnamon. They were riding in Essence's new 645 BMW. It was the same one she saw before they went down south. They were on their way to Essence's new Waters Edge condo on route 896. It was far from the city, but for $950 a month, and with the quality she was getting, there was no way she could turn it down.

"Damn, it feels good to have your own shit. I hope my furniture comes in time. I brought everything new. I'm starting fresh."

"I'm so happy for you, for us. We've come a long way. It seems like only yesterday when we were sleeping on mats with no box springs."

Sinnamon laughed as she thought on the days they had nothing. Life was once rough, but good now.

It Gets Dirtier

"I know right. Who would've ever thought, and just think, we're still young....not even old enough to drink. Bitches gone be hatin'." Essence giggled.

"They're going to keep on hating too. We have money, looks, nice things, and now all we have to do is get some businesses off the ground. Are you ready to invest your money? I'm looking into real estate."

Sinnamon began to get serious. They had a lot of money, but Sinnamon knew that with no income coming in, that money would be gone before they knew it.

"I'm not sure what I want to do Sin. Real estate sounds like the best move. I'm with you. We can do this together, I just don't want to make moves until we pull off this last caper." Essence said nonchalantly. For the last few days, she had her eyes on someone big.

"Last caper?" Sinnamon had forgotten all about Essence's idea of robbing one more person. She had hoped Essence forgot too.

"You didn't think I was playin' 'bout that, did you?" Essence looked over to Sinnamon.

"I was hoping you were over that." Sinnamon answered honestly.

"You haven't said anything about it."

"I know I haven't. I've been doing my homework though. I found a heavy hitter too. I know where his stash spot is and everything." Essence spoke with a smile on her face.

"Who is it?" Sinnamon asked, half-heartedly.

"Remember when I got that jewelry that we took from that dude Javar?" Essence glanced over at Sinnamon.

"Yeah, I thought you said you were going to sell it to Esco's friend Reef for the low." Sinnamon paused, and then thought a moment.

"No girl. I am not robbing one of Esco's friends. That's crazy."

"Girl, if you don't calm down. I ain't talking 'bout Reef. I kinda like him. I think he's into robbing people too. Anyway, he took me over to Bethal Villa and he sold it for me. I only wanted 80 stacks for

237

everything and the dude ended up paying Reef 100. I guess Reef taxed him.

"So you think the dude keeps all of his money in there somewhere?" Sinnamon doubted it.

"He got a bitch that stays there. I saw her grab a duffel bag from him the other day."

"So you've been watching him?" Sinnamon wanted to know.

"Watching him, I did more than that. I went out to eat with him and everything. Only one date though. Just to feel him out, you know, see if he runs his mouth and of course he did. Claims he got the city on smash with the dope."

"Who is he?" Sinnamon asked. She really didn't want to pull the caper, but hearing about it had her open. It was almost as if she couldn't help herself.

"He said his name is Mike, but they call him Sauce. I'm not sure if I've ever heard of him. You?" Essence looked over to Sinnamon once again.

"Not that I can think of." Sinnamon turned in her seat towards Essence. "So you want to rob somebody in Delaware again? Wilmington at that! Across the street from the police station? In hot ass BV?"

"Yep." Essence said simply.

"It better be worth it. Even if it's not, that's it. We're done. Agreed?" Sinnamon said.

"Agreed." Essence grinned from ear to ear, knowing her friend was with her.

Chapter 38

"So where do you wanna go tonight?" Sauce asked Essence as they rode down Market Street in his GS 400. This was his second date with Essence and he was hoping to score with her.

"I don't know, you tell me. I didn't have anything in mind. I just wanted to chill and clear my head, that's all." Essence spoke sweetly.

"You wanna just take a ride?" Sauce asked. He looked over at Essence and took in her beauty. He felt lucky to be in the car with her. If she played her cards right, she could be his misses. "So tell me about yourself." Sauce wanted to make small talk.

"There's not much to me. I'm a pretty simple girl. What do you want to know?" Essence looked in the side view mirror to see if Sinnamon was still following them.

"What's your background like? I mean, do you have brothers, sisters, are you from Delaware. You know, just the little things."

"Not to be rude, but I don't want to talk to you about my family. I don't know you like that. Let's chill. Matter of fact, do you think you can take me past BV so I can get some weed from my cousin?" Essence tried not to sound rude, but couldn't help it. Sauce immediately got an attitude. He wasn't used to anyone talking slick to him.

"Listen." Sauce said aggressively. "I don't know what's wrong with you, but please don't talk to me like some young boy. I don't tolerate disrespect. I will put you out right here and you can walk where ever you need to go." Sauce was fuming.

Sauce's reaction caught Essence off guard. She didn't view him as the aggressive type. He was so laid back on their first date. At the rate she was going, she was surely going to mess up her plans.

"I'm sorry Sauce. I'm just stressin' right now. I just have a lot on my mind." Essence massaged her temple to add effect. "I didn't mean to take my frustration out on you. Don't be mad." She purred.

Essences soft voice softened Sauce right up. He looked over at her and smiled. "It's cool. Don't even worry about it. My bad for jumping on you like that. I just get defensive easily." Sauce explained.

"I understand." Essence paused. "So can you still run me past BV?"

"I got you."

They were already over the Market Street Bridge, passing Rodney Square, so BV was only a few minutes away. They cruised in silence as they both thought on how the night may turn out. Their plans were a lot different from each other's. Essence looked in her side view mirror again. She watched as Sinnamon pulled past them and took the lead. Sinnamon knew where to go once she saw the direction they were headed.

Minutes later, they pulled around by BV. "Park next to that Caddy right there, my cousin lives in that house." Essence pointed to a house right across from one of Bethal Village apartment buildings. Sauce did as he was told. He looked at the Caddy and admired the rims that were on it. When the door flung open, he really liked what he saw. Sinnamon jumped out in the tightest fitting jeans she could find. They showed every curve.

"She looks good don't she?" Essence bought Sauce out of his daze. He was staring out his window so hard, he almost forgot

Essence was in the car. When he turned around to face her, he had the surprise of his life.

"Oh shit!" Sauce almost jumped out of his skin. His eyes opened wide from fear when he saw the .357 automatic. It was the same gun they stole from Flip.

"Just relax and don't make any dumb moves." Essence said calmly.

Sauce was frozen in fear. Sinnamon opened the driver's side door to let Sauce out. She held a large .40 cal in her hand as she signaled for him to step out the car. The girls knew that they had to move fast. Even thought it was late, a lot of people still walked the streets in that area.

"Come on." Sinnamon spoke through clenched teeth.
Sauce quickly got out the car. Sinnamon grabbed him by the arm and jammed the gun into his rib cage. Essence got out the car and grabbed Sauce by the other arm. The women guided him to the building that Essence saw him going into all the time.

"Which apartment is it?" Essence asked sternly. She was happy to make it into the building without being seen.

"3A." Sauce mumbled.

"You got the key?" Sinnamon asked.

"Right pocket" Sauce didn't care about them going into the apartment because he moved his stash two days before, to avoid a situation like this.

Essence retrieved the key from Sauce's pocket and opened the door. She was shocked to see that the apartment was completely empty. Not only did Sauce move his stash, he moved his friend too. He wasn't a rookie to the game.

"What the fuck is this?" Sinnamon screamed. She looked around at the apartment in disbelief.

"Where's the money at Sauce?" Essence was losing her cool.

"Ain't no money bitch. I don't know who did ya homework for you, probably that nigga, Reef. I heard that nigga be sending bitches at nigga's neck. I ain't dumb. I moved my shit not long after I bought that chain. I don't trust that nigga." Sauce said with a smirk on his face.

"Smack!" Essence smacked him hard in the mouth with her gun. The impact knocked his fronts out.

"Call me another bitch." Essence was heated. Not so much at him calling her a bitch, but she felt played. "Check the house." Essence told Sinnamon. She smacked Sauce again and again with the gun while Sinnamon searched the empty apartment. It didn't take long for her to come back empty handed.

"Ain't shit in here," Sinnamon said with a look of disgust on her face. This was the first time she was truly upset with Essence. "I thought you did your homework! This is some bullshit Essence. This is a waste of time, I'm out." Sinnamon was fuming. "I'll be in the car. Handle him."

Before leaving, Sinnamon smacked Sauce one good time with her gun and then disappeared out the door and made her way back to the Caddy.

Sauce laid on the floor, bleeding from cuts on his head, mouth and nose. Even through the pain, he managed to laugh. To him, the joke was on Essence.

"Oh, you think this is a game huh?" Essence yelled. She took her gun off safety.

"So what, you gonna shoot me?" Sauce asked. He began to get a little serious.

"I won't if you tell me where ya money is. Take me to it." Essence held the gun to his forehead.

"I can't do that." Sauce thought on what may happen if he took them to his stash. His friend her two kids that stayed with her. He couldn't put them in that type of danger.

"You sure?" Essence spoke in a calm voice this time.

Sauce looked Essence in the eyes and began to wish he never talked slick to her. Reality was checking in, and he felt himself about to check out. Essence's eyes spoke murder. Sauce closed his eyes and prepared to meet his maker.

"Boom." The gun shot echoed extra loud in the empty apartment, causing a few of the neighbors to wake up. Essence quickly ran out the apartment and out the building. She jumped into the car with Sinnamon and they pulled off, headed towards Essence's apartment.

"So was it worth it Essence? Was that last caper we just had to pull worth it?" Sinnamon was still heated as she drove. Not only did they not get anything out the deal, but Sinnamon also had to explain to Esco why she was coming in the house late. It was after midnight and she still had to drop Essence off and pick up her own car.

Essence put her hand up, signaling Sinnamon to stop. "Not right now Sin. I'm not for that shit right now." Essence looked out the window in a daze. She was pissed and embarrassed that she bought Sinnamon on a dummy mission.

"Fuck that, we're going to talk about this shit. You have me out here 12..." Sinnamon was cut off.

"I said not right now Sinnamon. Damn." A tear escaped from Essence's eyes. "Just drive and take me the fuck home. I'm not for your shit right now." Essence shrieked.

Sinnamon fell silent. There was no need to go on. She could tell her friend didn't need her to make her feel any worse. The damage was already done.

"Don't even worry about it. It's over now. We're just going to focus on our plans and move past this. We only had one robbery go wrong out of many. Our record is still good. Don't sweat it." Sinnamon spoke gently, trying to ease the tension.

Essence wasn't sure why she was taking the robbery so bad. It wasn't like that was her first murder. Something just didn't feel right in her stomach. Not only that, but she couldn't get the image of Sauce's pleading eyes out of her mind. She felt a little bad, and she had a bad feeling something wasn't right.

Chapter 39

The next morning, Sinnamon woke up early to cook breakfast for Esco and Shaquan. She was half tired, being that she didn't get much sleep. It was a little after 1:30 a.m. when she got in. To her surprise, Esco didn't say a word about it, he even agreed to take Shaquan to school for her.

"So what you got planned for the day?" Esco asked as he finished up the last bit of his food. Sinnamon made French toast, turkey bacon and eggs.

"Nothing, I just want to relax and get some rest." Sinnamon said with a sigh.

"I bet you do." Esco chuckled and shook his head. He felt some type way about her coming in late, but he wasn't going to say anything. He knew based on the lifestyle he lived, he was suspect to come in that same time or later.

"I hear that. It's almost eight now." Esco looked at his watch. "Be dress by one. I'ma pick you up so we can hang out for a minute. I wanna go to that little spot, 814, in town for lunch. Their fish is banging." Esco was referring to a little bar and restaurant on Wilmington's Market Street Mall.

"I'll be ready." Sinnamon agreed, seeing that Esco was demanding more than asking.

"Aiight, I'll see you around then. Make sure you ready too. You know how you women can be. Ain't that right Quan?" Esco slapped hands with Shaquan. He got Shaquan together and prepared to leave. "See you babe." Esco kissed Sinnamon on the forehead and left.

After Esco and Shaquan left, Sinnamon made her way to the bedroom to take a nap. She set her alarm for 12pm, and then stretched out in the big bed. As she laid down, she thought on last night's events, then about the events prior to that. Never in a million years did she think her life would end up like that. She quietly thanked God for allowing her to live through the mayhem. Her nightmare was finally over, and now she could live a regular life. All she had to do now was convince Esco to leave the streets. If something were to happen to him, she would really lose it. Twelve o'clock came in a blink of an eye. Sinnamon rolled over and turned her alarm off. She reached for the sky as she stretched and yawned.

"Damn that felt good." She spoke out loud.

Getting out of the bed was a job in itself. She didn't want to move. Reluctantly, she pulled herself up and headed to the bathroom. After a quick shower, Sinnamon did her normal routine. She oiled herself with Vaseline and then followed suit with her Victoria Secret lotion. When she was properly moisturized, she got dressed. Not in the mood for shoes at the moment, Sinnamon dressed in a pair of Seven jeans, a pink black and white Ed Hardy T-shirt with the matching hat. She pulled her ponytail through the opening in the back of the hat. She finished her outfit with a black pair of Dries Van Noten flats. By the time Esco arrived at home, Sinnamon was fully dressed and ready to leave. After grabbing her clutch, Sinnamon followed Esco outside and into a Dodge Charger.

"Whose car is this?" Sinnamon questioned when she got in.

"It's a rental."

"What's wrong with your car?" Sinnamon wondered.

"The nigga writing this book forgot what kinda car he got me driving." Esco answered, laughing.

Sinnamon cracked up. "I was wondering what happened."

Esco and Sinnamon made it to Club 814 in no time. They surprisingly found a parking space not far from the entrance. They made their way to the door, and then walked up the steps to the club. Being that it was so early in the day, there was no fee to get in.

"What's up Tony?" Esco slapped hands with the owner.

"Nothing much man, you?" Tony replied.

"Same thing, just another day." Esco pulled Sinnamon closer to him so Tony could meet her. "This is my Fiancé, Sinnamon. Make sure you treat her good if she comes in." Tony shook Sinnamon's hand lightly.

"Congratulations." Tony said to Sinnamon. He then focused his attention back to Esco. "You know I got you. She'll get VIP treatment."

Esco and Tony shook hands again, and then Esco escorted Sinnamon to a table in the corner. Being a gentleman, he pulled her seat out for her before he sat down.

"What's good in here?" Sinnamon was looking through the menu. This was her first time at 814. She always heard Esco talk about it though.

"Everything" Esco answered simply.

"That was a lot of help. What are you getting?" Sinnamon quizzed.

"Fish"

"Just order me the same thing." Sinnamon closed her menu.
Esco waved one of the waitresses over and placed his order. When she left, he made eye contact with Sinnamon. He had a few things he wanted to talk to her about.

"So what's up with you and Essence?" Esco asked.

"What do you mean?" The question caught Sinnamon off guard.

It Gets Dirtier

"I mean, what type of shit ya'll be on. First you send me 17 bricks from Atlanta in the mail. Then I spoke to Reef last night and he told me Essence sold a chain, watch, and bracelet for 80 stacks." Esco stared into Sinnamon's eyes for the truth.

Sinnamon immediately put her head down. She was hoping to never have this conversation with Esco. She was at a loss for words.

"Say something." Esco was getting irritated. "I'm trying to make sure you're safe. I already got a feeling on what ya'll up to. I just can't see it and if it's true, you gotta stop that shit."

"What is it that you think we do?" Sinnamon wondered if it was that obvious.

"I'm guessin' ya'll robbing niggas." Esco sat back in his seat and waited for her to respond.

"Listen babe, we did a few things that I don't want to talk about, but I'm done. I'm done with everything. I have a nice piece of money put away and I'm looking to invest it in something. And I want to start a business or something." Sinnamon spoke with passion.

"Baby, with the money you have and the money I have, I know we can do big things, but I need you to be there with me. You should stop what you're doing too."

Esco remained quiet, thinking about her request. He was officially a millionaire and had no reason to continue with the game. He just wasn't sure what he wanted to do.

"Since we've been engaged, I've been seriously thinkin' bout leaving the game."

"Don't think about it, just leave it. What is there to think about? Money's not an issue."

"Did you just walk away from ya hustle?" Esco wanted to know. He was looking for something to buy him time.

"Actually I did, dropped it at a drop of a dime. I made my money and I'm satisfied." Sinnamon said simply.

"It's not that simple for me. I've been doing this since I can remember, it seems like. I really have years in and it's not about money for me. It's almost like a way of life. It comes as second nature. Feel me?" Esco explained.

"I hear you but I don't feel you. Baby, I just want you to think on it okay?" She gave him the puppy dog look. "We'll be married soon and I really want to build something special. We already have Shaquan, and I'm sure we'll have kids. We need to build something for them."

"You right." Esco flashed a smile at Sinnamon. He loved the fact that she seemed to focus on all the right things. "This week and next week, you just look for what it is you want us to do and we'll take it from there." Esco paused and smiled again. "So how much money you got?"

Sinnamon chuckled lightly. "Look at you all nosey. I didn't ask you how much you have."

"I'm not you."

"Well, I have enough." Sinnamon teased. "Not as much as you though."

"Just wanted to make sure I was the bread winner." Esco joked.

"One more question." Esco got serious.

"What?" Sinnamon figured he was going to ask about the night before.

"Was that ya'll work with Dez and Spoon?" He heard a lot of different stories on it. His main concern was the fact that he heard about Dez's manhood being blown off. "Cuz that shit was crazy."

"Babe, this food looks good." Sinnamon said when the waitress sat their food in front of them. Sinnamon wanted to avoid the question. She didn't want to lie to Esco, but the truth was out of the question. She knew he would never tell, but some things you just take to the grave.

"You just gonna ignore that one huh?" Esco shook his head with a smile. He really like the fact that Sinnamon knew how to keep her mouth shut. She was more thorough than most of the niggas he knew.

It Gets Dirtier

Sinnamon grinned, and then dug into her food. The two of them talked about different investment plans as they ate. One thing they agreed on was to focus on Esco's music. They knew they could score big with that one. With all the money they had, the skies the limit.

* * * * *

"Last night a Wilmington man was found dead inside of an empty Bethal Village apartment on the eastside of the city. The man was pronounced dead at the scene at 12:43 a.m. He is the city's 16th homicide victim this year. Anyone with information, please call the Delaware Crime Stoppers. There's currently a ten thousand dollar reward for any caller that leads police to an arrest." The woman on the Six O'clock news said.

"Uh huh, I got that bitch now." Janeen said excitedly. She quickly jumped off her couch and grabbed her cell phone. "I can use ten stacks anyway." She smiled greedily as she dialed the numbers.

"Hello, yes, my name is Janeen and I have information on last night's murder." Janeen spoke through the receiver.

"Are you a witness?" The man on the other line spoke.

"I live right next door and-" Janeen was cut off.

"Next door, we knocked on everyone's door after we found the body. How come you didn't answer if you were there?" The man questioned.

Janeen fumbled with her words. She heard them knocking that night, but wasn't going to say anything at first. There were too many people around and she didn't want to be seen talking to the police. Besides that, there wasn't anything in it for her, but the 10 thousand dollar reward would be plenty; especially since she didn't like Essence anyway.

"I don't know. I guess I was scared." She answered.

"Okay, what did you see?"

"I heard a shot, and then saw a woman running out the apartment with a gun when I looked out my peep hole."

"Do you know the woman?"

"Yes."

"Do you have a name?" The detective began to get excited. Again he could get credit for solving a crime without getting off his ass to do any work. He loved Delaware and its many informants. They made his job so much easier.

"Yes, her name is Essence Taylor. We went to school together." Janeen's grin grew wider. She could feel the money in her palms.

"That's great. When do you think you can come to the station and make a statement?" The detective asked.

"Now, if you want. I live right across the street. Who should I ask for?"

"Ask for detective Johnson. You can call me Chuck though." Detective Johnson spoke smoothly.

"Okay, I'm on my way." Janeen hung up her phone, gathered her things and headed to the police station.

Chapter 40

"What's good my nigga?" Esco spoke into the receiver when the operator stopped talking.

"Chilling. Feeling good." Gage told him.

"Word. What got you so hyped?" Esco could hear the excitement in Gage's voice.

"I spoke to my lawyer today. He said I'm getting a new court date for sure. My appeal's finally gonna come through." Gage said excitedly.

"That's what's up. When you think you're goin' to court?" Esco asked. He was happy to hear the news.

"I don't know exactly when, but it should be soon. Barkstale already put the paper work in. The babe Shantel finally came clean and said she's the one that put the guns and drugs in my spot. Her fingerprints and everything were on them." Just telling the news made Gage feel free.

"I thought that bitch died. What made her come through?" Esco wondered.

"Man, I thought she died too. Come to find out her mom saved her. She was pregnant and everything. She said the little boy is mine. I'm waiting for the test results to come back." Gage answered.

"Don't she got the bug?"

"Yeah, but the boy don't."

"You think he's yours?"

"Es, I don't even care. On some real shit she just looking for a nigga to take care of the little nigga cuz she dyin'. I'ma do it if he's mine or not, just cuz she's settin' me free." Gage explained.

"You better than me," Esco told him. He would never do anything for a person like Shantel.

"I feel you cuz, but it's bigger than me and her beef."

"I feel you."

Gage continued to explain everything to Esco. He told him about the visit from Shantel's mom and everything. Esco told him about his plans of changing. He even thought on studying the Deen.

"You have three minutes remaining." The automated voice interrupted their conversation.

"Yo, I almost forgot to tell you, Flip got all shot up a couple weeks ago." Gage told him.

"For real, where at?" Esco asked.

"In one of their spots in ATL. They said it was a robbery." Gage explained.

"Damn, that's crazy. He alright?"

"He pulled through. He still in the hospital though."

"I'ma call that nigga when I hang up with you and see what's good with him. I ain't talk to him in a while."

"Alright man, be safe out there. Love ya dawg." Gage said.

"Love you too my nigga." Esco hung up and then dialed Flip.

"Esco," Flip spoke cheerfully.

"What's good nigga? I just spoke to Gage and he told me what happened. Why ain't you call me?" Esco questioned.

"Man, I've been fucked up. A nigga almost died down this bitch. Word." Flip said seriously.

"You know who did it?"

"Some bitches." Flip answered nonchalantly.

Esco thought for a minute. The thought of Sinnamon and Essence pulling the trigger crossed his mind. He quickly shook it off. The world can't be that small, he said to himself.

"You knew em?"

"Not really. I'll run into them though." Flip said simply.

"I hear that. What's up with Mills?"

"Man I don't know what's up with that nigga. After I got hit up, he's been actin like a sucka. Talkin' bout let the shit ride and what not. Between you and me that nigga bitching. Either that or he played a part in the shit." Flip wasn't really feeling Mills at the moment.

"You know that nigga didn't have nothin' to do with that shit. He ain't the snake type." Esco tried to convince Flip.

"I don't see him bein' on that type time either but shit just looks funny. I mean, the nigga was supposed to be with me when it all went down, but all of a sudden he had some B-I to take care of. Then after I get hit, he talkin' that bullshit. Shit just seems suspect." Flip adjusted himself on his bed. The thought of Mills stabbing him in the back made him uncomfortable.

Esco took in what Flip was saying. He didn't know what to think. Mills was his boy and he couldn't picture him doing it, but he did have to admit, things looked shaky. He began to think how he would react. Mills talking like he didn't want to ride would bother him too.

"So what's good with everything else?" Esco switched subjects.

"Things in slow motion right now. I should be out the hospital in a week or so and then it's back to business as normal. You know Gage fuck around and be home soon."

"Yeah, he was telling me. That's good money." Esco replied.

"He said he ain't fucking around though."

"I can't blame him, not after comin' off a 56 year stretch. They tried to finish that nigga. Real rap, I was thinkin' about callin' it quits myself. I'm 'bout to get married soon and..."

"Married? Damn nigga. When that happened? Last time we spoke, you ain't even mention having a girl." Flip was happy for his boy.

"Yeah man, it was a spare of the moment thing. That's why I'm 'bout to take my money and invest in some legal shit. The game don't last forever." Esco said seriously.

"You niggas kill me. All this money! I don't see how ya'll can even think about walking away. You sound like Mills. You nigga's crazy. I'ma do this shit 'til the Feds come or niggas kill me." Flip just couldn't see past go. He was stuck on the streets.

"What's the point of making money if you can't enjoy it? Nigga you the one crazy, talkin' bout the Feds and dyin. I ain't trying to see neither. I got money. More than enough and anything after this is straight greed."

The more Esco spoke to Flip, the more he realized he should've been gave up the streets. Why not stop when you have everything?

"Whatever floats your boat. I'ma do me. Listen though, just get at me later. I'm 'bout to get some rest so I can heal faster. The faster I heal, the faster I can get that money ya'll niggas don't want." Flip said with an attitude. He couldn't see that his friends were finally growing up. He was the only one stuck on his young boy shit. The sudden change in his boys made Flip began to feel bitter.

"Do you cuz. I'll check back with you in a couple of days to make sure you straight." Esco said sincerely and then hung up the phone. I needed to hear that, Esco said to himself. He laid back on his couch, and then turned his music back up. He was listening to a track he laid for his 'Most of the Monster' CD. The beat was nice and mellow. He got it from a dude named Malik Phillips that he met through his boy lil Kenny. The CD was definitely going to be a hood classic.

"Baby come on with me, and baby you will see. Better Daaayzzzz better Daaaayzzzz, let's leave it all behind baby we will find better daaaayzzz." Esco smiled as he listened to the hook to the song. He was definitely looking for better days.

Chapter 41

"Boom, Boom, Boom." Was the sound of the battering ram against Essence's door. Four days since Janeen made her statement and the police finally found Essence's new place. It was 5:30 a.m. when the SWAT team barged in.

"Get the fuck on the ground...now! Let me see your hands. Let me see your fucking hands!" The lead officer yelled at the top of his lungs. He was wearing a helmet and carrying a shield with a large gun sticking through the slot.

Within seconds, ten more officers filled the condo, wearing similar gear. Most of the officers carried modified weapons that were equipped with flashlights or infrared beams. They all held their firearms pointed at Essence. One officer dragged her out of her bed and onto the floor. He held her face down as he cuffed her hands behind her back. Lucky for Essence, she was dressed in a pair of sweatpants and a tee shirt.

After lifting Essence off the ground, they escorted her out of her condo and into a waiting police cruiser. The officers then went to work on her belongings. During the search, they left nothing unturned and managed to break any and everything that was breakable. Most of the officers loved that part of their job. A few of them even stole a few items they knew had nothing to do with the case.

It Gets Dirtier

After an hour of searching, the officers were disappointed that they didn't find anything that linked Essence to the murder. She wasn't as dumb as they expected. The clothes she wore and gun were already history. With no physical evidence, you would think she would be set free, but not in Delaware. Delaware system is if a person said you did something, then you did it until proven otherwise. You will be arrested, thrown in jail, and it's up to a jury of your so-called peers to determine your fate.

As Essence sat in the back of the police cruiser, she kept a blank face. No one told her what she was being charge with or anything. She didn't bother asking either. In her heart, she already knew what was going on, so on her way to the police station, Essence just stared out the window. She knew that would be the last time she got to take in the scenery for a while.

At turnkey, Essence was placed in a cold cell by herself. The only thing in the cell was a metal bed with no mat, and a dirty metal toilet with a sink attached. She wasn't even given toilet paper. For the first half hour, Essence paced back and forth in the small cell. Chill bumps covered her body and her nipples hardened because of the cold air. She was past uncomfortable. After a while she laid on the metal bunk with her hands behind her head and got as comfortable as she could get. Before she knew it, she was asleep.

"Clank, Clank, Clank." A detective banged loudly on the metal bars of her cell.

Essence sat up on the bunk and looked up at the tall lanky detective. He stared her up and down with his poppy eyes. At first look with his beard and style of dress, you would've thought he was a street player, and not a detective, but instead of a chain around his neck, he proudly wore his badge.

"Well, well, well. What do we have here? Murder one! I love my job." The detective wore a huge smile across his face. "Oh, let me introduce myself. I'm detective Johnson, but you can call me Chuck."

Detective Johnson said sarcastically. He opened the door to the cell, cuffed Essence and then walked out. She followed behind him without saying a word.

"Awful quiet there aren't you?" Detective Johnson still had his silly grin across his face. Essence rolled her eyes and remained silent.

On the elevator ride up to the interrogation room, Detective Johnson couldn't help but stare lustfully at Essence. She had a beauty no one could deny. She on the other hand, looked at him in disgust. There was nothing she hated more than cops and snitches. Once they reached the proper floor, the elevator doors swung open. Essence and Detective Johnson were greeted by his partner. He too had a street look to him, wearing a thick beard, and several scars that looked like stab wounds. He had a look of a real gangster. He even sported a nice pair of shades.

"Detective Burtin my man. How you feeling today?" Detective Johnson greeted his partner. They slapped hands and exchanged laughs. They were really happy about their new arrest.

"How are you Ms. Taylor? I'm detective Burtin. If you want, feel free to call me Crumb. You already met my partner Chuck and we're working your case." Detective Burtin spoke politely. He stuck out his hand to shake Essence's. When he realized she wasn't able to shake it, he led her to a little room with a desk and a small seat. He uncuffed one of her hands then cuffed the other to the desk. He and Detective Johnson took seats across from Essence.

"First let me tell you now, you are under arrest for the murder of Michael McFinnly A.K.A. Sauce." Detective Johnson went on to read Essence her Miranda rights.

"So, is there anything you would like to say regarding this matter?" Detective Burtin asked softly. He was playing the role of concern.

"We're here to help you help yourself. Can you tell us if there was anyone with you during the crime or did anyone put you up to it? Tell us anything."

It Gets Dirtier

Essence sat with her head down. She was tired and not for the games. All she wanted was a phone call and some sleep. She never thought she'd say it but she was ready to go to jail. Turnkey's holding cell was the worst. Finally looking up at the two detectives, she just stared at them.

"So you're not going to say anything?" Detective Burtin asked.

"Can I have my phone call now?" Essence said dryly.

"Oh, you want us to give you a phone call but you don't wanna answer any questions? Do you know you are facing life without the possibility of parole? Life! As in forever, you'll never come home and what do you need to make a call for? Ain't like you're getting a bail," Detective Johnson said harshly.

"My partner's right. With a murder one charge, you will never see the streets again, but with the right info you could easily cop out and get less time. Do you have kids?" Detective Burtin was digging for a weak point.

"Listen. I have nothing to say. Just please take me to a phone and then do what it is that ya'll do." Essence looked both detectives coldly in the eyes.

"Alright, suit yourself. It's your life, not mine. When you're ready to talk, contact us and until then, enjoy the carpet munchers in W.C.I." Detective Burtin said spitefully. He was pissed. Time and time again, he broke down so-called thugs in the streets, but he couldn't get a peep out of a woman.

Essence was cuffed once again and escorted to her holding cell. After about an hour in the cell, she was finally allowed to make a call. She dialed Sinnamon.

"Sin, it's me Essence. I got arrested." Essence spoke weakly.

Sinnamon's heart dropped to the bottom of her stomach. "For what?" She asked.

"Murder" Just admitting she was arrested for murder made Essence emotional. A single tear escaped her eye. Sinnamon was silent for a moment. She didn't know what to do. Essence was her best friend and not only that, but every murder Essence committed, she was right there. Sinnamon began to cry lightly, but quickly got herself together.

"Don't worry about it Essence. I'm going to get you the best lawyer I can get. You'll be home in no time. Everything's going to be okay." Sinnamon said sincerely.

"I know, I just don't know what's going on. This is crazy. They about to send me over to W.C.I., I'll call you when I get there." Essence was trying to hold herself together but found it difficult to hold back her tears.

"Okay, I love you girl. Call me." Sinnamon began to cry as well. She could hear the pain in Essence's voice.

After hanging up the phone, Essence wiped her face and followed an officer to get her fingerprints done. When they were finished, she was escorted back to her cell where she cried herself to sleep. A murder charge was a hard pill to swallow. Before being transported to W.C.I., she got herself together and prepared to show no emotion in the jail. She refused to show any sign of weakness.

* * * * *

Gage laid back in his bunk, still not believing what was written in black and white; 99.9 percent. Now he knew without a doubt that Hakeem was his son. He replayed his sexual encounter with Shantel over and over again. They only had sex one time and he pulled out and ejaculated on her face and chest. How did she get pregnant? He thought to himself.

"Damn, that bitch must've been fertile." Gage spoke out loud.

"What you talking 'bout cuz?" Gage's celly, Shatter asked.

Shatter was also waiting for an appeal to go through. He was serving a life bid for a murder that he didn't commit. He was one of many Delaware inmates found guilty without any physical evidence against them. The only thing linking him to his case was so-called witnesses that just so happened to be potential suspects and convicted felons. They had every reason to lie.

"I'm that baby's papi." Gage mimicked the men from the movie "Life."

"Get the fuck outta here." Shatter was shocked. He couldn't believe the news himself. After Gage gave him complete details of the night, he would've never guessed it.

"No bullshit. Look." Gage passed Shatter the paper.

"You know what you have to do now. When you go home, be the best father you can be. Teach him to be a proud Muslim and keep him away from the streets. You yourself gotta make sure you live right. He's gonna be on your every move." Shatter spoke seriously, and gave Gage his paperwork back.

Gage laid back on his bunk and thought on what Shatter said. Shatter was 100% right. Gage was now a father and had to play his hand right. He would not want his son to grow up and do the things he's done. Gage laughed to himself.

"I got a son." Gage smiled.

Chapter 42

"You should skip town." Esco told Sinnamon. He watched as she paced nervously back and forth.

"Where am I going to go? I don't have any family anywhere. I don't know what to do." Sinnamon whined.

"Just calm down, pack up some things and I'm going to take you down North Carolina. Right now, I don't think they're looking for you but you need to leave before they do." Esco explained.

"North Carolina? Who's down there?" Sinnamon asked.

"My Aunt Mae, she'll take good care of you too." Esco told her.

"What about you? Are you going to stay with me?" Sinnamon whined. She didn't want to go down there by herself.

"I'll come down there when I can, but I still have business I need to finish up here. Plus, while I'm here, I'll be able to keep tabs on what's goin' on and let you know if it's safe for you to come back up here or not." Esco paused and grabbed Sinnamon's hands. He looked into her eyes. "Just trust me, everything will work out baby. Don't be afraid, okay? You trust me?"

"Yes."

"Aiight then, let's pack up." Esco gave Sinnamon a soft kiss on the lips.

It Gets Dirtier

Sinnamon had everything packed and they were on the road with-in an hour. Esco knew in a blink of an eye, your house could be surrounded and you'd be walking out in cuffs. Being that school was in, Sinnamon asked Ms. Jones to care for Shaquan and she agreed without questioning. The desperate look in Sinnamon's eyes was enough for her. That and the twenty grand she gave her didn't hurt.

They made their trip in Sinnamon's Bentley with Esco behind the wheel. He knew the way there like the back of his hand. He made the trip so many times, that he brought himself a small home down there. Being that he was only there occasionally, he let his Aunt Mae move in.

The eight-hour trip to North Carolina seemed to fly by. Esco and Sinnamon really enjoyed each other's company. They talked about everything from growing up to the present. The more they talked, the more they seemed to have in common.

"We here now." Esco told Sinnamon when he saw the Eden North Carolina sign.

"It looks country babe. Where do you have me?" Sinnamon took in the scenery of the small town. There were dirt roads, ranch houses, and farm animals were walking around. It was the total opposite of the city.

Esco laughed at Sinnamon's reactions. He remembered having the same impression when he first went down there when he was younger. At first, he hated it, but eventually he grew to love it.

"It's not as bad as it looks. I ain't sayin' it ain't country, but it's not what it looks like. It's a little city area not far from here, and don't be fooled, these country boys be getting' that paper down here. You'll see the cars and shit." Esco explained. There were a couple of dudes he even did business with in the area. Esco pulled into the driveway of a white and blue ranch style house. From the outside, there wasn't much to it, but it was nice. When Esco blew the horn, a heavyset woman came out with open arms.

"Hey baby!" Esco's Aunt Mae looked Sinnamon over and then

gave her a warm hug.

"How are you Ms. Mae?" Sinnamon spoke politely.

"Aunt Mae. Just call me Aunt Mae baby." She told Sinnamon.

"Ira, what are you eating up dere in Wilminton? You need to put some meat on dem bones." Aunt Mae pinched Esco's arm.

"I'm eating good Aunt Mae, you know I ain't never had a problem with that." Esco said happily as they went into the house.

"I don't know, Ira." Aunt Mae turned to Sinnamon. "Do you know how to cook?"

"Yes ma'am." Sinnamon answered with a smile. She got a kick out of Aunt Mae calling Esco by his real name. Back in Delaware only a few people called him Ira. "Tell her Ira." Sinnamon teased.

"She can cook a little somethin', somethin'." Sinnamon nudged him on the arm playfully.

"Well honey, I'ma makes a woman outta you before you leave here. Teach cha the old fashioned way." Aunt May took a seat in her favorite rocker. Esco and Sinnamon sat on the couch in front of the big screen TV.

Sinnamon looked around the living room. She spotted pictures of Esco and his mom back in the day. She admired the cherry wood china cabinet in the dining room. Sinnamon got up to get a better view of the figurines in the china cabinet. The house was small, but very homely.

"I made them myself." Aunt Mae said proudly when she saw Sinnamon looking at the figurines.

"Oh my God, you made them?" Sinnamon said surprised. They looked professionally crafted. "They are beautiful."

Sinnamon, Esco, and Aunt Mae talked for a little while longer. Mainly Aunt Mae, telling stories about Esco when he was younger. Sinnamon got a kick out of it too. She now had a few things to tease Esco about. When the conversation died down, Esco and Sinnamon made their way to Esco's room to get some much-needed rest. Esco spent the next two days with Sinnamon. They did a little shopping, went to the movies and did everything else they could do in two days. The time went by fast. Before they knew it, Sinnamon was dropping Esco off at a small airport so he could go home. He had to put his ear to the streets and find out what was going on.

* * * * *

Once back in Wilmington, Esco got straight to business. He had a fresh 200 bricks from his Texas plug waiting for him. Only paying $12,500 a brick and selling them for $22,500, he was going to walk away with a nice profit...two million to be exact. After talking to Sinnamon, he had no plans on breaking things down this trip. He wanted to get rid of everything ASAP. There was no more time for games, everything had to go. He dialed his heavy hitters to let them know he was back in town. After a few runs, Esco was 20 bricks lighter and 200 grand richer. He felt like a million dollars. He put his cash up and then made his way to the Ave to holler at his boy Gunner. Gunner had a few bitches pumping for him around BV, so if anybody knew something, he knew Gunner did.

"What's good my nigga?" Esco slapped hands with Gunner and gave him a brotherly hug.

"Same shit, just another day. Tryin' to get this gwap." Gunner told him. They stood out front of the barbershop watching the young boys in the trap. Gunner played it smart, he didn't want the spotlight. His motto was cop heavy, break it down, and pass it out. Then pick the money up later. He was keeping his hands clean.

"You heard 'bout that nigga Sauce getting rocked?" Esco questioned.

"Yeah, that shit's crazy. That nigga got slummed by a bitch. I guess everybody's playing for keeps these days. He was in the way anyhow." Gunner spoke with no compassion.

"You ain't lyin'." Esco laughed. "Listen though, you ain't hear nothing else on it? My peoples got booked for that shit and I'm tryin' to see what happened."

"I never cared to ask about the shit. I ain't really dig the nigga like that. Home girl did me a favor. When I go back and check on my squad, I'll see what's good for you. You know them nosey bitches be knowin' everything." Gunner said nonchalantly.

"That's good lookin'." Esco slapped hands with Gunner and then jumped back in his car. He turned his radio up and let himself blast through his speakers.

"Let me tell you what I feel like/ what I do in real life/ since I rap and I'm real/ then I'm real nice."

It was still daylight and he had one more stop to make before going in. He had to take a trip up Philly to see his lawyer. That's who he was going to put on Essence's case. For certain charges, Esco didn't trust Delaware lawyers. Not that none of them weren't good, he just didn't like the politics involved. Not many people beat murder cases in Delaware. Once booked, you're in for the ride.

Esco made it to his lawyer in a half hour. Once in the office, Esco took a seat in a plush chair, sitting across from the lawyer's desk. Before sitting, they shook hands.

"So what seems to be the problem? You're not in any trouble are you?" Mr. Goldstein spoke in a deep tone. He was about 5'7" with a heavy frame. His skin was light brown and he sported a salt and pepper George Jefferson hairstyle- bald on the top with hair on the sides.

"Naw, I'm in the clear on this one." Esco laughed. He was happy not to be the one in trouble for a change. "A friend of mine caught a murder charge, I was hopin' you could help her."

"Her?" Mr. Goldstein was surprised.

"Yeah, same thing I thought. So what's this gonna run?" Esco asked.

"Depends on how far it goes. When did she get arrested?"

"A few days ago,"

"Did she have a prelim?"

"No, not yet,"

"She going to trial or copping out?"

"She gotta make it home."

"How 'bout this, pay me ten grand now and I'll do the prelim, do some of my own investigations, and see what type of fight I can put up. Then we can go from there. Is that okay with you?" Mr. Goldstein waited on a reply.

"Cool with me." Esco dug in his pocket and pulled out a stack full of hundreds. He counted out ten grand and paid Mr. Goldstein.

"When can I expect to hear from you?"

"Today's Monday, give me till about Wednesday or Thursday."

"Aiight let me know if they're looking for any other suspects too." Esco requested as he got up.

Mr. Goldstein looked at Esco and shook his head. He assumed he might have played a part in the murder. It didn't make him any difference though, as long as the money was green.

Chapter 43

"Damn, it feels good to be out that fucking hospital." Flip said. He was finally home, but still recovering. The doctor told him to make sure he took it easy and go to his therapy sessions and in no time, he'd be 100 percent.

"Mills said call him." Monica told him.

"I don't feel like talking to that nigga right now." Flip informed her.

"I'm tryin' to get some one on one with you."

"One on one with me," Monica spoke seductively. It's been a few weeks since they had some alone time. Besides, a few oral pleasures she gave Flip in the hospital, they had no sexual contact, and Monica's chocolate body was burning with desire. She stood in front of Flip as he laid back on his big La-Z Boy recliner.

"Yeah some alone time with you," Flip said with a smile. He put his hands in his pants and fiddled with his stiff flesh, as he admired Monica's sexiness. She was built like Megan Good, but had the complexion of Keisha from Belly. With her chinky eyes and long straight hair, she had an exotic twist.

"You want some alone time with me or her?" Monica lifted up her skirt, put her right leg up, and sat her foot on Flip's armrest. Moving her panties to the side, she exposed her bald soft area. Using both

267

hand, she parted her second pair of lips and gave Flip a view of her pink, wet area.

"Yeah, I need to see her about somethin'." Flip licked his middle and pointer finger and then let them dance in her moisture.

Monica let out a soft moan. "Umm I missed you baby." She whispered. Monica took off her shirt and began to massage her perky B-cups. She fiddled with her nipples like she was trying to find the right radio station. Flip loved her small dark, black nipples. He called them his black berries. Flip tried to take off his pants, but Monica stopped him.

"Relax baby. Let me take care of you." Monica gently pushed Flip back into his chair. She slid him out of his pants and then took his hard flesh into her mouth. She flicked her tongue around the tip of his manhood. The feeling sent chills down his spine. After a good tease, Monica began to slowly rock Flip's mic. Her head bobbled up and down to a beat of its own. Flip put his head back and held his mouth open. He was stuck. Monica let her saliva trickle down his shaft as her head went up, then slurped it all up when she went down. She almost made Flip cum when she deep throated him down to the base of his manhood, and stuck her tongue out, letting it play with his balls. With brains like that, it was easy to say she was a genius.

Before Flip managed to explode, Monica stood up on the lazy boy and squatted over top of him. She grabbed his manhood and lined it up with her opening. Slowly, she guided herself down his pole, and when she reached the bottom, she slowly rose up. It was all in the legwork. As Monica got her eagle on, Flip laid back in a world of his own. He loved when she took control. Her ride game was like no other. Flip watched as she bounced herself to an orgasm. Monica's cum slowly trickled down Flip's manhood. Her legs buckled and she dropped to her knees, leaving Flip deep inside her.

"I love you baby." Monica said sweetly. Flip kissed her softly on the lips and then on her neck, making his way to her black berries.

His tongue danced with her nipples as he massaged her back with both hands. Monica began to rock back and forth.

"Ride that dick baby." Flip moaned.

Monica rocked faster and faster. She dug her nails into Flip's chest. "You feel sooo good." She moaned and grinded harder.

Flip held on to Monica's waist as she began to ride him like a mechanical bull. He began to tense up, and felt his toes tingle and his manhood got even harder.

"Yes baby, cum in me." Monica knew Flip was about to cum.

Flip grabbed Monica's waist hard and held her down on his manhood. His entire body relaxed as he released himself inside of Monica. She slowly rocked back and forth as his flesh jumped around inside of her.

"Damn. I love you." Flip smiled ear to ear.

* * * * *

Essence sat in her cell fuming. She couldn't believe Sinnamon wasn't answering her phone. How could her best friend leave her out in the cold? Something has to be wrong, she convinced herself. Essence was in a cell by herself so she laid in her bed and began to cry. That's all she really did since being locked away. Crying herself to sleep was her medication. Essence didn't really cry over being locked up because she wasn't scared. She was more confused, not knowing anything about her case and then Sinnamon was MIA. She wondered if Sinnamon got locked up as well. If so, who would hire her lawyer? Essence jumped up when she heard keys at her cell. She quickly wiped her eyes and waited for the door to swing open.

"Your lawyer's here." A light-skinned female office said nicely. She was one of the officers that Essence liked.

"Officer Jones, is it a PD or a paid lawyer?" Essence asked.

"I think it's a paid lawyer. If he's a PD, I never seen him before."

A smile broke across Essence's face, she jumped up quickly and followed behind Officer Jones. The officer let her into the interview room and closed the door. Essence was glad to see he was black.

"Are you a PD or lawyer?" Essence questioned before taking a seat.

"I'm a lawyer out of Philadelphia. One of the best, I might say. There's no need to worry. You're in good hands." Mr. Goldstein chuckled. "I'm Jerome Goldstein." Essence was relieved to know she had a paid lawyer. She was scared to have a PD, because she knew they were known to send people up the river without a boat or paddle.

"Who hired you?"

"Ira." He replied.

"Ira?" Essence looked puzzled.

Mr. Goldstein chuckled again. "Esco,"

"Oh." A smile broke across her face. She was embarrassed that she didn't know his real name.

"He called me yesterday and told me to tell you that your sister's okay and she said she loves you and not to worry." Mr. Goldstein informed her.

That brightened Essence's day. She knew he was talking about Sinnamon.

"So how does my case look?" Essence got to business.

"Honestly, I don't even see how you got arrested. The Delaware law is something else. Based on the reports I have, there's no physical evidence, just one witness that didn't even see the actual crime. She only claimed she spotted you run out of the apartment with a gun." Mr.Goldstein said.

"Who's the witness?" Essence asked.

"I don't have a name yet. In the paperwork it says she lives in the building, a neighbor that saw you through a peephole. If they don't have anything else, I'm going to move for a suppression hearing. You'll be home in two or three months, I may even beat it at your prelim." Mr. Goldstein said confidently.

"You're sure it's that simple?" Essence was surprised.

"I'm positive, once we find out who the witness is, I'm sure she'll change her statement." Mr. Goldstein was used to dealing with thugs so he knew in cases like this, witnesses rarely show up at court. "If she doesn't change her statement, then we'll go to trial. I'm excellent at destroying people's credibility.

"Sounds good to me."

Mr. Goldstein went on to interview Essence. He asked about her background and other basic information. He then asked about where she was when the murder took place and if she had an alibi. After the interview, both Essence and Mr. Goldstein left feeling good about the case. Essence would be home soon.

* * * * *

"Yo Es, come holla at me, I'm up the way." Gunner told Esco over the phone.

"Aiight," Esco hung up, he was just wrapping up a deal with his boy Reef. A dude Esco did business with was short on the paper he owed him. Mac brought two bricks for 45 grand every week and Esco always fronted him an extra one for twenty-five. The last two times, Esco went to pick his money up, Mac was short five grand. Mac was in the hole ten grand altogether and Esco was tired of the games.

"I'ma meet the nigga around back street, after I serve him, handle him. I'm only giving him two bricks this week. I told him he couldn't get no fronts 'til he paid his debt, so I'ma hit you with 25 stacks and you can keep the two birds." Esco and Reef sat in Reef's car.

"I'm cool with that. We'll just meet after it's handled." Reef said coolly. He loved putting in work. Two bricks and twenty-five grand was a nice come up.

"Aiight cuz, I'ma hit you up when I'm ready." Esco slapped hands with Reef and then exited the car and jumped into his. Esco made his way to Concord Ave to talk to Gunner. He figured Gunner had some information for him regarding Essence's case. When he pulled up, Esco spotted Gunner standing in front of the barbershop. Seeing Esco, Gunner stepped in the street and jumped in Esco's car. Esco pulled off.

"What's good cuz?" Gunner spoke and slapped hands with Esco.

"You tell me." Esco replied.

"Some bitch name Janeen called the police on ya peoples." Gunner got to the point.

"Yeah," Esco shook his head.

"I know where the bitch stay too. Dumb bitch, went bragging to some broad round there 'bout getting a ten stack reward for turning ya peoples in. She told the chick why not get the money, ain't like she wasn't gonna get caught anyway."

"Motha Fucka's trip me out. That's cool though, good looking too." Esco had circled the block. He pulled over in front of the barbershop.

"If you need me, let me know. I already got the drop on the bitch. I hate snitches anyway." Gunner slapped hands with Esco and then made his way out of the car.

"That's a bet, I'ma holla at you when I see how I want to play this shit." Esco told him. He put his car in drive, then quickly back in park when he spotted his boy, Clark. "Clark Bar," Esco yelled through his driver side window. Clark was kicking it with one of the local babes from around the area.

"What's good?" Clark slapped hands with Esco when he made his way over to the car.

"Don't forget, we gotta put that song on wax tonight." Esco reminded Clark.

"Which one, bobble head?" Clark asked with a smile.

"Yeah." Esco laughed. The song was a hood remake of 'Same Girl' by R. Kelly and Usher. Only they were talking about a babe that gave them oral pleasures.

"Ya new name is bobble head, bobble head!" Clark sung a line from the song and burst into laughter. "I might call that bitch tonight."

"You crazy as a motha fuck." Esco was all smiles. "I'ma holla at you later on tonight though." Esco and Clark slapped hands and Esco pulled off. He had more business to tend to.

Chapter 44

"Hey baby, I missed you so much." Sinnamon jumped into Esco's arms and began to kiss him all over his face. It's been almost two weeks since he left her in North Carolina. He was there now making a business run.

"I missed you too." Esco kissed Sinnamon on the lips, and then placed her on her feet. It was a little after 11 p.m. and Sinnamon was fresh out of the shower. She had on a terrycloth robe and matching slippers. Her hair was curly from being washed.

"I have something to show you." Sinnamon grabbed Esco by the hand and led him into the bedroom. When they reached the room, Sinnamon shut and locked the door. Taking off her robe, she laid on the bed butterball naked. Esco smiled with approval.

* * * * *

The next morning, Esco and Sinnamon woke up in each other's arms. After having sex the night before, they fell asleep without a word. Esco didn't even get a chance to tell Sinnamon about Essence's case.

"Babe." Esco nudged Sinnamon to wake her up. She turned her back towards him and pulled the covers over her head.

It Gets Dirtier

Esco crept out of the bed with a plan in mind. He grabbed one end of the covers and yanked them off of Sinnamon. The sudden air sent chill bumps all over her naked body.

"Wake ya ass up." Esco was full of laughter.

"You're always playing." Sinnamon snapped. She reached for more covers but was unsuccessful. Esco tossed them across the room.

"What, what do you want Ira?" Sinnamon couldn't help but laugh, seeing Esco with a silly grin on his face.

"You up now?" He asked, still smiling. He took a seat on the bed next to Sinnamon.

"Yes baby, I'm up." Sinnamon laid her head on his lap.

"I spoke to the lawyer. Essence is straight. They only got one witness. She'll be home in no time." Esco said smoothly.

"Witness?" Sinnamon thought back to that night, she didn't remember seeing anyone. Then she thought on the saying, someone's always watching.

"Yeah, some bitch name Janeen. They say she turned her in for the reward money. She don't hold no weight though. She didn't even see what happened. She just happened to look through the peephole when she heard the gunshot." Esco explained.

"I remember Janeen. She used to pick on me. I can't stand that bitch." Sinnamon thought on all the trouble Janeen gave her over the years.

"Well, don't worry about her. Essence will be home in no time." Esco assured her.

"So are they looking for me?" Sinnamon asked. She was ready to go back home.

"Naw, the girl only identified Essence."

"So I'm leaving with you?"

"I want you to stay down here for a little while longer. At least until I get everything out the way. I'll be done my work soon, Essence will be home, and we can go live that normal life you wanted." Esco told Sinnamon.

"So what about Janeen, how are you going to make sure the situation with her is going to work out?" Sinnamon wanted to know.

Esco gave her a devilish smile. "Don't worry 'bout all that. Just know she ain't comin' to court."

I know she's not Sinnamon thought to herself, she too had plans for Janeen.

"Okay baby." Sinnamon said sweetly.

"Well, I gotta shoot back up top. I'll be back down here in a few days to check on you." Esco began to put his clothes back on.

"You're leaving already? It hasn't even been twenty four hours babe." Sinnamon whined, putting on her robe.

"I know but I gotta handle what needs to be done. I'll be back before you know it."

"You promise?"

"Yeah girl, I promise." Esco kissed Sinnamon on the forehead and prepared to leave. Sinnamon followed him to the front room.

"See you in a couple of days Aunt Mae." Esco kissed her on the cheek.

"You're not going to stay and eat? I'm gonna cook in a few." Aunt Mae said.

"Naw, I don't really have the time, I gotta catch this highway." Esco made his way to the door. He hugged and kissed Sinnamon one last time.

"Love you baby." Sinnamon said sweetly.

"Love you too."

Once Esco left, Sinnamon began to pack her things. She wanted to catch Janeen before Esco did. There was no way she was going to let Janeen get away with putting Essence in jail. She already got away with years of disrespect. Sinnamon felt Janeen was a problem she needed to handle herself. She always knew the tables would turn one day, and she'd have the upper hand.

It Gets Dirtier
* * * * *

"So you really plan on leaving the game alone?" Flip asked. He and Mills were at the same house that Flip got shot in.

"Yeah, it's 'bout time I call it quits." Mills shot the 3 ball in the corner pocket.

"So it's that easy for ya'll? I don't understand it. All this cash easy money too. You, Esco, and Gage all talkin' that same bullshit. I can't see me leavin' this shit 'til I'm in a box. I'm telling you, I'll be pumping from behind the wall if I ever get knocked." Flip said with arrogance.

"You just gotta know when enough is enough. I guess right now, it's not enough for you. I'm done. I'm good, and I'm satisfied. Money ain't an issue, it'll never be." Mills hit the 8 ball in the side pocket, ending the game. "I'm already on the run. Insha Allah (God willing), I don't get caught up behind that. I'm hoping to reach the statute of limitation thing I heard about. I got too much to lose right now. I'm livin' better than I ever thought possible. Nigga's dream to live how we live, I used to dream 'bout this shit and I ain't tryin to give it all up to be in jail, lookin' at pictures, tellin niggas how I used to be ballin'. Feel me?" Mills explained.

Flip knew Mills was making sense but he wasn't ready to let the streets go. "I hear you nigga, but I don't feel you." Flip re-racked the balls.

"You still riding up top with me to see bout Gage right?" Flip changed the subject.

"Yeah, I'ma just have to garb up in the courtroom, just to be safe." Mills answered.

"Smart move. What time you trying to leave?"

"You said tonight right?"

"Yeah."

"I'm riding with you."

"Aiight." Flip cracked the balls to start a new game.

Chapter 45

"Damn Esco you really ain't gonna hit me with the other bird." Mac whined. Esco sat in the driver's side of his car counting the money Mac just gave him.

"Listen, you should be happy I'm not just takin' ya money and tellin' you, you beat. You keep fucking wit my paper like shit's a game." Esco didn't even bother looking at Mac. The sight of him may cause him to shed his blood right in his car.

"It's me though dawg. You know I'm good for a couple dollars. I know that shit ain't hurtin' you." Mac wasn't giving up.

Esco cut his eyes over at Mac. "Don't tell me what's hurtin' me nigga. My money is my money. I don't give a fuck if it was $10, you owe me, I need all mines. You fucking crazy tellin me 10 stacks ain't hurtin' me. You got me fucked up. Yo just get the fuck out of my car before I forget I halfway fuck with you." Esco was heated.

Mac looked at Esco to see if he was serious. When he saw the fire in Esco's eye, he knew it was time to stop playing games. He only held on to the money he owed Esco because Esco used to mess with his little sister and felt he was in the safe. Esco was like family in his eyes. They did business together for the last four years.

"My bad S. I'ma get that money to you by tonight. I didn't know you really wanted it." Mac sighed.

It Gets Dirtier

He tried to give Esco a five, but only received a cold stare. Mac stepped out of Esco's car with a sad look on his face and a footlocker bag full of cocaine. He had a feeling he may have just lost his plug. He watched Esco pull off. On his way back to his car, Mac noticed a man in a wheelchair coming down the street towards him. Mac immediately felt sorry for the man and watched how he struggled to maneuver his chair over the cracks and grooves in the sidewalk.

Suddenly the man's chair tipped over and he fell violently onto the ground. "Aww shit." The man yelled out in pain.

Mac quickly threw the bag with his coke in his backseat and made his way over to help the man.

"Let me help you up my man." Mac said in a friendly tone. He reached down to grab him.

"Naw, I got it." The man said with a sudden burst of energy.

"I'm just makin' sure you okay." Mac said. He figured the man was one of them physically challenged people that didn't like help they didn't ask for.

"I'm good, but you ain't." The man pulled out a .44 magnum bulldog revolver. "Esco said don't worry 'bout ya tab."

"Boom, Boom." The shots from the large gun entered Mac's face and out the back of his head. He fell back, tripped on the curb and landed on his back. Blood formed a puddle underneath him. Reef got up and dusted himself off. He quickly checked Mac's pockets and took his keys. Reef then folded up his wheelchair, hit the trunk button to Mac's Buick and threw the chair in it. He hopped in the car and pulled off.

* * * * *

When Sinnamon made it to Delaware, she went straight to Essence's condo to switch cars. She was hoping it wasn't towed away. Pulling into the development, Sinnamon spotted the Caddy in the parking lot. She pulled up beside it, hopped out her Bentley and jumped into the Caddy, headed to BV.

It Gets Dirtier

Twenty minutes later, Sinnamon pulled into the same parking space she did the night Essence killed Sauce. She spotted a couple of dudes sitting on the steps of the apartment building that Janeen lived in.

For a minute, she contemplated on what she wanted to do, but with no other choice, she exited the Caddy and sashayed over to the group of men.

"Do you know which apartment Janeen stays in?" Sinnamon asked no one in particular.

All the men stared at her lustfully. They all debated on talking to her. The ring on her finger had them second-guessing, and she had a look on her face like she wasn't for the games. Which she wasn't, her visit was strictly business.

"Yeah, ma, she lives in 3B. She ain't there though. I think she went to the store or sometin'." A light skin man with a New York accent answered.

"Thanks. I'll come back then." Sinnamon turned to walk away.

"Hey ma, you forgot to leave me ya number." The light skin man said quickly.

"Good one baby, but I'm already taken." Sinnamon flashed her ring.

"I respect that. If you change ya mind, I'm Slice, if you need to come find me, gorgeous." Slice watched Sinnamon lustfully as she walked away.

When she got back into the car, Sinnamon checked the clock. It was only 9pm, she had plenty of time. With nothing else to do Sinnamon checked into the Court Yard Marriot Hotel to take a catnap. She didn't want to let Esco know she was in town, so going home was out of the question.

Sinnamon woke up around one o'clock in the morning. Dressing herself in all black, she was dressed to kill...literally. Sinnamon exited her room, took the elevator downstairs, and left the hotel. She walked down the street to where she parked her car, got in and pulled off.

It Gets Dirtier

This time when Sinnamon was back around Janeen's neighborhood, she parked a couple blocks away. She put on a blond wig that she bought in North Carolina; it was supposed to be a bedroom treat for Esco. Then she applied a light color foundation on her face to give her a complexion of a white girl. When Sinnamon checked herself out in the mirror, she was satisfied with how she looked. She put her hood over her head, held her head down and headed to Janeen's. When she finally made it to the building, Sinnamon was relieved that no one was on the steps this time. She quickly entered and made her way to 3B. Once there, she pulled out her credit cards and went to work on the door. She was in three minutes later.

Asleep in her bedroom, Janeen didn't hear a thing. Sinnamon moved around in the apartment like a ninja. She spotted a large wooden African sculpture on the coffee table and picked it up. It was the shape of a half naked woman, holding a basket on her head. Sinnamon rubbed on the jagged breast of the sculpture. This should do the trick. Sinnamon found Janeen's room and entered it quietly.

The light from the TV flickered enough for Sinnamon to see Janeen sleeping with a scarf on her head. Sinnamon hovered over top of her and took her first swing. It felt good. She was going to enjoy this. The blow woke Janeen up, but was followed by another that put her back to sleep. As Sinnamon repeatedly smacked Janeen with the sculpture, blood flew everywhere, including all over Sinnamon. As Sinnamon brutally beat Janeen, she thought about all the names she called her over the years, all the jokes and the pain. She hit her harder and harder. Finally, the sculpture broke, leaving a dagger like piece in Sinnamon's hand. With one thrust, Sinnamon buried the sculpture deep into Janeen's chest.

Sinnamon looked down at Janeen and almost lost her lunch. She was so in a zone she didn't realize how much damage she did. Janeen was beat beyond recognition. Her face was smashed in. The job was done. Sinnamon left just as quickly and quietly as she came.

Sinnamon made it back to the Caddy without being seen. She

hopped in and made her way back to Newark to her car. Once there, she removed her bloodstained clothes and placed them in a bag to dispose of them. She hopped in her Bentley and made her way back to the hotel to take a shower. When she was all cleaned up she made her way home, ditching the clothes along the way. When she entered her house, she was greeted with a .40 cal in her face.

"It's me baby, it's me." Sinnamon said quickly. Her heart pounded rapidly in her chest.

"Damn girl. What chu doing here? I was about to send you on your way." Esco put his gun back into his waistband. He had fallen asleep on the couch watching TV.

"I missed you baby. I didn't want to stay down there if I didn't have to." Sinnamon spoke with an innocent voice.

"Whatever, you better call before you come in next time." Esco told her playfully. The two of them embraced, and then went to the bedroom.

Chapter 46

"Mr. Parker, what I have in front of me right now is hard to believe. I don't even know what to say. I don't know whether to blame the law enforcement agencies that arrested you, or to think you somehow managed to manipulate the system." The Judge looked at Gage with a frown and then back at his papers. "I have reviewed these papers over and over again, and there's nothing in here that can give you a retrial." Gage felt his hopes vanishing. "I have no choice but to let you go.

You're dismissed of all charges, but Mr. Parker, be careful. I really don't believe what's in front of me so if you ever come back in this court again, I will give you all the time I legally can. You are free to go." The Judge banged the gavel.

Gage sat in his chair speechless. He wasn't expecting all of that to go down. His lawyer told him he was going to set a new trial, not go home. The Judge wanted to give him a trial, but on what? Shantel admitted that she put everything there. Her fingerprints were even on the guns. Not only that, but she was even ready to go to jail for the part she played. When the Bailiff escorted Gage out the courtroom, he look back to see Arrissa, Flip, Esco, and a Muslim woman all hugging one another. Gage shook his head at them with a smile on his face. He was free.

It Gets Dirtier

* * * * *

"Yo, they let me go dawg. Can you believe it, I'm free." Gage said excitedly to Shatter, when he entered the cell. Gage began to pack his things.

"Say word." Shatter finished his last push-up.

"Word..."

"Alhumduallah, you better take this blessing and run with it." Shatter told him.

"No doubt. You know you next baby. I'ma keep it tight with you till then." Gage said sincerely.

"Parker, get your shit and come on." A CO yelled.

"Listen man, be safe out there. I love you dawg. Don't come back." Shatter told Gage. Shatter couldn't wait for his turn.

When Gage made it out the gates, Arrissa greeted him. They hugged one another tightly and held on like there was no tomorrow. Tears dropped from her eyes, she was so happy. "I told you I was going to get you home." She whispered in Gage's ear.

"I love you. You hear me?" Gage said, still embracing Arrissa.

"I love you too." They finally broke their embrace and Arrissa guided Gage to her car. It was a black on black M45 Infiniti.

"Damn baby, this how we doing it?" Gage admired the car.

"You told me to get something nice." Arrissa was happy to see Gage liked the car. "This car is definitely nice." Gage said as he got in on the passenger side and began to fool around with the many buttons.

Arrissa pulled off smoothly.

"Mrs. Carter called me not too long ago." Arrissa informed Gage.

"Yeah, what she say?" Gage was still cheesing. He was happy to be free.

"She said all of Hakeem's things are packed for us to come get him, but before we get him, Shantel wants to see us." Arrissa said reluctantly. She wasn't really trying to see Shantel.

It Gets Dirtier

Gage sucked his teeth, "I know baby. I don't want to go either but it's the right thing to do."

"Well lets' go straight there and get this over with. I'ma feel crazy in there with her laid up like that." Gage could only imagine how Shantel looked, lying in the hospital, dying from Aids. Then the fact that he set her up to get it made it worse. Both Arrissa and Gage were nervous to see Shantel, because they both felt guilty.

* * * * *

When they reached Shantel's hospital room, they knocked lightly on the door. They could hear the monitor's beeping as they walked in. Shantel was lying down watching TV. She was hooked to an IV and wore an oxygen mask over her face. The sight was heart breaking. Arrissa's eyes began to water. Shantel had lost well over fifty pounds and the burns from Arrissa's hot mix left her face disfigured. She was far from the beauty they both remembered. Gage and Arrissa were shameful for their actions.

Shantel took the mask from her face. "I didn't think ya'll would come." Shantel smiled weakly. "I know I'm a mess, but I'm okay with it." She sat herself up in her bed. "Happy to be home?"

"I can't even explain how I feel." Gage said happily.

"I'm sorry for putting you through that. I was just so mad." Shantel explained. Gage didn't know how to respond so he remained quiet.

"I wanted ya'll to come out here so I could let ya'll know that I was sorry for everything that I've done, and I want ya'll to know that I forgive ya'll for what ya'll done to me. God has worked on me and I want to leave this earth with a clean slate." Shantel focused in on Arrissa. "Arrissa, I still love you like a sister, no matter what. I pray that one day you forgive me for what I did to you and your unborn child. I acted out of rage. I truly am sorry. This may be a lot to ask, but I'm asking you to love my child, the way you would've loved yours.I'm not going to be here soon Rissa. If you can find it in your heart to be his mother and tell him the good things about me. Let him know I was beautiful and tell him about our friendship."

284

It Gets Dirtier

Arrissa was touched by Shantel's words. She began to cry like a baby. "I do forgive you." She hugged Shantel, dripping tears on her.

"Don't cry girl. You're going to get me all emotional." Shantel said, releasing tears of her own. "Gage, I know you're going to be a great father. I just want you to put what went on between us behind us, and bury it with me. I don't want our son to know about this mess, and please forgive me enough to tell him only good things about me. Can you promise me that?" Shantel begged. She knew Gage had a hard heart.

"Shantel, I forgave you the moment you forgave me. You came through and you set me free, and gave me a chance to be the father I never had. I will do everything you ask of me and more. What happened between us will stay behind us." Gage paused. He took Shantel's hand into his. "I am truly sorry for all of this, and I really want to thank you for letting me know you forgave me."

"You're welcome." Shantel said weakly. Gage, Shantel and Arrissa talked for another two hours about the good old days. Shantel really needed a visit like that. Besides her mother, she didn't have anyone else. Gage and Arrissa agreed to make visits often. When it was time to go, a burden was lifted off everyone's chest.

* * * * *

"So how does it feel to be home?" Mills asked Gage. Mills, Esco, Flip and Gage were at Gage and Arrissa's house talking. Arrissa had managed to get her and Gage a nice home in Bear, Delaware. Mills gave Arrissa all of Gage's money and he, Esco and Flip all gave Gage a piece of the profits from everything they made. Gage didn't have as much money as them, but still had over a couple million.

"I can't even express how I feel. I mean, I knew this day would come eventually, but it's so overwhelming. I really didn't expect it so soon." Gage explained.

"So what's your plan?" Flip asked.

"Well you see I got little man now, and the wife." Both Arrissa and Hakeem were upstairs. "So I'm chillin'. Thanks to ya'll and a few investments, money's not an issue. I'ma just continue to humble myself and worship Allah. I want to teach my son the Deen." Gage explained.

"I hear that. I guess I'ma be out on the street solo then. Mills and Esco hanging it up too." Flip said.

"That's Alhumduallah. Flip you should go ahead and give it up too." Gage suggested.

"Naw, I'm good. This is the path for me. I love my life." Flip spoke in ignorance.

"I'll pray for you Flip. Insha Allah (God willing), you'll see it's another way. Can't keep doing the same things over and over, eventually you'll get tired of it though."

"Yeah man, you ain't lyin' bout that cuz I'm damn sure tired of it. I'm 'bout to get married soon, probably have some babies and what not. I'm chilling." Esco said. He looked at his watch. "Speaking of which, I need to go ahead and make my way home before the Misses start buggin'"

"So who is she anyway?" Flip asked.

"Her name is Sinnamon. Bad little thing too, I'll introduce ya'll to her before ya'll leave. When ya'll leavin' anyway?" Esco asked.

"Probably not for another week, Mills and me gonna go up Philly for a while and party with some of my peoples. Then we gonna kick it with ya'll another day before we go head and take it back down south." Flip said.

"Aiight, that's a bet. I'll holla at ya'll tomorrow." Esco slapped everyone's hand, then left.

Chapter 47

The next morning, Esco was up early in his living room doing pushups. This was a regular routine for him. He always worked out in front of the TV, watching the news. That's how he stayed up to date on what went on around the world.

"In Wilmington, a gruesome discovery of a woman's body was found last night in her Bethal Village apartment. Authorities were called to the home of Janeen Freeman after complaints of a foul smell coming from her apartment. A maintenance man found the woman beaten to death in her bedroom, she was identified through fingerprints. She is the city's 17th homicide this year. Not even two weeks ago, a man was found shot dead in the same building. Police do not believe the murders are related. They are however looking for Freeman's boyfriend, Shawn Jackson for questioning. Anyone with information regarding Jackson's whereabouts is encouraged to call the police." A picture of Janeen's boyfriend came on the screen.

Esco couldn't believe his luck. That was 50 grand he was saving and another problem out the way. He ran up the steps to tell Sinnamon. The thought of her doing it didn't even cross his mind. Who would think a woman could commit a murder that brutal.

"Baby, that bitch dead." Esco shook Sinnamon awake.

"What are you talking about?" Sinnamon rolled over and yawned.

"The girl that told on Essence, that shit was on the news. Her boyfriend beat her to death." Esco explained.

Sinnamon sat up in her bed. A smile crept across her face. "For real, her boyfriend killed her?"

"No bullshit, I just saw it."

"That's good, so Essence coming home today right?"

"Should be, I'ma call Goldstein and let him know this shit happened, right on time too because her preliminary hearing is today. They're gonna have to throw this shit out." Esco said happily. "Without Janeen there was no case."

Sinnamon just smiled. She grabbed Esco and pulled him to her.

"Lay down with me."

* * * * *

"Essence bag and baggage." Officer Jones was at her cell.

"I'm ready." Essence was already packed and ready to go. Earlier that day it only took about five minutes of Goldstein talking for her case to be dismissed.

"You weren't playing were you?" Officer Jones smiled brightly. She had taken a liking to Essence and was happy to see her go.

"I would've left from the court house if they'd let me. I don't need any of this shit." Essence left the cell, leaving her commissary items behind. The only thing she packed was her state clothes, blanket and sheets.

On the other side of the wall, Sinnamon greeted her. They hugged and kissed one another on the cheeks. They were happy to see each other.

"Welcome home sis." Sinnamon said. The two of them got into Sinnamon's car. Essence couldn't keep the smile off her face. She was home.

"That's crazy how that shit happened to that girl. I almost feel sorry for her." Essence said, looking out the window.

"Shit happens, besides, I don't see how you could feel sorry for her, she got what she deserved. I couldn't stand that bitch." Sinnamon spoke with venom.

Essence looked over at Sinnamon. She studied her facial expressions.

"What?" Sinnamon said. A smile broke across her face.

"You did that shit? You are truly crazy." Essence said laughing.

"Thank you though."

"I didn't do that one." Sinnamon smiled. "Anyway, where you trying to go?"

"The mall."

Chapter 48

"Look at this shit right here." Flip smacked the newspaper with is hand. He couldn't believe his eyes. He and Mills were sitting in the car about to go see Esco.

"What?" Mills didn't know what Flip was talking about.

"Essence Taylor was released from W.C.I. after the witness wa found beaten to death by boyfriend." Flip read the paper out loud.

"So what that mean?"

"Look nigga." Flip showed Mills Essence's picture. "That's one of the bitches right there. Them whores from Delaware. I'ma off that bitch!"

Flip was excited that he would finally get his revenge. "I ain't leavin' till I find both them bitches. I'ma ask Esco do he know them." Flip pulled off to meet up with Esco. Mills looked at the paper in disbelief. What a coincidence. The girls were living on his turf and he never even seen them before. Mills had mixed emotions. He wanted to get at them, but then at the same time, he just wanted to walk away from it all.

"This is crazy." Mills said out loud, still not believing the news.

"Damn nigga, you don't sound happy like me." Flip looked over at Mills.

"Naw, I'm ready, I just can't believe this shit." Mills replied.

"Well just know it's on site with them bitches. I'm glad I bought my .40 wit me." Flip patted the gun that was on his waistband. "I can't wait for this shit." Flip turned off on Governor Prince Blvd., headed to the projects where Esco was waiting. Mills and Flip were supposed to meet Sinnamon and her friend before the three of them went to hang out.

When Flip turned on Bower's Lane, he got the shock of his life. He pulled over a half block away from where Esco was chilling, talking to Sinnamon and Essence. Watching them laughing and enjoying themselves had Flip heated. He pulled his .40 cal out and cocked it back.

"I can't believe this shit." Flip said angrily. He felt Esco set him up.

"What the fuck is good with you?" Mills looked at Flip like he was crazy. He was so busy trying to think of an excuse to leave Delaware to avoid murdering the girls that he didn't even see them standing there with Esco.

"You don't see that shit?" Flip pointed his gun in the direction of Esco and the girls. "That snake ass nigga. I'ma kill all three of them." Mills finally spotted Esco with the girls. At first, he didn't know what to think. Then he began to reason. If Esco knew what happened and that the girls were responsible, why would he invite us down there to meet them? It didn't add up. "Flip, chill for a minute." Mills said calmly.

"What the fuck do you mean chill. Those bitches tried to earth me." Flip screamed.

"I know and we gonna get 'em, but you can't knock Esco off in the process. Let's wait."

"Wait for what? That nigga probably the one that sent them, how else would they find us outta all the niggas in Atlanta." Flip fumed.

"If he knew what was going on, why would he tell us to come down here?" Mills asked.

"I don't know and I don't care." Flip had his mind made up.

It Gets Dirtier

"Flip, use ya head my nigga. Use ya head! Its broad daylight, we in hot ass Riverside and we don't even know what's good." Mills explained. Just then, a cop car rode past them. "See what I'm saying. Besides that, Esco ain't no dumb nigga. If he had somethin' to do with it this might be a trap." Flip thought hard on what Mills was saying. He didn't know what to think. Part of him didn't care about the police or any trap, murder was his only option. Then his common sense kicked in and he knew he'd go to jail if he aired things out right then and there.

"You right." Flip pulled off and left the projects. A million thoughts crossed his head. he felt something wasn't right.

"Let's just go somewhere and think things over. Then we'll handle them. I know they probably just bitches that stay down there. I know ain't neither of them his girl." Mills said confidently. Mills flipped open his phone. "I'ma call him and tell him we'll get up with him later."

"Whatever." Flip had a lot on his mind. He didn't know who to trust or what to think. Deep in thought, he turned his radio up. The perfect song was playing.

"Somethin' goin' on, I feel funny can't tell me nothin' different, my nose twitchin' intuition settin' in like Steve's vision...." Beanie Segals' 'Feel It in the Air' played through the speakers.

Flip didn't know what was going on. All he could do was paint a picture from what he'd seen. The game was dirty, how else could he think. Still in a zone, Flip jumped on I-95 north, headed to Philly. He and Mills rode in silence. Ya hand shake ain't matching ya smile. Flip said in his head with Segal.

Chapter 49

"Yo Newz, I don't know what's good my nigga, but something don't seem right." Flip explained to one of his young boys. Newz was a tall dark-skinned 19 year old that was ready to bust his gun whenever. When he was around, most of the time it was bad news. That's how he got his name.

"You want me to off him right now?" Newz pulled out a nickel plated 9mm Beretta. "I'll off him and lite this whole crib on fire."

Mills was down stairs in the living room in Flip's old house in Philly. Never in a million years would he have guessed what the conversation was about directly above him. He sat, sipping on a Heineken and some Remy, oblivious to what was going on. He would never guess Flip doubted his loyalty.

"Naw. I'm not sure if he had anything to do with it yet. Just smack him with the hammer, knock him out, and tie him up down in the basement. I'ma go pick up Shawn Bone while you handle that. Then we gonna shoot back down Wilmington and handle them bitches." Flip directed.

"Aiight cool." Newz said. He and Flip walked down the steps. Newz joined Mills on the couch.

"Yo, I'll be back. I'm 'bout to go get some weed." Flip told Mills.

It Gets Dirtier

"Aiight." Mills had his eyes locked on the TV. He wasn't paying Newz any attention. After Flip left, Newz waited patiently for Mills to drink a little more. He looked at him with a cold heart. He wanted to kill him. Ten minutes later, Newz got tired of waiting. Sitting right next to Mills, made his move easy. With one quick blow, Newz smacked Mills in the bridge of his nose with his Beretta.

"Aww shit." The blow caught Mills by surprise. He held his nose as blood poured from it.

Newz began smacking Mills relentlessly with the gun. He almost got carried away. Once he saw Mills wasn't moving, he grabbed him by his ankles and dragged him down the steps to the basement. When he found some duct tape, he wrapped it around Mills' mouth, sealing it tight. Newz had to wrap it around three times for it to stay put. Mills blood made it hard for the tape to stick.

Once his mouth was covered, Newz taped Mills' hand together and then his feet. Not satisfied with his job, Newz began to wrap his entire body with tape. When he was done, Mills resembled a mummy. Newz made his way back up stairs to wait for Flip and Bone.

About ten minutes later Flip and Shawn Bone came through the door. "Bone lover." Newz said as he slapped hands with his long time friend.

"What's good nigga?" Bone said breaking their brotherly hug. Bone was a brown-skinned young boy that stood 5'9". He had a small frame but the style of a Pit bull, little but vicious. Him and Newz together was a problem. Flip put them on his team a couple years ago.

"Where dat nigga at?" Bone asked with a smile.

"That nigga wrapped up down stairs." Newz said proudly.

Flip, Bone, and Newz went downstairs to see Newz's handy work. Bone fell out laughing when he saw Mills. "Damn cuz, what's this? The return of the mummy." Bone cracked.

It Gets Dirtier

Flip walked over to Mills and smacked him awake. Mills looked up at Flip with blood shot eyes. In his mind, he knew he would die. All he could do was pray.

"I apologize for this Mills, but I don't know what to think. I'ma handle shit down Wilmington and see what's good, then I'ma decide what to do with you. Hopefully, you in the clear." Flip said. He didn't want to kill Mills but would if he had to.

Flip and his young squad made it to Wilmington in about a half hour. They made their way to the projects where they saw Esco and the girls earlier that day. Flip noticed the Caddy out there, they decided to wait and see what was what.

*****

"I'm pissed to be back in this place." Essence was upset to be back in Sinnamon's project home. She missed her condo.

"It's only for a little while. I got all your money in a deposit box in the bank. It won't take you long to get another place." Sinnamon assured her.

"You're right." Essence sighed. Sinnamon's phone rang.

"Hello." Sinnamon answered.

"You ready?" Esco asked on the other end.

"Yeah."

"Well, I'm 'bout to pull up out front. Come get Quan and take him to Ms. Jones." They were going to the movies.

"Okay."

*****

"I think that's the boy Esco right there." Flip told the young boys when he saw Sinnamon's Bentley pull up. They watched as Esco got out the car and open the passenger door to let Shaquan out. Just then, Sinnamon exited the house and knocked on Ms. Jones' door. The three of them watched as Sinnamon kissed the little boy and he disappeared in the house.

"That's one of the bitches. The little boy must be her son." Flip said, thinking of a plan.

"Well, let's get 'em now." Newz said impatiently.

"Naw. We gonna let Esco and the bitch leave. It's too hot round here to just run up on them. That bitch Essence probably in the house by herself. We can off her and then go next door and kidnap the other bitch's son." Flip told them.

"Then what? I ain't tryin' to baby sit too long." Bone said.

"Leverage my nigga. It's always good to have leverage. Besides, I wanna give Esco a chance to clear the air. See if he love his bitch or his niggas, or at least his money. We'll find out where Esco and the bitch stay at when funeral time comes." Flip had a master plan.

"Well, let's move out." Newz said when he saw Esco and Sinnamon pull off. He put his hoodie on and pulled his gun out. Flip and Bone followed suit.

"I got the bitch ya'll get the boy." Flip ordered.

"Aiight." Bone and Newz said in unison. They exited the car and made their way to the houses.

"At the count of three, we gonna kick the doors down." Flip told them. "One, two, three."

"Boom!" Both doors flew open.

Flip entered the house with his gun pointed. Essence was on the couch watching TV. She was frozen in fear. She immediately recognized Flip.

"Remember me?" Flip said with a smile. Essence closed her eyes.

"Boom, Boom, Boom!" Flip sent three rounds into Essence's chest. He walked over to her and fired another round.

"Boom." This one went into her head.

Flip tucked his gun and walked out the door. He was met by Bone, carrying a crying and kicking Shaquan.

"Boom." Bone and Flip heard a shot, and then Newz came walking out the house quickly. The three of them made their way to the car. It was still running.

296

It Gets Dirtier

"I had to kill that crazy old bitch." Newz laughed. "She really tried to fight me."

Flip peeled off and they headed back to Philly. "One down. Two to go. Things are gonna get messy when it hits the fan."

TO BE CONTINUED...

So Real You Feel You Lived It!

Street Knowledge Publishing LLC
1902-B Maryland Ave
Wilmington, DE 19805
TOLL FREE: **1.888.401.1114**
www.streetknowledgepublishing.com

Date: _____

Purchaser _____

Mailing Address _____

City _____ State _____ Zip Code _____

Qty.	ISB Number	Title of Book	Price Each	Total
	978-0-9822515-6-0	Bloody Money	$15.00	
	978-0-9822515-9-1	Bloody Money 2	$15.00	
	978-0-9799556-4-8	Bloody Money 3	$15.00	
	978-0-9799556-0-0	Tommy Good story	$15.00	
	978-0-9822515-0-8	Tommy Good Story II	$15.00	
	978-0-9746199-1-0	Me & My Girls	$15.00	
	978-0-9746199-0-3	Cash Ave	$15.00	
	978-0-9822515-1-5	Merry F$$kin' Xmas	$15.00	
	978-0-9799556-0-7	A Day After Forever	$15.00	
	978-0-9822515-3-9	A Day After Forever 2	$15.00	
	978-0-9746199-6-5	Don't Mix the Bitter with the Sweet	$15.00	
	978-0-9799556-9-3	Playing For Keeps	$15.00	
	978-0-9799556-3-1	Pain Freak	$15.00	
	978-0-9799556-5-5	Dipped Up	$15.00	
	978-0-9799556-6-2	No Love No Pain	$15.00	
	978-0-9746199-4-1	Dopesick	$15.00	
	978-0-9799556-7-9	Lust, Love & Lies	$15.00	
	978-0-9746199-7-2	The Queen of New York	$15.00	
	978-0-9746199-8-9	Sin 4 Life	$15.00	
	978-0-9822515-4-6	A Little More Sin	$15.00	
	978-0-9746199-5-8	The Hunger	$15.00	
	978-0-9746199-3-4	Money Grip	$15.00	
	978-0-9822515-7-7	Young Rich and Dangerous	$15.00	
	978-1-944151-26-3	Street Victims	$15.00	
	978-1-944151-28-7	Street Victims II	$15.00	
	978-1-944151-30-3	Street Victimes III	$15.00	
	978-1-944151-32-4	A Small Wonder	$15.00	
	978-1-944151-45-4	Coup De Grace	$15.00	
	978-1-944151-47-8	Burton Boys (May 2017)	$15.00	
	978-1-944151-56-0	Burton Boys 2	$15.00	
	978-1-944151-58-4	Burton Boys 3	$15.00	
	978-1-944151-00-3	Dirty Living	$15.00	
	978-1-944151-65-2	Watch What You Say	$15.00	
		Total Books Ordered	Quantity	
			Subtotal	

SHIPPING/HANDLING (Via U.S. Priority Mail)			
$7.20 for 1st book, $2.00 for each additional book			
Institutional Check & Money Orders ONLY		Shipping	
(No Personal Checks Accepted)		Total	
	Total	**$**	

It Gets Dirtier

Street Knowledge Publishing LLC
1902-B Maryland Ave
Wilmington, DE 19805
TOLL FREE: **1.888.401.1114**
www.streetknowledgepublishing.com

Date: _____

Purchaser _____

Mailing Address _____

City _____ State _____ Zip Code _____

Qty.	ISB Number	Title of Book	Author	Price Each	Total
	Butterfly Collection				
		Beautiful Demise	K.D. Harris	$13.99	
		Scarred	K.D. Harris	$13.99	
		Pressure (Coming April 2017)	K.D. Harris	$13.99	
		Dying to Fit In (Coming June 2017)	K.D. Harris	$13.99	
		Legacy (Coming August 2017)	K.D. Harris	$13.99	
		Classy Clique (Coming Sept. 2017)	K.D. Harris	$13.99	
		Caged Secrets (Coming Nov. 2017)	K.D. Harris	$13.99	
		Messy Media (Coming Dec. 2017)	K.D. Harris	$13.99	
	SKP Erotica				
	978-1-944151-04-1	Beyond Measure	K.D. Harris	$15.00	
	978-1-944151-06-5	Beyond Measure II	K.D. Harris	$15.00	
	978-1-944151-62-1	Beyond Measure III (April 2017)	K.D. Harris	$15.00	
	978-1-944151-08-9	The Games We Play	K.D. Harris	$15.00	
	978-1-944151-02-7	For The Love Of It	K.D. Harris	$15.00	
	Eric B Crime Novels				
	978-1-944151-20-1	That Was Dirty	Wasiim	$15.00	
	978-1-944151-22-5	It Gets Dirtier	Wasiim	$15.00	
	978-1-944151-24-9	As Dirty As It Gets	Wasiim	$15.00	
	978-0-9799556-8-6	Money and Murder	Fred Brown	$15.00	
	978-1-944151-35-5	Money and Murder II	Fred Brown	$15.00	
	978-1-944151-39-7	Money and Murder III	Fred Brown	$15.00	
	978-1-944151-49-2	Scandalous Ties	Jermaine "Ski" Buchanan	$15.00	
	978-1-944151-51-5	Scandalous Ties II	Jermaine "Ski" Buchanan	$15.00	
	978-1-944151-52-2	Scandalous Ties III	Jermaine "Ski" Buchanan	$15.00	
	978-1-944151-55-3	Scandalous Ties IV	Jermaine "Ski" Buchanan	$15.00	
	978-0-9799556-2-4	Courts in the Streets	Kevin Bullock	$15.00	
	978-0-9822515-5-3	Courts in the Streets II	Kevin Bullock	$15.00	
	978-1-944151-43-0	Courts in the Streets III	Kevin Bullock	$15.00	
		Total Books Ordered		Quantity	
				Subtotal	
SHIPPING/HANDLING (Via U.S. Priority Mail) $7.20 for 1st book, $2.00 for each additional book Institutional Check & Money Orders ONLY (No Personal Checks Accepted)				Shipping Total	
		Total		$	

Made in the USA
Middletown, DE
22 February 2021

34150349R00179